NO CRONE UNTURNED

A SPELL'S ANGELS COZY MYSTERY BOOK 3

AMANDA M. LEE

WINCHESTERSHAW PUBLICATIONS

PROLOGUE

ELEVEN YEARS AGO

I was late.

I wasn't particularly worried about it. I lived in a group home, after all. I was due to age out ... and soon. I only had until my high school graduation. There was very little they could do to me. If they wanted to kick me out two weeks early it wouldn't be the end of the world. I had nowhere to go and no idea what to do with myself, but that wasn't going to change between now and my removal date. I was living on borrowed time, and it wasn't the best feeling.

My boots thumped the ground as I trudged the sidewalk, the shadows on either side causing me to watch my surroundings carefully. Very little frightened me. I'd seen too much in my almost eighteen years ... even though I couldn't remember everything I'd seen.

I was an orphan, or at least that's what they called me. I had no idea if my parents were dead or simply woke up one day, said Scout Randall was too much work, and abandoned me in front of a fire station. That's where I was found, and the only thing I knew with absolute certainty was that I was truly alone.

I didn't have a name, so the firefighter who found me gave me one. Scout, from his favorite book. I never did figure out where the Randall came from. Of course, I didn't ask. It didn't matter.

I grew up in the system, shuffled from home to home. I never had a bad placement. Not really anyway. No one wanted me long-term, though. I couldn't decide if that was a good or bad thing. When you grow up in the system you hear these stories about children finding forever homes and being happy. To me they were always fairy tales, because I'd never known anyone in the system to get a happy ending ... and that included me. Still, other kids remained hopeful. I'd given up that dream a long time ago.

All I wanted was to survive.

A furtive noise caught my attention and I flicked my eyes to the tree on my right. I had very good survival instincts. Of course, I had a little something *extra*, too. I was magical. That wasn't a word I threw around lightly — or wanted to dwell on. I knew it made me an enticing target for those who might want to use my powers for evil. I learned at a young age to keep my abilities to myself to avoid unwanted attention.

Despite my best efforts, I recognized there were people who suspected. The firefighter who found me always made it a point to check in. I think he believed I was somehow his responsibility, which was ridiculous. As far as I was concerned, he'd done his job when he turned me over to his superiors. He owed me nothing ... and yet he still visited once a month and always asked if anything peculiar had happened since his last visit.

He brought me presents, including candy and toys, when I was younger. As I grew older, the gifts became more thoughtful. He knew I liked to read and bought me an e-reader. He loaded it with books he thought I should read and then gave me a gift card to fill it with books I wanted to read. He told me over and over again that books were the key to adventures. As fond as I was of him and the time we spent together, I had news for him. The key to adventure was getting out of this hole.

In truth, I'd given up even trying to find a home several years before. I was never that into it, all the pomp ... and circumstance ... and pretending that was associated with adoption events. I was always the suspicious sort, so I was never one to open up to relative strangers. I didn't want to pretend to be something I wasn't. I didn't want to open up. I needed to protect myself ... so that's what I did.

I was sixteen when they tried the last home placement. Thanks to my magic I knew right away it wasn't the place for me. I could sense danger there. It didn't come from the husband, but emanated from the wife. She was mentally ill, wanted to purge young minds and bring them to a certain way of thinking, and her method involved four church visits a week. I didn't even spend a full night in the house. I simply left and walked to the previous group home I'd been housed in. When Steven, the man who ran the home, found me sitting on the front steps the next morning, he didn't look surprised.

He asked me what had happened. I thought about not telling him no matter how much he declared it to be important, but ultimately I knew other children might not be able to figure out their plight in that home (it might not be immediately obvious after all) until it was too late. So I told him the truth and he squeezed my shoulder. He promised me it was going to be okay and he would find a different place. I responded that I didn't want a different place, that I wanted to spend my last two years in the home.

He looked conflicted at first, as if that flew in the face of every-thing he'd ever learned. Ultimately, though, he saw something in my eyes that convinced him I was telling the truth. After that, the group home was my home. He talked various foster fathers into teaching me a variety of things, including mechanics and home repair. He knew from the other homes I'd stayed in that those were the things I was most interested in, so he arranged various unofficial classes.

Over the years, Steven and I had developed a fairly easy rapport. Still, he didn't like it when I was late. I was hardly going to break my leg trying to race to get to him, though. I had only two weeks left ... and I had to think.

I'd dreamed of being out of the system for so long that I thought I had things figured out. In truth, the closer I got to my discharge date, the more fearful I became. I knew I wanted to be free, hit the open road and see the world. But I had no money. I did have an interesting skill set thanks to Steven. I could fix almost anything, and he'd taught me several coping methods to deal with my temper. I could make it ... as long as I found a job. That was easier said than done. I had no references, no parents, and most business owners weren't likely to be thrilled about opening their doors to someone like me.

I had to come up with a better plan. I was running out of time.

I picked up my pace. Steven would likely still be up and I wanted to brainstorm with him. He often had good ideas, but he made me ask for his help. He stressed that. He said I was independent, which was a good thing, but it would be my downfall if I didn't get it together and try to open my heart to people. I thought that was a lot of nonsense, but I needed him to help me figure things out. It was humbling to admit, but there it was.

I was more than halfway home now. I'd been at the library researching jobs in the area on the internet when it closed. I hadn't realized it was so late. I'd gone down a rabbit hole and emerged only when they kicked me out.

It was early spring and the nights were crisp. I didn't feel the cold as I increased my pace. All I could think about was what I was going to do in two weeks. I would be completely on my own then and was at a genuine loss. Steven reassured me that he would be there when I needed help — we'd grown closer than he usually allowed with his charges — but I was determined to do this on my own. I didn't want to need people. That was the whole point of growing up.

I was two blocks from the group home when the hair on the back of my neck stood up and saluted. Instinctively, I slowed my pace and began scanning the bushes on either side of the road. The magic allowed me to protect myself. Of course, I carried myself in such a way that strangers had stopped approaching me when I was fourteen for the most part. I wanted it that way.

This was different.

"I know you're there," I said after a beat, completely stopping my forward momentum and glaring at a clump of trees about thirty feet away. There was no movement, nothing to hint that I wasn't alone. But I knew. There was a predator lurking, and he thought I was easy prey. Well, I'd show him what a true predator looked like.

4

"You might as well come out," I called out. "I'm not an idiot."

There was silence for a moment, then the rustle of leaves. When a figure finally materialized on the other side of the trees, it wasn't what I expected.

It was a man ... kind of. He couldn't have topped five feet no matter how much you stretched him, and that included the shoes he was wearing that looked to have heels. He wore a weird little suit with patches at the elbows of the blazer. He sported a bald head — the moon bounced off it — other than about three wispy fibers that could probably be described as hair if someone was hard-pressed. One eye sort of sagged, giving him the appearance of winking.

"Cripes," I muttered under my breath. "What happened to you?"

The man drew himself to his full diminutive height and puffed out his chest. "Nothing happened to me. What happened to you?" He seemed insulted that I would dare call him on the carpet for being a creepy stalker.

"Why are you hiding in the bushes?" I demanded, folding my arms over my chest. "Are you a pervert or something?"

His eyes flashed. "Of course I'm not a pervert. What a question to ask. I wasn't hiding, by the way. I was ... taking a nap."

That was the lamest excuse I'd ever heard. "You were taking a nap in the bushes? Are you homeless? You don't look homeless. You're weird-looking, but that jacket looks expensive, despite the patches."

The man's features blazed with annoyance. "I will have you know, young lady, that this jacket was designed by one of the finest tailors in all of England."

Oh, he was British. That explained it. Well, maybe. "What century was the jacket made?"

"This century. It's a new coat." He sniffed as he straightened. "Who are you to judge what other people wear anyway?" He gave my hodge-podge of clothing a once over. "You look like you shop at a second-hand store."

"That's because I do shop at a secondhand store." I didn't really care that he was insulting my clothing. I'd never been one for fashion. Sure, I had dreams of buying my own leather coat one day — something black and rugged that made me look tough — but I was resigned to that taking a while. I still had to get a job ... and a roof over my head ... and food would be nice. "You still haven't told me why you're hiding in the bushes."

"I wasn't hiding in the bushes," he shot back. "I don't understand why you keep saying that. I was hiding in the trees, not the bushes."

"Oh, well, that's so much better," I drawled. I was growing bored with the conversation. Still, I knew that I couldn't simply leave him to ambush some other unsuspecting victim. "You look like a pervert, so that's what I'm going with."

He made a squeaking noise that sounded like disgust. "I'm not a pervert! Stop saying that."

"I don't know anyone else who would hide in the bushes after dark. I mean ... I guess you could be a robber. If that's your thing, you're going to be disappointed. I don't have any money."

"I don't want your money. Really, what an undignified thing to say."

I had to give him credit. Even though he was hiding in the trees like a freaky criminal, he was making a good effort to put me on the defensive. It was an interesting trick. "I'm running late. I have to be going." I moved to step around him. I thought he would let me pass rather than mess with me. Instead, he reached out and grabbed my arm, wrapping his spindly fingers around my wrist as he started to chant in a language I didn't recognize.

"What are you doing?" I jerked my arm from his grasp, causing his eyes to widen further as he squeaked again. I fixed him with a dark glare. "What did you just say?"

"I didn't say anything," he lied. "You're hearing things."

"I'm not hearing things." This was no longer fun. "What language was that?"

"I have no idea what you're talking about." He stared at the sky. "You're starting to become a nuisance so ... off with you." He made small shooing motions with his hands. "I'm sure someone is missing you. Not someone bright, mind you, but someone all the same."

Someone was missing me. Steven. I didn't want to disappoint him.

It was rare that I could say that about anyone, but he was all I had. Well, Steven and the firefighter who refused to write me off. They were it.

That didn't mean I could simply turn my back on this idiot. "That sounded like a spell," I pressed, my eyes narrowing. "Were you casting a spell on me?"

This time when the man's eyes landed on me he was incredulous. "What are you?" His tone was accusatory.

"An Aquarian," I replied. "Some people think that makes me aloof, but I happen to like the fact that people annoy me."

He rolled his eyes. "That's not what I was asking." His eyes drilled into me. "What are you?" He asked the question in such a manner that there could be only one answer. I knew what he was digging for, but even if I had the answers he sought I wouldn't share them with him.

"What are you?" I shot back. "I mean ... other than a creepy stalker who likes to hide behind bushes and attack teenage girls. Wait ... you weren't whacking off in there, were you?"

I didn't think his eyes could bulge out of his head any further, but I was wrong. He seriously looked as if he was going to pop a gasket. "That is undignified!"

"So is your face," I argued. "Seriously, I'm not leaving here until you tell me what you were doing."

"I ... you ... ." He looked flustered. Then he straightened. "I don't have to tell you anything. You're not my superior."

"No, but I am a teenager who was accosted by a strange guy hiding in the bushes. I can call the police. I'm sure they would love to know what you were doing." In truth, I had no intention of calling the police. I mistrusted them more than tiny little men in bad suits who hid in the bushes. He didn't need to know that.

"I wasn't hiding in the bushes!" he exploded. "I was in the trees, and I wasn't hiding. I was ... communing with nature."

"Yeah, that sounds like code for whacking off."

"I just ... you are an undignified girl." He took an exaggerated step away from me. "I'm not a pervert. I know what you're thinking, but you're wrong."

"Uh-huh." The more he talked, the more convinced I was that he was most definitely a pervert. It ultimately didn't matter. I was late ... and he wasn't my problem. "If someone goes missing from this area tonight, I'm giving your description to the police. You've been warned."

"Oh, well, that's fair," he barked as I resumed my trek to the group home. "I'm pretty sure you're judging me on my appearance, and that's wrong. I don't know who raised you, but you need a manners adjustment."

"I'll take that under advisement." I didn't look back until I made it to the end of the block. Once there, I looked back to the spot where I'd left him. He remained, but he wasn't alone. Another man had joined him. This one was tall and dressed all in black.

As if sensing me watching, he slowly turned until his gaze snagged with mine. Even though there was too much distance between us for me to see his eyes, I got a flash of clear blue and a chill went through my body. Whoever this man was, he wasn't good.

I felt caught, as if I should call for help and confront him. He seemed to grasp my predicament because he burst out in a mocking laugh and shook his head.

"Perhaps we will meet again one day," he called out. "No further communication need be attempted tonight. You should feel lucky."

That wasn't the word I would use to describe how I felt. "Maybe you should feel lucky," I shot back. "I'm terrifying."

"So my associate has told me. For now, you're safe. You should go home."

"That's the plan." I continued staring. "What are you?"

"I asked that question first of her," the little guy complained. "She won't answer."

"Perhaps that's because she doesn't know," the dark man said. "Either way, she's ... interesting." I couldn't see his predatory smile but I could feel it. "Go home. I believe we will meet again. This isn't going to play out tonight."

I felt as if I should be relieved, but I didn't know why. "You won't like it if I see you again," I promised finally. I liked pretending I was a badass and I wasn't going to break my streak now. "I'll be your worst nightmare."

The dark man shrugged. "We shall see. Either way, not tonight. Go home. Think about how lucky you are."

"Maybe you should think about how lucky you are."

He laughed, the sound echoing through the darkness. "Perhaps I will." He raised his hand and waved. "Until we meet again."

Yeah, yeah, yeah. I was sick of strange men tonight. I was completely and totally over them.

ONE

PRESENT DAY

"Oh ... my ... gawd! What is that? Is that pee? I think it's pee."

I shifted my eyes to my co-worker Marissa Martin and did my best not to roll my eyes ... or laugh. Making fun of her misfortune at a time like this wasn't a good thing. Still, it took every ounce of self-control I had to swallow the chuckle that threatened to bubble up.

"It's not pee," I assured her quickly. "There's no way it's pee. I mean ... it's a bog. There's water in a bog, not pee."

Marissa narrowed her eyes to dangerous slits, which only made the crow's feet at the corners more pronounced. She was in her forties but pretended to be almost a full ten years younger ... although she was the only one falling for her act. "It smells like pee."

She wasn't wrong. The unmistakable scent of urine permeated the air. I was trying to figure out where it was coming from when she took an unfortunate step and splashed into the murky water that encroached from the east. That only made the scent bolder.

"I think it has something to do with swamp gas," I said pragmatically. I wasn't an idiot and knew that it would be best for everybody concerned if I managed to convince her that it really was just off-color water. I had a feeling I knew what else was lurking in the swamp ... and it wouldn't be pretty if she found out.

"Swamp gas?" The face Marissa made was so absurd I had to bite the inside of my cheek to keep from laughing out loud. I had no idea why her reaction tickled my funny bone the way it did, but I was so close to losing it that I was one misstep away from toppling over a line that would result in a lot of screeching ... and probably more foot-stomping, which certainly wasn't going to help the odor problem.

I nodded and flashed a tight-lipped smile, hoping I came across as intelligent rather than an out-and-out liar, because in truth everything I was about to tell her was a falsehood. Er, well, I guess technically it could've been true. I really didn't know. I was just making it up as I went along. Odds were that I would stumble upon at least one true statement.

"This is a swamp." I gestured toward the small water source. It was in the middle of the woods, a good twenty miles from Hawthorne Hollow, a small paranormal hamlet in northern Lower Michigan. "The water here doesn't get enough sun because of the trees." I gestured toward the leafy branches above. "Because of that, the water grows stagnant."

It sounded plausible so I kept going. "When water becomes stagnant, it takes on a urine scent because of the lack of photosynthesis. It's not pee. It just smells like pee."

Marissa furrowed her brow. "Is that true?"

I bobbed my head. "Absolutely. Would I lie to you?" The answer was yes, but she didn't need to know that.

"But ... I thought photosynthesis was what happened to plants."

Crap. I was betting on her not knowing that. She wasn't exactly book smart. To be fair, she wasn't street smart either. She was an all-around pain in the behind as far as I could tell. That didn't mean I wanted to tick her off.

"What do you think is below the water?" I asked, making things up as I went along. "No, I'm serious. We're in the middle of the woods. There are plants in the woods. This swamp is also in the middle of the woods. That means the swamp is littered with plants."

"Oh." She nodded sagely. "That totally makes sense. I get it now."

That made one of us. "I'm glad. Now, focus on your work. There's a bog monster in here somewhere and we have to find it."

As if on cue, there was a shrill chuckle on the far side of the swamp. I swiveled quickly so I could look in that direction, narrowing my eyes as I searched for a hint of movement. I found nothing, and yet my senses told me what I was looking for was located on that side of the water.

"Ugh." I groaned. The creature was playing with us. There could be no other explanation. He'd somehow moved to the opposite side of the water without me noticing. How did he even manage that?

"Do you think that was him?" Marissa whispered. She was all business now that we'd made first contact with our target.

"I think it's unlikely to be anybody else," I replied dryly, wrinkling my nose as I got a particularly nasty whiff of the urine scent Marissa had spent the last twenty minutes going on and on about.

"Where?" Her voice was barely a whisper.

"If I knew where, he'd already be dead," I muttered.

"Well, excuse me for living," Marissa snapped, her eyes flashing. "It was just a question. There's no reason to be ... surly."

I knew better than to argue yet I couldn't seem to stop myself. "Surly?" I arched a confrontational eyebrow. "I'm pretty sure I wasn't being surly."

"And yet I'm sure you were. You're always surly. The only people you're ever nice to are Raisin and Gunner. I have no idea why you've taken such a shine to Raisin because she's young and annoying ... and not in a fun way like Lindsay Lohan. As for Gunner ... well ... we all know why you're nice to him."

Thankfully there were no lights in the bog other than the moon, which occasionally shone through the rustling leaves above. I could feel my cheeks burning. In addition to being another co-worker, Gunner Stratton was my boyfriend ... though I was loath to use that word. It made me feel much younger than I actually was. "I'm confused how Lindsay Lohan was ever fun," I hedged.

"Um ... didn't you see *The Parent Trap*?"

I racked my brain. "Actually, no. I don't think I've ever heard of that movie. What's it about? Is she some sort of alien who lands in a town and traps all the parents?"

The look Marissa shot me was full of dumbfounded surprise. "Um ... no."

"Huh. That's too bad. That sounds like my kind of movie."

Her eyes slanted as she tilted her head to the side, considering. "Are you seriously telling me you haven't seen *The Parent Trap*?"

"Not only have I not seen it, I've never heard of it."

"It's by Disney. Actually, there are two of them. The first came out a long time ago, long before I was born. The second was out when I was finishing college."

I did the math in my head and managed to keep a straight face. "And when was that again?"

Annoyance rolled off her in waves. "Forget the movie. You're missing out, though. Lindsay Lohan plays a set of twins separated at birth who meet up at summer camp. When the twins realize they were separated for their whole lives, they launch a plan to switch places and reunite their parents. It's a magical movie."

It sounded like nonsense. "Yeah. I'll have to take your word for it."

The eerie laughing returned, causing the hair on the back of my neck to stand on end. This time it was much closer.

Marissa drifted closer to me, her eyes wide as she searched for hints of movement. "Do you hear that?"

"The nightmarish laughing from the bog monster? Yeah. I hear it." I heaved out a sigh and looked left and right. I wasn't quite sure what I was searching for — something to help with the lighting problem couldn't possibly hurt — but I came up empty on all fronts. "We need to hurry this along. I don't want to be out here all night."

Marissa, obviously nervous, kept darting her eyes from one location to the next. I'd never seen a bog monster — and apparently neither had she — and I had no idea which direction the attack would come from. "Let me guess: You have plans with a certain special someone."

The look she shot me could be construed as sweet, but I knew better. She'd had issues with my relationship with Gunner from the start. She was far too old for him — though she liked to play the age game more than anybody I'd ever met — but that didn't seem to be a deterrent. Her nose was clearly out of joint when it came to me and Gunner.

"I do have plans with a certain someone," I agreed, grinning in a manner that I knew would set her teeth on edge. "His name is Merlin and he likes to eat food out of a can more than a bag, has eight different catnip toys to rub his head against and get high, and purrs while watching movies with me. I don't think he'll be a fan of *The Parent Trap*, but I guess it's not out of the realm of possibility."

Marissa made a face. "You're talking about your cat."

"I am."

"So ... you're not hanging out with Gunner tonight?" She almost looked hopeful.

Technically, Gunner and I hadn't made plans for tonight. Of course, we hadn't made plans any night for the past two weeks and we'd still spent every spare moment together. We were in that heady beginning of a relationship that saw both partners smelling roses and seeing shooting stars at every turn. I thought I hated gooey people like that ... until I became one of them. Still, I didn't see the point in sharing my personal business with Marissa.

"Not last time I checked," I replied breezily, jerking my head to the left when I heard scurrying feet. Again, I didn't see anything. I sensed a presence closing in, though, and it was ... odd. That's the only word I could muster to describe it. "How big is this monster supposed to be?" I asked finally.

Marissa held out her hands and shrugged. "How should I know? I've never seen it."

That brought up an important question. "Who has seen it?"

The question clearly caught Marissa off guard, because she opened her mouth to answer and then snapped it shut. "Well ... I don't know. Rooster just said he needed two people to come out and fight a monster that someone saw while camping. I didn't ask who that someone was. You volunteered to take it on and I did the same because ... um ... I like fighting monsters in the woods," she added.

That second part was a massive stretch. In fact, I would've gone so far as to call it an outright lie. We both knew the only reason she volunteered was because she thought Gunner would go with me and she wanted to make sure that didn't happen. She was nothing if not transparent.

"Yeah, well ... ." I broke off when I heard it again. The pitter-patter of little feet. Like ... very little feet. "Okay." I planted my hands on my hips and scanned the bushes to the east. "Listen, I know you're out there. I also know you're tiny. I don't know what your plan is, but I'm like three feet taller than you so there's no way you can overpower me."

"Three feet." Marissa's lips twisted as laughter bubbled up from the bushes in question. "That means this thing is only like two and a half feet tall."

"Maybe a little closer to three feet, but you're basically correct," I countered, glaring at the rustling bushes. This thing hadn't shown itself yet but it was only a matter of time. "I guess I could just start shooting magic wherever I think it might be."

I was a trained witch, though I still flew by the seat of my pants most days. I was big on experimenting and had no problem throwing around a bit of magic ... except for the fact that I didn't want to hit some innocent animal. Sure, I was a badass biker witch, a member in good standing of the Spells Angels, but I also liked bunnies and raccoons. I was a softie when it came to animals, which is exactly how I ended up with a stray kitten taking over my new home. See, I was fine taking out monsters. Fluffy things were another matter.

"You should definitely start throwing around some magic," Marissa agreed. "The sooner we finish this, the sooner we can head back. Well, not together or anything. I can head back to The Cauldron and you can go home and hang out with your cat."

My lips quirked. "Right."

"You like your cat. You just said so."

"I do like my cat," I agreed. "I might stop in at The Cauldron for a quick drink or something, too." The Rusty Cauldron was our home base. Sure, we had office space, but there was something more satisfying — and relaxed — about meeting in a bar.

"Oh, you don't need to go to The Cauldron," Marissa countered. "It's a weeknight. There's nothing happening there on a weeknight. The only reason I'm going is because I left my tablet behind the bar. I need to pick it up and then I'm heading home, too."

That was a bald-faced lie. I'd seen her tuck that tablet into the storage bin on her motorcycle before we headed out to take on the bog monster. She must not have remembered that I was standing right next to her when she locked it away.

"A drink sounds good," I persisted, swiveling quickly when I heard rustling leaves again. This time I actually managed to see some movement. The bog monster was now directly in front of me, though I still hadn't managed to get a clear view of him.

"You could always have a drink at home," Marissa suggested.

"Yes, but it's not nearly as fun to drink alone." I lifted my hand, purple magic erupting from my fingertips as I stared at the spot where I knew the bog monster waited. "I prefer being sociable when I drink my bourbon."

Marissa scowled. "I've yet to see you be sociable since you arrived ... and that was weeks ago."

"Oh, I'm a social butterfly," I countered. "I ... ."

The bog monster picked that moment to erupt from the bushes. He hopped out, allowing me to see his real form — which reminded me of a leprechaun without the charm (and clothing) — and then growled as he doubled in size and started glowing.

"Holy ... !" Marissa squeaked as she scrambled to escape from the creature.

I was expecting it to attack. We'd invaded his territory, tromped all over his home base, and insulted his urine-scented splash pad. There really was only one way for him to respond.

He grew to the size of a small giant, showing off a pair of razor-sharp teeth, and then reached out to grab me with spindly hands that boasted ragged fingernails. I didn't wait for him to put his hands on me. Instead, I shot out a bolt of magic that caught him dead center in the chest. Like a deflating balloon, he started to shrink.

"Oh, no," the creature complained in a shrill voice. "Witches. I hate witches."

I smiled and raised my hands a second time. "Then you should've left the campers alone," I offered. "We wouldn't have even come out here to get you if you'd kept your presence quiet."

"What fun is that?"

He had a point. "Sorry about this, but it's part of the job." I jolted another bolt of energy into him, grimacing as his cheeks expanded in an unhealthy manner. He suddenly looked as if his skin was too tight for his body. "Uh-oh."

"Is he supposed to look like that?" Marissa asked just as the creature exploded.

I'd realized what was going to happen a split-second before it came and managed to throw up a shield spell. That meant I wasn't covered in bog monster goo in the immediate aftermath. Marissa, on the other hand ... .

"Oh, my ... !" She let loose an unearthly screech when she realized what had happened.

For lack of anything better to do, I scratched my cheek and shrugged. "Well, that was a learning experience. I didn't know he was going to explode that way. Um ... sorry?"

Marissa's eyes promised bloody retribution. "I'm going to kill you."

While I knew she meant it, I also understood that I was ten times stronger than her. There was nothing she could do to me. We both knew it. "There, there." I stopped myself before I patted her shoulder and got bog monster goo on me. "Whew. Now you smell like pee."

"Ugh. I really hate you."

SHE WAS STILL COMPLAINING WHEN WE RETURNED to our motorcycles five minutes later. We'd been forced to park near the road and hike in because there was no easy access to the swamp from the lonely highway. I was thankful to find our rides untouched, though I had the distinct impression someone had been loitering near them during our absence.

"Do you feel that?" I asked, glancing around.

"Feel what?" Marissa was still wiping viscous green goo from her face. "All I feel is disgusting."

"I ... don't ... know." I scanned the landscape in every direction, stopping when I looked to the east and found a huge house on a bluff overlooking the forest. "Has that always been here?"

Marissa's expression was twisted. "Are you serious? It's a house. It's an old house to boot. It's been there for as long as I can remember."

"I didn't see it when we parked."

"Did you look in that direction?"

That was a good question. "I guess not." I stared at the house. At one time it was probably quite the showplace. It looked like a mansion with a unique view ... that had been forgotten about thirty years earlier. Even though I couldn't see it up close and personal, I had no doubt the roof was sagging and the inside needed a definite polish. Still, the bones of the house were impressive. "It's a Victorian."

"It's a shack," Marissa shot back. "It's been abandoned for years. Someone should really tear it down. The only people who ever visit are the kids who like to party. It's kind of a death trap these days."

I was curious. "How do you know that?"

"Because there was a wendigo living in there about four years ago and we had to take it down inside," Marissa replied. "The house is ... gross. Not as gross as me right now, but disgusting all the same."

"Oh." I couldn't help being a little disappointed. There was something about the house that called to me, though I couldn't put my finger on what. "That's kind of a bummer, huh?"

"Yes. I'm still horrified about it." She rolled her eyes and inclined her head toward her bike. "Can we leave now or should we continue to talk about the abandoned house in the middle of nowhere for the rest of the night?"

I blew out a sigh. "No, we can go."

"Thank you for your permission."

I tugged on my helmet, straddled my bike, and started it on the first try. I was more than ready to leave, yet something pulled my attention back to the house. I couldn't see anyone. There were no lights. The electricity probably wasn't even on. Despite that, I couldn't shake the feeling that someone was watching us from the murky windows.

"Let's go," Marissa barked. "I can't wait to tell Rooster how you fouled up this one."

Ah, she was a true joy. Still, I'd had fun tonight. Yes, I have a weird sense of humor. That's simply who I am.

Scout Randall, abandoned girl and witch extraordinaire. I was really starting to come into my own.

TWO

*M*arissa beat me back to The Cauldron. It wasn't that
she was a better driver as much as she had an agenda.
Also, I remained distracted by the house. I stopped at a certain point
on the road and stared at the imposing shadow, willing a light to come
on or some sort of movement to catch my attention, anything really
to give me an excuse to go inside. That's what I really wanted, because
I couldn't shake the feeling that someone was watching me from the
bluff.

Marissa lost patience with me when I dawdled upon our
initial escape. She still had bog monster coating her and was furious. She wasn't exactly what I would call a fun person to be
around on a normal day ... and this was pretty far from a
normal day.

Marissa had cornered our boss Rooster Tremaine and Gunner at
the bar when I strolled through the door. They were doing their best
to keep from touching her because of the green goo coating her from
head to toe. She gestured wildly and cast me an evil glare as I greeted
the room.

"I want something done about it," she sneered as the talking
ceased. Only members of our group were in the bar. That was hardly

surprising given the fact that it was a weekday and Hawthorne Hollow wasn't exactly a hotbed of activity.

"Good evening, all," I drawled, smiling brightly. "What were you all talking about?"

Gunner shifted on his stool so his back was against the bar and he faced me. He took a long pull from his beer and grinned. "Oddly enough, we were talking about you."

"I thought that was your perpetual state these days."

His grin only widened. "Pretty much."

"Oh, shoot me now," Marissa groused as she rolled her eyes. The goo was turning an odd blue color as it dried, which made her look like a demented Smurf. "Why don't you two just mount each other and get it over with?" Her agitation was on full display, and while she usually enjoyed pointing it at me, Gunner was almost always spared. Not today, though.

"I've considered it," Gunner said dryly, unruffled. "But my father is the chief of police and he's always looking for a reason to mess with me. I don't really fancy having a public indecency charge on my record — though I'm not ruling it out."

"Your wit is astounding," Marissa snapped.

Gunner's smile never faltered. "Believe it or not, you're hardly the first person to tell me that." He shifted his eyes to me. "I hear you blew up a troll. That sounds ... neat."

"Yes, and I'm anxious to hear about it," Rooster enthused. "I've never seen a troll."

"It wasn't a troll," I countered, giving Marissa a wide berth as I took the stool next to Gunner and greeted the bartender, Whistler, with a happy smile. I nodded at his silent question and he grabbed me a beer from the cooler. "It was something else."

"Um ... it was a troll." Marissa's tone was disdainful. "I think I would know because ... um ... look at my outfit. It's ruined because you decided you just had to blow up the troll instead of, I don't know, stabbing it or something."

She was a total trip and she made me smile. "You don't know the outfit is ruined," I countered, opting to see if I could push her further

... just for kicks and giggles of course. "A little Tide and a dash of bleach and that shirt might be right back to normal."

"I doubt it," Bonnie Jenkins, a fellow Spells Angels co-worker, said from a nearby table where she was playing solitaire. Her attention appeared to be focused squarely on the cards, but I knew better. She was clearly monitoring the conversation, mostly because Marissa tended to bother the entire group with her whining. "I'm pretty sure there are entrails permanently fused to the hem on the side over here. I don't think bleach will fix that."

"Oh. Ugh!" Marissa was beside herself. "I want some punishment here, Rooster." She was bordering on screechy. "For once, I want you to actually put your foot down and handle this situation. She's out of control."

There was no doubt who Marissa was referring to. I, however, couldn't muster the energy to care. I was over her ... although I remained bothered by the events of the evening. Oddly enough, what happened with the bog monster was low on the list of things perplexing me.

"I want to get back to the monster," Whistler countered.

"That's what I just suggested," Marissa snapped.

The curmudgeonly bartender ignored her and remained focused on me. "If it wasn't a troll, then what was it?"

That was a good question. "I think it might've been a mutated leprechaun, but I'm not sure."

Gunner's eyebrows shot up his forehead. "A leprechaun?"

"Yeah. It had the same size body ... and was green. It was off, though. It might've been something else entirely. I think there was some lizard in it, like a chameleon or something. It was naturally small but changed its appearance at the end."

"It changed appearance?" Rooster looked intrigued. "How did it manage that?"

I shrugged, unsure. "Chameleons can change color. This thing changed its appearance. I didn't waste much time asking questions. I just reacted ... and that was it."

"Yes, she reacted by blowing it up," Marissa drawled. "If you'll notice, she blew it up in such a way that I got coated in dead troll and she's pristine. I very much doubt that was an accident."

"I didn't do it on purpose," I protested, finally reacting. "It really was an accident. I had no way of knowing that he would blow up that way. It was only at the last second that I realized and threw up a shield spell ... but I kind of forgot to cover you."

The way Gunner pressed his lips together told me he was trying to hold it together. He was a master at covering his emotions, which made me think he really didn't care if Marissa saw his mirth.

"This is not funny," Marissa hissed, pinning him with a dark look. "I know you're all ... lusty ... where she's concerned, but this is a real issue. I deserve a little respect."

"Lusty?" Gunner finally shifted his eyes from me and focused on Marissa. "I don't believe that word has ever been used to describe me. Horny? Absolutely. My grandmother said I was a horny little devil when I was a kid because I had so many girls hanging around the house. Lusty, though, that's a new one. I think I like it." He winked at me as I rolled my eyes.

"You just had to drop in the part about all the girls hanging around your house, didn't you?" I challenged. "Just for the record, that's a bit annoying. Nobody likes a braggart."

Whistler raised his hand. "I happen to love a braggart ... especially when he's got sexy stories practically coming out of his ears like Gunner. You have to understand that the boy is something of a legend in these parts."

Instead of puffing out his chest and reacting like a normal man might have, Gunner's cheeks flooded with color. "That's a bit of an exaggeration," he reassured me quickly. "I mean ... that's not exactly true. I dated a few girls as a teenager. I'm hardly a legend."

"Oh, now he turns modest," Whistler intoned.

"Shut up." Gunner jabbed a finger in the older bartender's direction. "You're going to get me in trouble. Women don't like it when other females are mentioned in conjunction with their men. It creates static."

Whistler's expression was blank. "Says who?"

"Says anyone who has ever tried to keep a woman happy."

For some reason, the way he phrased his response made me smile. "Is that what you're doing?" I teased. "Are you trying to make me happy?"

"Every moment of every day."

When I risked a glance back at him, I found he was sober ... and seemingly intense. "Okay." I patted his wrist to ease the moment. "I was just messing around. I don't really care about all the teenage girls who panted after you back in the day. You've got one of those faces. I already figured that was the case."

"And besides, she's snagged you now and it's obvious you're smitten," Bonnie added, still playing with her cards. "You're not exactly setting the female population of Hawthorne Hollow's hormones on fire like you did back in the day. It's fine. Scout isn't the insecure sort."

To my surprise, Gunner frowned. "Um ... I could totally set hormones on fire if I wanted."

His reaction made me snort. "I think you hurt his feelings, Bonnie."

She merely shrugged. "Live and learn."

Thankfully the front door opened at this point, drawing everyone's attention. Ruthie "Raisin" Morton practically flew into the room, her curly hair — which she called red but looked more purple to me — was standing on end and her eyes were so wide I thought they might pop out of her head.

"Guess what?" She was sparkly as her gaze bounced between faces.

"Um ... I think I'm going to guess that you're not supposed to be here," Rooster supplied. He was calm and yet stern at the same time. Raisin was a regular fixture with our group, but she was not allowed at the bar after dark. She knew it, and more importantly, we all knew it. He was about to go big brother on her, and I very much doubted it would be pretty.

Ruthie offered up a haphazard hand wave. She'd never been one to follow rules and apparently she had no intention of starting today. "You guys are the only ones here. It's not as if somebody is going to get arrested or anything. Chill out."

Rooster worked his jaw. He was genuinely fond of Raisin, to the point he'd painted himself as something of a surrogate father for her. He tried to ride a fine line of disciplinarian and encouraging force. He didn't always straddle it in the best manner. "We've talked about this," he stressed.

"We have," she agreed, matter of fact. "You've talked and I've listened. I know I'm not supposed to be here after dark, that Whistler could get in trouble with the police because I'm underage. The thing is, the police in this town don't care about me. Also, Chief Stratton won't give me grief because Gunner can talk him out of writing up one of those ticket things for Whistler. We're totally fine."

Gunner's relationship with his father wasn't always easy. They had an interesting dynamic, one that often resulted in arguments ... and a bit of petulance on Gunner's part. I had no doubt the elder Stratton loved his son. He wasn't great at showing it, though, and Gunner was bitter about certain aspects of his childhood. What they really needed was family therapy, though the odds of that happening were slim.

"First, it's not Gunner's job to smooth things over with his father," Rooster countered. He'd adopted his "I'm the boss and you have to listen to me whether you like it or not" face and it always made me laugh to see it, because it seemed out of place. "You need to follow the rules instead of assuming Gunner will fix things if you don't."

Raisin made a protesting sound. "But it's not even a big deal," she persisted, refusing to let it go. "It's not as if I'm drinking. In fact, I'm not here to do anything bad ... like ask about monsters or magic or anything either." Her eyes momentarily flicked to Marissa. "But I am kind of curious about what happened to her."

Marissa shot her a warning look. "Don't worry about it," she growled. "It's none of your concern."

"If you say so." Raisin shrugged and turned back to Rooster. She'd adopted what I liked to think of as her "puppy dog" face and she was pulling out all the stops to get Rooster to line up with her way of thinking. "I'm just here to remind you that my play is coming up. It's right around the corner, in fact. We're deep in rehearsals now. You guys bought tickets weeks ago ... opening night is actually in a few days and I thought I should maybe remind you that it's going to be a really cool night."

Ah, well, that explained it. Ever since Raisin had been cast in the school play, she'd turned into something of a nervous wreck. She was excited ... and afraid ... and giddy depending on the day. The thing she wanted most was for us to be there. Her grandmother would be in the first row, of course, but other than that Raisin had nobody in her corner. She needed us.

"We'll be there," I reassured her with a firm smile, a flash of light catching my eye through the window. I grabbed my beer and slid off the stool, making sure I didn't touch Marissa as I moved around her on my way to the window.

"I know you said you would be there," Raisin hedged. "I just wanted to make sure you didn't forget or anything. I mean ... I know you guys have other stuff going on, like whatever is all over Marissa."

Marissa growled. "Oh, just keep bringing it up. I love talking about it ... especially since it's clear Scout isn't going to be punished for what she did."

"Why would Scout be punished?" Gunner challenged. "She killed the monster, saved the day, and you're perfectly fine."

"There are entrails in my hair," Marissa snapped.

"Yes, but once you shower it won't be a big deal," Gunner persisted. "I'm getting sick of you going after Scout every time a takedown doesn't go the way you think it will. She's doing the job and you're complaining. That's the real travesty here."

"Oh, puh-leez." I wasn't facing Marissa so I couldn't see her eye roll, but I could picture it in my mind's eye and it would've made me laugh if my attention hadn't been directed at something else.

"What do you see?" Bonnie asked from behind me. She'd abandoned her game and joined me at the window.

"It's storming," I replied at the exact moment a terrific bolt of lightning flashed through the window. It was quickly followed by a rumble of thunder strong enough to shake the ground.

"What's going on?" Raisin asked, her voice quaking. Her excitement about the play had quickly diminished in the face of the storm.

"It's okay," Rooster reassured her, easily sliding back into protective mode. Sure, Raisin wasn't supposed to be here, but it was hardly the first time she'd broken the rules. She wasn't hanging out at a bar because she wanted to get drunk. She was here because she loved and needed us ... and it was our job to reassure her that things were going to be okay. That's what Rooster was doing now as he slid his arm around her shoulders in a reassuring manner. "It's just a storm."

"I didn't realize it was supposed to storm," Gunner noted as he moved to my other side, his eyes transfixed on the window. The lightning show was truly impressive, seemingly one flash after the other, with barely a twenty-second break between ... sometimes less. "I watched the forecast this morning and it didn't mention a storm."

Whistler snorted disdainfully. "Yeah, being a meteorologist must be the best job in the world. It's the only career where you can be wrong ninety percent of the time and nobody calls you on it."

Rooster joined in on the meteorologist hate as he kept Raisin anchored to his side. I tuned them out and focused on the storm.

"What are you thinking?" Gunner asked, his voice low. He looked concerned.

"What makes you believe I'm thinking anything?" I challenged. In truth, I didn't have an answer for him. I wasn't really thinking anything ... and yet I was perturbed all the same.

"I know you," he replied simply. "You've got that look you get."

That didn't sound complimentary. "You know me, huh?" I did my best to turn my expression flirty. "What am I thinking now?"

"That you can distract me with sexy talk to get me to drop this," he replied without hesitation, causing my smile to slip. "Seriously, what's wrong?"

I shrugged. "I don't know. I just have a weird feeling."

"Do you think it has something to do with the bog monster?"

I tilted my head, considering, and then shook it. "No. I don't know that it has anything to do with anything. I just ... have a feeling."

"Is it a good feeling? I like when you're feeling good." Now he was the one with the flirty smile.

"I don't know." I held out my hands. "It's just a feeling right now."

He studied my face for a moment and then nodded. "Well, I guess it's good I brought my truck. We can load up your bike and ride home in relative safety. We can drop Raisin off on the way and lecture her again about hanging out in bars." He raised his voice for the last part, which caused Raisin to scowl and Rooster to snicker.

"That's a fine idea," our boss enthused. "Sounds like a perfect end to a perfect evening."

I wasn't sure I agreed with the "perfect" part, but I didn't exactly have anything to complain about. Well, at least not yet.

THREE

*G*unner gave Raisin the talk on the drive to her house. She pouted for the entire ride, which caused me to have to hide my smile. It wasn't that he broke her down as much as he reminded her that Whistler could get in real trouble if the wrong people figured out that Raisin was at the bar. She didn't like the lecture, but she nodded.

Then he built her right back up.

"We're really looking forward to your play," he said when we were idling in front of her house.

"Really?" Her eyes sparkled. "I mean ... you're not just saying that?"

I vehemently shook my head. "Absolutely not. There's nothing I like more than good theater."

She shot me a sidelong look. "Name one play you've ever been to."

"*Hamilton. Wicked. The Cursed Child.*"

Her eyes went wide. "Seriously?"

I nodded. "You guys don't have much theater, but there's plenty in Detroit. I've been to the Fox Theatre and the Fisher many times."

"That is so cool."

I considered suggesting a trip south when we could manage it to take her to a show, but I held my tongue. Before getting her hopes up I had to clear it with her grandmother and get the time off. The invitation would have to wait until I had calendars all lined up. "I think you're going to be the star of your play," I assured her. "We're all going as a group and you'll have a huge cheering section."

"Probably the biggest cheering section," Gunner agreed.

"Not the biggest." Raisin made a face. "Shiloh Walker has, like, four brothers and sisters and a bunch of cousins and uncles. They'll all be there for her."

"Yes, but you have people going who aren't required to because of blood," I reminded her. "Your cheering section is better."

She brightened immediately. "Yeah. There is that."

Gunner waited until she was in the house to put his truck in drive. "Have you really been to a lot of theater productions?" he asked as he pulled onto the highway.

I nodded. "I'm more than just a pretty face."

He grinned as he reached over and collected my hand. "I guess so. You're definitely layered."

"Just wait until you learn about my penchant for animals-eating-people movies."

"Oh, yeah?"

"I can't get enough of them."

"You're multifaceted weird."

"Absolutely."

THE RAIN DISSIPATED DURING THE NIGHT and the morning air smelled fresh when I woke the next day. Gunner was still passed out, dead to the world, so I took the opportunity to have my coffee on the front porch. Merlin tried to join me, but I was afraid he would wander into the woods and be attacked by a bigger predator — he was still a kitten after all — so I latched the screen. He proceeded to howl and throw himself at the door to force my hand.

I pretended I didn't notice.

"Good morning," Gunner murmured when he joined me thirty minutes later. He was shirtless, his hair mussed, and he looked incredibly appetizing. His morning stubble was always a turn on, though I had no idea why. It baffled me. He pressed a kiss to my forehead and then sat in the chair next to mine. "Why are you up so early?"

That was a good question. I didn't have an answer. "I don't know. Just woke up early."

He arched an eyebrow. "Nightmares?"

"No." I shook my head. My dreams had been tumultuous, but I wouldn't call them nightmares. "Just ... restless."

He studied me for a long moment, took a sip of his coffee, and then shifted before finally speaking. "You know, this relationship thing works best when we talk to one another. I know neither of us are exactly experts, but it might be worth a shot."

I heaved out a sigh. I knew what he was doing, and I wouldn't necessarily disagree. That didn't mean I was in the mood for a heavy discussion. "I just feel like something is going to happen," I said finally.

"Between us? If you get your cute little behind back inside I can guarantee something happens."

He made me laugh, which was probably his goal. "I think I'll stick with my coffee for now." I shot him a pointed look. "And, no, I wasn't talking about us. I think things between us seem solid."

"They do. That's what worries me. I'm not sure you do 'solid.'"

That might've been true in the past. But now, well ... I was comfortable. It was a weird feeling for me. "I'm pretty happy for now. If things change, you'll be the first to know."

"Fair enough." He sipped his coffee again. "You were jacked up during the storm some last night. Does this have something to do with that?"

I opened my mouth to answer, uncertain, and then shrugged. "It's just a feeling I have. I don't know how to explain it."

"Are you afraid of storms?"

I shot him a withering look. "Um ... I blew up a bog monster last night. I'm pretty sure that storms are low on my list of things to worry about. Well, except for tornados. I'm not a big fan of storms that can do lasting damage."

"I agree with you there." He pursed his lips. "I trust your feelings.

You're one of the most intuitive people I've ever met. If you think something bad is about to happen, I have to think you know what you're talking about."

"Yeah, well ... that's just it. There's nothing to point us in a direction. I'm simply uneasy."

"Well ... ." Whatever he was going to say died on his lips when his cell phone rang. He grumbled as he got to his feet and headed inside to retrieve it. He'd already answered and was talking when he rejoined me. "Are you sure?" He sounded annoyed as he listened. "No, Dad, I'm not suggesting you don't know what a murder looks like. I was asking about the paranormal aspects."

I sat up straighter, the hair on the back of my neck rising. Could this be the start of it? Was this part of the reason I couldn't shake the sense of dread that had been threatening to swallow me whole for the past ten hours?

"Fine." Gunner blew out a sigh. "We need to shower. We'll meet you in town in an hour." He didn't disconnect. Instead he waited. "Oh, don't be a pain," he said after a moment. "I don't care if you want to make fun of us for being domestic. I'm not sixteen. That won't work on me." More silence. "Oh, whatever. You're the worst father ever."

He ended the call and turned his attention to me. "There's a body downtown."

I'd already ascertained that. "I take it we're heading to town."

"Yeah. I think we're needed."

"Then I guess we should hit the shower."

Gunner let loose an annoyed sigh. "And there went my plans to get you back into bed."

Despite the serious turn the conversation had taken, I was amused. "It's still early. You might get your wish by the end of the day."

"There's something to look forward to."

GRAHAM STRATTON WAS A BULL OF A man. Looking at him was like looking at Gunner in thirty years. I wasn't unhappy with the image. Gunner was named after his father but refused to go by the moniker. In fact, he was distinctly uncomfortable with it. It always amused me when Graham poked his son by using the name ... or a variation of it.

"Hello, Junior," he called out as we approached the scene behind the library. The area had been taped off and he was the only one standing nearby.

Gunner scowled. "Do you have to call me that?"

"Yes. It irritates you."

"And that's the only reason you do it, right?"

"Pretty much."

"You suck." Gunner growled and slid his eyes to me as I struggled not to smile. "I know you're enjoying this. Don't bother denying it."

I pretended I didn't hear him and focused on Graham. "What have you got, Chief?"

Graham's eyes lit with amusement as he looked me over. Unlike his son, his relationship with me was somehow warmer ... and I was still trying to figure out why. He seemed to like me, which ran counter to everything I'd heard about him. Gunner told me his father would never approve of anything he did, yet Graham appeared to like his son's girlfriend. The whole thing was a riddle.

"Good morning, Scout." He looked me up and down. "You look lovely this morning."

I was dressed in my usual jeans and T-shirt, so I knew he was throwing out the compliment simply to rankle Gunner. I decided not to get involved in that aspect of their relationship. "Thank you. What's with the dead girl?" I inclined my head toward the body on the ground. A sheet covered it, but there could be no confusion as to what was underneath.

Graham's smile faded. "Honey Martelle."

Gunner shifted. "You're kidding."

Obviously he knew our victim. "Are you telling me this woman's real name was Honey?" I was appalled at the thought. "Who would name their kid that?"

"I don't know, *Scout*." Graham pinned me with a look. "Sometimes people name their kids weird things."

I didn't look away. "My parents didn't name me Scout. A fire-fighter did, after a character in his favorite book. I have no idea what my real name is."

He shifted from one foot to the other, uncomfortable. "Actually, I believe I already knew that. I didn't mean to bring it up again."

"Yes, because I'm an abandoned child and I have tender feelings," I drawled. "You must be very careful not to upset me."

He rolled his eyes. "You're a real piece of work."

I couldn't argue with that. Still, he'd called us down here for a reason. "Why do you need us? I'm gathering this isn't a run-of-the-mill murder."

"Not even close." Graham was grim as he knelt next to the body. He took a moment to look around to make sure we hadn't garnered any looky-loos and then peeled back the sheet from the head and neck. "Does this look normal to you?"

The question didn't require an answer. I was horrified by what I saw, but I kept my expression neutral. Honey — and no matter what he said, that was a stupid name — didn't have a throat. It appeared to have been completely ravaged. There was blood everywhere, including all over her shirt ... and her green eyes were open and sightless.

"Oh, geez." Gunner looked pained. "I can't ... what did this?"

"Why do you think I called you?" Graham challenged. "This is your realm of expertise. I'm just a lowly cop."

"I don't know what did this," Gunner countered. "Unless ... do you think this has something to do with your bog monster?"

When I glanced at him, I found him watching me with keen eyes. I knew what he was really asking. Was this why I'd been so keyed up? It seemed a likely option.

"I don't see how the bog monster could've done this," I replied. "I mean ... I blew him up. You saw Marissa. There's no coming back from that."

"Maybe there was more than one," Gunner suggested. "Maybe the second one saw you take out the first and decided to come to town to exact some revenge."

That was entirely possible, but it didn't feel right. "The people who reported the bog monster said he was stealing food and biting legs when people tried to swim. They didn't mention anything about ripping out throats."

"He could've upped the ante because he was enraged."

"I guess." I rolled my neck, unconvinced. "I don't think we're dealing with a bog monster."

Graham held up his hand to silence us. "Do I even want to know what the two of you are talking about?"

"Probably not," I replied. "It doesn't matter anyway. No backwoods creature that only attacks people away from the lights of the town did this. We're dealing with something else."

"What?" Gunner asked. "You were upset this morning. Is it because of this?"

"It's not as if I knew about this," I shot back. "If you're insinuating I did, you're wrong."

He held up his hands. "I'm not trying to pick a fight with you. I'm not blaming you. I'm trying to figure this out."

"Geez, I see you two need to work on your interpersonal skills," Graham muttered.

I would've snapped at him, but he wasn't wrong.

"Leave her alone," Gunner growled.

"Actually, that was a dig at you, son."

"Then ... leave me alone."

I ignored the father-son sniping and moved closer to the body, dropping to a crouch for a better look. "When is the medical examiner coming?" I asked when there was a lull in the insults.

"He's running behind," Graham replied. "It's going to be a good two hours, and since all of my officers are either patrolling or off, that means I'm stuck here babysitting a corpse."

"Oh, poor you," Gunner drawled. "How will you survive?"

"I could put you on the ground next to her," Graham shot back. "I mean ... you two used to date and all. Maybe it will make you nostalgic for old times."

I sensed rather than saw Gunner's head snap in my direction. I pretended not to have heard the comment. It's not as if I didn't know Gunner had a past. Sure, I could've gone without knowing that he dated a woman named Honey, but that was hardly high on our list of concerns.

"Why did you have to bring that up?" Gunner hissed. "I mean ... are you trying to hurt Scout?"

"Of course not," Graham shot back. "I was trying to annoy you."

"Well, good job." Gunner shot his father a sarcastic thumbs-up as I waved my hand over the wound and unleashed a bit of magic.

Graham snapped his head in my direction when he realized what I was doing. "Don't mess with the body!"

"I'm not messing with the body," I reassured him. "I'm trying to see under the blood. I'll put it back."

"Put it back?" He furrowed his brow, confused. Then, as the spell began to take hold, his eyes widened. The blood that had been there moments ago disappeared, leaving behind a clear view of what was left of poor Honey's neck.

"What is that?" Gunner asked, squinting as he tried to make out the remnants of what used to be unmarred skin and bone. "Are those ... teeth marks?"

I nodded, lifting my phone so I could take a photo before dropping the magic and returning the blood to where it had previously rested. "Vampires," I said succinctly. "We're dealing with vampires."

Graham was all business. "How can you be sure? I mean ... the neck thing would seem to be a giveaway, but I know other creatures that kill by ripping out throats."

"The two puncture wounds are distinct," I replied. "She was fed on before being drained."

"Will she turn?"

I hesitated before answering. "I don't think so," I said finally. "I don't see any blood around her lips. She would have to feed on the vampire to turn. I guess it's a possibility, but I don't think that's what we're dealing with."

"Should I stake her just in case?"

I shrugged. "I don't know. Do you want to stake her? I might wait

36

to see if she rises, because she might be able to describe her assailant. Then we would know who we're looking for. I don't want to tell you how to do your job or anything, though."

He scowled. "You know, the more time you spend with my son the less cute you become."

"Oh, that's not true," Gunner countered. "I think you're adorable when you irritate my father."

I was in no mood for their shenanigans. I had other things to worry about. "If it's a lone vampire, he should be easy to dispatch," I mused, mostly to myself. "If it's a nest, though ... ."

"Have you dealt with many nests?" Graham asked, his eyes somber.

I nodded. "There are a lot of abandoned buildings in Detroit. They make for great nest locations ... for vampires and wraiths. I've wiped out a few nests in my time. The biggest was sixty vampires."

Gunner was taken aback. "Are you serious? We rarely see them here. This is more shifter territory."

"Which is why most vampires would want to stay away." I grunted as I stood, something occurring to me. "Tell me about the house on the hill."

Gunner and Graham adopted twin looks of confusion, their eyebrows drawing together as their foreheads wrinkled.

"What house on the hill?" Gunner asked finally.

"The one out by the swamp. It's on a bluff. Marissa said it was abandoned, but last night I could swear someone was near our bikes while we were gone, and I felt as if someone was watching me. I brushed it off as nerves after my fight with the bog monster, but what if it's something else?"

Gunner tilted his head, considering. "I know the house you're talking about. As for history, I don't know it. It's been empty for as long as I can remember."

Graham volunteered, "I can't remember the family's name, but I can look it up."

I nodded encouragingly. "Do that. While you're at it, see if the deed has changed hands recently. I swear someone is up there."

"That should be easy enough." Graham folded his arms over his chest. "What are you going to do?"

I offered him a blinding smile. "Why, break into the house, of course. I'm pretty sure something evil is up there. If not vampires, it might be something else that needs to be taken down. It's worth a look."

"You can't just tell a police officer that you're going to break into a house," Graham complained bitterly.

"I just did and I seem to have survived," I noted, earning a wink from Gunner, who was back to enjoying himself. "It's abandoned, right? I'm technically not breaking and entering if nobody lives there."

"Yeah, that's not how it works."

"Let's pretend it is ... at least for today."

"Whatever. My son has definitely been a bad influence on you."

"I'll take that as a compliment."

FOUR

*G*unner didn't even bother putting up a fight about our destination. Instead, he took the lead when we rode out to the house. He knew where the driveway was, and we parked directly in front of the rundown manor and removed our helmets.

"This place doesn't look abandoned," Gunner said as he eased off his bike, his eyes trained on the upstairs windows, which consisted of intact stained glass. "Those windows weren't there as recently as a few months ago."

I hadn't seen the stained glass windows the previous evening. It was dark and I was too far away. Up close, though, they were interesting ... and a bit disturbing.

"That's a pentagram." I pointed toward the window in the nearest turret. "Why would anyone want to advertise like that?" When he didn't immediately respond, I turned in his direction and found him watching me with an unreadable expression. "What?"

He shook his head and merely smiled. "I didn't say anything."

"You're thinking something ... and I'm guessing it's not complimentary."

"That's where you're wrong." He folded his arms over his chest, looking smug. "I was just thinking you're the only person I know who would've picked that pentagram out of the pattern. I mean ... I see it, but only after you pointed it out. Not everyone seems to think penta-grams are advertising either."

Oh, that was just ridiculous. "Um ... I'm sorry, but in what world is window pentagrams not advertising?"

"You don't know that it's a purposeful symbol. It could be an acci-dent, something that merely popped out of a different design."

"Yeah, because that's likely in a paranormal vortex."

His forehead wrinkled. "A what?"

"A paranormal vortex," I repeated.

"I don't know what that is."

"It's this place." I didn't see any reason to keep the information from him. Frankly, I didn't understand how he hadn't figured it out. "This entire area hums with energy. It's the reason paranormals are drawn here. How can you not know that?"

"Because I don't think it's really a thing."

"Uh-huh." He was cute but there were times I worried he was slow. Okay, not really, but he didn't always catch on straight away when it came to magic. Of course, he'd grown up here. Sometimes the hardest things to see are the ones right in front of your face. "I guess if you don't believe that means it can't possibly be true."

"I didn't say that. I've simply never heard of it. I want you to explain it to me."

"It's a magical convergence." I shifted my eyes back to the window. I didn't see any movement, but that didn't necessarily mean anything. "Hawthorne Hollow is one. The very land we're standing on is magi-cal. The rivers and waterways are flush with power. I'm sure there are magical caves around here to boot, but I haven't had time to go on a search yet.

"Paranormal vortexes are rare," I continued. "This is the only one I'm aware of in Michigan, but I know that Salem is one. New Orleans is another. There's a place in Kentucky, too, and northern California. I guarantee there are other places overseas, like Stonehenge."

"You think Stonehenge is a paranormal vortex?"

I didn't like his tone. It was clear he was having fun with me. I could take the teasing, but I wasn't in the mood for it today. "I've never been there, but it's totally on my bucket list. Haven't you ever asked yourself why those stones were erected the way they were? And how?"

"I haven't really thought about it."

"It's the magic. It draws believers. It also draws other creatures. There are magical places in the world that can do that."

"And you're saying Hawthorne Hollow is one of them."

I nodded. "I don't know why ... or even how, but this is definitely a paranormal vortex."

"Well ... that's interesting."

His tone was enough to make me grind my teeth. "I don't need the mocking," I shot back. "You don't have to believe me, but a modicum of respect would be nice."

He balked. "Hey, I respect you more than any other person. You've seen the way I am with my father. I treat you ten times better than him."

"I'm assuming the sex has something to do with that," I said dryly.

"Oh, no. Don't go there." He wagged a finger. "You're more than just sex to me. You're endless sarcasm, too."

I didn't want to encourage him, but I couldn't stop from laughing. "Good to know. I ... ." The sound of a door shutting jerked me right out of the verbal foreplay and back to the present. When I stared at the house, I couldn't see anybody. What was a walkway at one time was completely overgrown. The hedges had lost all shape. The only reason to believe anyone was nearby was the new windows.

And then it happened.

"Can I help you?"

I heard the voice before I saw the face. It was a tad nasal, altogether whiny really. I didn't see an actual person and braced myself to take on an invisible enemy ... and then I saw a tuft of hair that just happened to be on an ear.

"What the ... ?" Gunner, the macho type, extended an arm to push me behind him as the very top of a head became visible over the bushes. "Get back."

"Have you ever considered that you should get back? I mean ... no offense, because I know you're big and tough, but I'm totally more powerful than you."

He slowly slid his eyes to me, apparently forgetting about the terror heading in our direction. "Oh, really?"

I nodded. "Yeah. I can show you later if you want."

"If it involves you getting naked and pretending to be a superhero, I'm all for it."

His response took me by surprise. "I ... wait. I'm not dressing up like a sexy Wonder Woman just so you can be kinky."

"Your loss. Now ... *shh*." He pressed his finger to his lips and turned back to the creature that was moving to intercept us. Once free of the bushes, it wasn't a monster we faced.

"Oh, it's a little person," Gunner said a little louder than would've been considered polite. He dropped his pugilistic stance and grinned as the short man headed in our direction.

"I don't think you're supposed to say 'little person,'" I argued as I continued to watch the interloper with mistrust. Unlike Gunner, I wasn't a proponent of the "size matters" club. I'd seen tiny little demons rip off limbs in five seconds flat while the big ones simply stood there and looked stupid. I wasn't ruling out a dangerous encounter, though I was mildly mesmerized by the way the sun glinted off our new friend's bald head.

"Oh, really, smarty?" Gunner challenged. "If I'm not supposed to say 'little person,' what am I supposed to say?"

"I believe it's polite not to comment at all," the newcomer said, pulling up short as his gaze bounced between us. "May I help you?"

He wore a suit, though I figured it had to have come from the children's section of a department store. It was a little worn around the edges and had patches at the elbows. Oddly enough, it looked familiar, but I couldn't place where I thought I'd seen it before.

Gunner cleared his throat. "I apologize for trespassing and stuff, but ... um ... we thought we saw someone hanging out here, and since the house is abandoned, we wanted to check it out. Could you tell us why you're living in an abandoned house?"

It seemed a perfectly reasonable question, but there was an absurdity about it that caused me to bite the inside of my cheek to keep my laughter in check. For his part, the little guy didn't look amused.

"First, this is not an abandoned house," he started, adopting an air of superiority that would've been hard to carry off even if he was a foot taller. "My mistress owns this house."

"Your mistress?" I cocked an eyebrow. "Does that mean you're cheating on your wife? If so, I have to say, I don't generally get this whole philandering thing. If you want to sleep with someone else, you should do your wife the honor of getting divorced."

The look he shot me was withering. "She's not my mistress. She's my mistress."

I glanced at Gunner. "Did he just explain something?"

The tiny man let out a sigh that fluttered his lips. "Perhaps we should start over again," he suggested. "My name is Bixby. I'm the man of the house, but only in the sense that I'm running it for my mistress — my employer, not my paramour."

"Oh." Realization washed over me. That made a lot more sense. "I get it now."

Bixby didn't look as if he cared whether or not I understood. "Now, why don't you introduce yourselves or I'll assume you're idiotic robbers and cut you off at the kneecaps."

Oh, that was kind of cute. He actually believed he was capable of that. "I'm Scout Randall." I didn't extend my hand but did offer up a weak smile. "This is Gunner Stratton. We're local."

"How lovely for you," Bixby drawled. "I assume you're dating given the witty repartee I overheard from the house. I hope you're not related in some fashion. Given the way you act, I can't rule it out."

It took me a moment to unravel what he was saying. "Did you just insinuate ... ?"

Gunner squeezed my wrist to cut me off. "So, how long has your mistress owned this house?" He was focused on getting information, which was important, but I couldn't overlook the incest remark. Bixby might've been tiny, but he had a sharp tongue ... and I kind of wanted to strangle him with it.

"It's a recent acquisition," Bixby replied primly.

There was something about him that seemed so familiar ... and then I remembered. "Hey, I know you."

Gunner couldn't hide his surprise. "You know him? Please don't say he's an ex-boyfriend."

I didn't respond to the ludicrous assertion, instead focusing on Bixby. "You hid in the bushes and tried to attack me when I was a teenager." As far as accusations go, it was a strong one.

Bixby was taken aback. "I most certainly did not."

"You did. I remember you. I was walking to the group home. I remember I was worrying at the time about what I was going to do. I was due to age out of the system in a few weeks and I was terrified what that would mean. It's not as if I ever had a lot of help but I was used to a roof over my head. I was pretty certain I was going to be homeless."

Gunner slid me a sidelong look. "Were you?"

"Not really."

"Not really?" He made a face. "What is that supposed to mean?"

"It means not really," I shot back. "My group home leader allowed me to stay for a few months until I got a job and wasn't so afraid. He was a good guy."

"So ... you weren't homeless."

"Not then, no."

"But you were homeless at one point?" He seemed fixated on the topic.

I shot him an incredulous look. "Can we talk about that later? This guy was loitering in the bushes when I was a kid. I sensed him and ... ." I trailed off when I remembered the rest of the story. "There was a guy with you. He was dressed all in black. You were trying to procure me for him."

Gunner's eyes went wide. "Procure you? Do I even want to know what that means?"

"Probably not." My mind was a jumbled mess and when I pinned Bixby with my scariest look he didn't so much as avert his gaze for a split second.

"I believe you have me confused with somebody else," Bixby said.

"Um, no."

"I think I would remember hiding in the bushes. It's something I don't do."

"Oh, you remember." I narrowed my eyes. "Do you work for a vampire?"

Gunner's mouth dropped open and he let loose a hoarse chuckle. "Oh, my. You'll have to excuse my girlfriend. She likes messing with people ... and we just watched a vampire movie last night. It must've got the creative juices flowing." He slipped his arm around my waist and shot me a pointed look. "Apologize to the nice man for saying he hid in the bushes and tried to jump you."

There was absolutely no way that was going to happen. "Yeah, I'm good." I pulled away from him and snapped my eyes to the front of the house when I heard the door shut a second time. The individual who glided out this go-around was much taller than Bixby. It was also a woman.

"Oh, it looks as though we have visitors." The woman was blonde, a good two inches taller than me, and dressed in an expensive ensemble that probably cost more than a year's rent at my first apartment. She graced us with a sunny smile as she padded down the walkway in fuzzy high heels that boggled the mind because they were so tall. "Hello. I love meeting new people."

She said it with such enthusiasm that I was instantly suspicious. What? Nobody loves new people.

Gunner took control of the conversation before I could stick my foot in my mouth again. "Yes. We just met your ... man. Um ... I'm Gunner Stratton." He went through the motions to introduce us a second time as I openly glared at Bixby. For his part, he steadfastly kept his eyes a good two feet in front of me, so no matter how I shifted I couldn't catch his gaze. The little monster was playing games with me and I didn't like it.

"I'm Melody Summers." She offered Gunner an intimate smile as she shook his hand. She was practically purring when they touched. "I'm new to the area."

"Um ... hi." Gunner seemed caught off guard at the way she greeted him and lost his sense of conversational direction.

I rolled my eyes at the exchange. Melody was pretty, ridiculously so, but that didn't mean she wasn't employing a freaky pervert. "And I'm Scout Randall." I slapped Gunner's hand away and placed mine in her hand. "I'm so happy to meet you."

"Scout?" Melody's smile was fluid when it switched to me. "That's ... an interesting name. Were your parents literary fans?"

"I honestly have no idea." I dropped the handshake and flicked my eyes back to Bixby. "Did you know your butler — or whatever he is — used to hide in bushes and try to entice female teenagers about ten years ago?"

Gunner choked on a nervous laugh as Melody furrowed her brow.

"Excuse me?" Melody was clearly caught off guard. The question was enough to have Bixby making eye contact, though.

"She's mistaken me for someone else, mistress," he reassured his boss. "I did no such thing."

"Oh, you did." I was annoyed with his reaction. "You were with a dark guy and loitering in the bushes just north of Detroit. He gave you a lecture when you failed ... and tried to be witty with me. Do you really think I don't remember you?"

Bixby let loose a heavy sigh. "I don't know what to tell you, miss. We've never met."

My temper was on full boil now. "Are you actually telling me you went after so many girls ten years ago that you can't remember me?"

"I'm telling you that you've mistaken me for somebody else."

"I have not."

Melody cleared her throat to get my attention. "Um, Scout, correct?" She had a conciliatory smile on her face.

"I just told you my name, like, thirty seconds ago. You were like, 'Oh, your parents were literary fans' and everything."

Melody's smile never wavered. "Right. Well, I think I'm going to talk to you now." She turned her full attention to Gunner. "Are you familiar with the area? I just inherited the house from an uncle I didn't even know was still alive because he fell out of touch with the rest of the family decades ago. I fell in love with the place despite the state of disrepair. I plan to restore it to its former glory ... although I think that's going to take some time. You're the first person I've met since arriving. Maybe you could give me a tour of the area."

Gunner looked caught off guard. "Oh, well ... ."

"You don't have to worry about Bixby going with us," she said, trailing her fingers up his forearm and earning a hateful stare from me for her efforts. "It can be a private tour."

"Yeah, Gunner," I drawled. "It can be a private tour."

After what felt like a great deal of time — it was probably only three seconds but, seriously, he should've moved faster — he yanked his arm away and immediately started shaking his head. "I'm with her," he blurted out, jabbing his finger in my direction. "Um ... me and her."

I shook my head. "Geez. Your father is right. Our communication skills seriously are lacking." Even though Gunner clearly needed help with the aggressive female, I had other things on my mind. The biggest being Bixby. He was back to acting innocent. "I remember you," I hissed. "You're not fooling anybody with this little act ... and I'm not saying little in a derogatory way because you're ... ." I held my hand about two feet off the ground for emphasis. "I'm going to prove who you are."

"I'm certain you will, miss," Bixby supplied, an air of pity surrounding his words, as if he was simply trying to placate me. "Perhaps you should have some lunch or something. You seem like you might be feeling lightheaded."

Before I could respond, Melody let loose a warm chuckle. "Oh, I think I'm really going to like this town."

FIVE

J was still fuming about Bixby when we left twenty minutes later. I would've preferred scouting out the property a bit longer, but Melody's constant surveillance, along with Bixby's presence, ensured that wouldn't happen. Melody refused to stop throwing herself at Gunner and he grew increasingly uncomfortable. When you coupled that with the way I kept accusing Bixby of being a slimy pervert ... well, things deteriorated quickly.

"She's obviously not a vampire," Gunner noted as he grabbed his helmet and stared at me from across his bike seat.

"You don't know that," I grumbled.

"It's daylight, baby. Vampires can't go out in daylight."

He had a point ... which was beyond frustrating. "Well, maybe they're both working for whatever vampire is controlling them." I thought back to the shadowy figure I saw when I was a teenager. "Maybe it's the same guy. He said he would likely see me again."

Gunner's eyebrows hopped. "Are you suggesting that they're here for you?"

Was I? That seemed a bit haughty. "No." I immediately started shaking my head even though I wasn't sure how to answer the question. "That's doubtful. I'm sure it's a coincidence."

"Didn't you once tell me you don't believe in coincidences?"

That was true. "Yeah, but ... not this time. I told you this place is a paranormal nexus. The power circulating here is enough to draw a vampire."

"We didn't see a vampire."

"I just told you that Bixby freak was with a vampire when I was a teenager. Haven't you been listening?"

He held up his hands and gave me an exaggerated stare. "Okay. Calm down. There's no reason to get worked up."

That was easy for him to say. "Really?" I was legitimately torqued where he was concerned. "You don't think there's a reason for me to be worked up? For crying out loud, that guy was hiding in the bushes and wanted to jump me."

"But ... how can you really be sure about that?"

"I was there!"

"And it was ten years ago." He used his most reasonable voice, which only served to irritate me further. "Have you considered that maybe you're confusing him with somebody else?"

"Um ... you've seen him. How would I confuse that guy with anybody else?"

"He looks like a normal guy."

"Oh, he does not. He's, like, five feet tall and wears the suits with the patches." I trailed off when I realized it was the patches that had jogged my memory. "I know it's him. You might not want to believe me — and I think that has a little something to do with your new girl-friend and the way she kept rubbing your arm to distract you — but I know what I know ... and I know that guy is trouble."

Gunner didn't bother to hide his eye roll. "Oh, please. I was just being polite. I wasn't flirting with her. You should know that."

"Right. You weren't flirting." That was the most ludicrous thing I'd ever heard. "That's why you forgot I was even with you for half of the conversation."

He made a protesting sound. "I did not. I was simply trying to be a polite guest. We looked like idiots going there the way we did. I mean ... she probably thought we were there to rob her."

"She didn't think that. She only came out because it was obvious Bixby wasn't going to be able to control us. She needed to use her feminine wiles to draw you in."

The expression on his face would've been funny under different circumstances. "Her feminine wiles?"

I bobbed my head without hesitation. "That's what I said. She used her feminine wiles and you were a big pile of goo."

"Um, first of all, I'm never a big pile of goo. Secondly, if I were to turn to goo — which I won't because I'm manly and tough — you'd be the one doing the turning."

The sentiment was almost sweet. Almost. "I was there. I saw how you reacted to her. It was a little sickening."

"Whatever." He offered up a dismissive hand wave. "I'm not getting into an argument with you about this. I'm not interested in anyone but you. I'm pretty sure I've proved that the past couple of weeks."

And I was pretty sure that his tongue would've hit the ground if it were long enough when he got a gander at Melody. That hardly seemed worth arguing about, though, when we had Bixby to discuss. "I'm telling you there's something wrong with the little guy."

"And I think you're exaggerating. Just because he reminds you of someone you saw once ... ."

"No. I know it was him."

"But ... ."

"I know it was!" I stomped my foot for emphasis, glaring. "Don't tell me what I don't know. I saw him. I remember that night because ... I was afraid. I thought I was going to be tossed out on the street in two weeks and had no idea what I was going to do."

Gunner's expression softened. "I'm sorry about that." He moved closer and slid his arm around my shoulders. "That must've been terrifying. I can't imagine how you made it through that. My father is a pain in the behind, but I never once worried about being homeless."

I thought about fighting the hug but it felt good to give in and lean for a moment, so that's what I did.

"I'm sorry about fighting," he said after a beat. "That's the last thing I want."

That made two of us, and still … . "You were hot for her. Admit it."

"No. I'm hot for you. I'm not going to lie about liking blondes." He gave my hair a soft tug. "But she does absolutely nothing for me. You do everything."

It was hard to argue with him when he put himself out there like that. Sure, under different circumstances I might've tried, but that felt unnecessary now. "It doesn't matter."

"It matters." He moved his hand to the back of my head and tipped it up to stare into my eyes. "You really are all I want."

Frustrated, I blew out a sigh. "I can't even yell at you when you say things like that."

His grin was wide and mischievous. "Why do you think I say them?"

"Because you're a butthead." I rubbed my forehead and tried to regroup. "I know you think I'm mistaken, but I swear that's the same guy from when I was a kid."

Gunner hesitated before answering. "So we'll look him up. Bixby isn't a common name. And we should be able to find information on his mistress too. We'll figure it out."

That was all I really wanted to hear. "Great. I'm looking forward to grinding his face into the dust."

He smirked and leaned forward to give me a quick kiss, happy that the crisis had been averted. "That's my girl."

WE HEADED TO MABLE'S TABLE FOR AN early lunch. The owner of the establishment, Mable, waved when she saw us and directed us toward a corner booth. I was just about to slide in across from Gunner when someone cleared a throat behind us.

"Why don't you guys sit on the same side so you can paw each other under the table?" Graham suggested, his eyes lit with amusement. "I'll take the other side."

I wasn't even certain how he'd managed to sneak in behind us. Suddenly, I felt off my game. "How long have you been there?" I glanced around, annoyed. "Have you been following us since we were outside?"

My reaction obviously wasn't what he was expecting, because he furrowed his brow. "I was already here. I was in the bathroom."

Oh, well, that made me feel better.

"I saw you when I was coming out. I figured I should share some information with you."

"Sounds good." Gunner grabbed my arm and directed me to slide to the inside seat. "We're getting a big lunch because Scout is clearly starving and hunger clearly makes her a bit crazy."

"Why do I have to sit inside?" I asked.

Gunner's face was blank. "Why does it matter?"

"Because everyone knows the aisle position is the one of power. The person who sits on the aisle controls the bathroom ... and basically the other person. Men like to make women take the inside position. It's sexist."

He stared at me for a long beat, blinking, and then shook his head. "Geez. You're a lot of work this morning." He slid into the far seat and held up his hands. "Happy? Now you have the power."

"Thank you." I smiled serenely as I met Graham's amused gaze over the table. "What?"

Graham merely shook his head. "Nothing."

Gunner handed me a menu and changed the subject. "Is Honey off the street?"

Graham nodded, turning grim. "She is. The medical examiner did a cursory examination before hauling her away. He says I probably won't get a full report — and that's minus any toxicology results — until tomorrow."

"Sounds like the medical examiner's office is on their game," Gunner drawled. "Did he say anything good?"

"Just that he believes her death may be an accident."

I jerked up my eyes from the menu, dumbfounded. "Um ... did he not see the wounds on her throat?"

"He did. He thinks she might've been attacked by an animal."

"What animal could kill her in that manner?"

"A bear, for one. A wolf for another."

"Bigfoot," Gunner added, causing my forehead to wrinkle.

"Did you just say Bigfoot?"

He laughed at my discomfort. "I used to be obsessed with Bigfoot when I was a kid. I love the legends ... and this area is thick with fun stories. When things were bad when I was younger, I used to imagine myself running away to live with Bigfoot in the woods."

Instinctively, I reached over and covered his hand. I might've been abandoned by my parents, left to fend for myself in a harsh world, but he'd known his mother ... and she had tried to hurt him. Not all aches were equal, but everybody had scars. "That sounds fun."

He squeezed my hand. "It definitely sounded fun."

"Oh, geez." Graham rolled his eyes. "I see you two are all lovey-dovey again. How did that happen so fast?"

Gunner shrugged as I went back to reading the menu. "I like to think she simply can't stay angry at me."

When Graham didn't immediately respond, I tore my gaze from the food offerings and found him staring at me.

"It's hormones," I volunteered without hesitation. "When we're around each other, the relationship is so new everything becomes chemical. That's the way of the world."

"Ah." He seemed amused by my response. "Good to know."

"Isn't it, though?" I beamed at him before pointing toward something on the specials menu. "I know we're here for lunch, but what is a country omelet skillet?"

Gunner's eyes widened in amusement. "Oh, I didn't even see that. It's my favorite."

"Yes, but what is it?"

"Potatoes. Scrambled eggs. Onions. Green peppers. I like to add tomatoes, something I think you would like. Then it's smothered in sausage gravy."

It sounded disgusting enough to be awesome.

"It's very good," Graham agreed. "I didn't see that on the menu when I was getting coffee earlier. I might order one myself."

"What'll you have?" Mable asked as she finally made her way to the table. She was the craggy sort, rarely in a good mood, and yet she inspired loyalty from half the town, including Graham and Gunner. They both adored her.

"The skillet." Gunner gestured toward the specials menu. "I know it's a little late and you're probably focusing on lunch but Scout has never tried it."

"Oh, right. This is all about Scout." Mable winked at me. "You can all have the skillet."

Gunner's smile was so wide it threatened to swallow his entire face. "Yay! I want a glass of water and some coffee, too. Thank you."

"I'll have the same," Graham supplied. "Put it on their tab. My son is buying."

Gunner scowled but didn't put up an argument.

Mable turned her expectant eyes to me. "I'll try the skillet. Gunner said you could add tomatoes."

"Absolutely."

"Thank you."

Mable ripped the sheet off her pad and handed it to her daughter Mindy as the young woman moved to pass by. "Put this in for me," she ordered.

Mindy's eyes widened. She was the whiny sort and she annoyed me to no end on a regular basis ... and it wasn't because she had a crush on Gunner, although that might've had a little something to do with it. "Why do I have to put it in?"

"Because I want to talk to the sheriff about the dead body this morning," Mable replied with faux sweetness. "You're already heading in that direction so I figured there was no harm in you carrying a piece of paper for the rest of your trip."

The look Mindy shot her mother was withering. "Maybe I want to hear about the dead body. Did you ever think that? I mean ... Honey was in school with me."

"Yes, I remember," Mable said. "You were crushed beyond belief when you heard Gunner and Honey were dating. I believe you locked yourself in your room for a week and pushed pins into a voodoo doll to get them to break up."

Mindy's mouth dropped open. "I can't believe you just said that," she practically shrieked.

Mable rolled her eyes. "Put in the order and stop your bellyaching."

The more time I spent around Mable, the more I liked her. The same could not be said for her daughter, who took the order from her mother and stomped off with an extra huffy sway to her hips.

"It's fun to torture our kids, isn't it?" Graham said, grinning as Gunner shook his head.

"It's definitely fun," Mable agreed. "But I do want to hear about Honey. While I wasn't particularly close with her, I never thought of her as a troublemaker. Do we have something we should be worried about?"

Graham hesitated and then held his hands palms out. "I don't know. I know that's not the answer you want to hear but it's the only one I have. The medical examiner seems to think she was attacked by an animal."

Which was the most ludicrous thing I'd ever heard.

"Do you think that?" Mable asked pointedly.

"I don't know." Graham looked legitimately baffled. "I mean ... some of the bears have been coming closer to town, but they don't usually attack humans. The same with the wolves, unless they're rabid, and we haven't had an infestation to worry about in years."

"What about you?" Mable's eyes landed on me. "Do you think it's an accident?"

I had no idea why she focused on me, but I simply shrugged. "I'm not an expert."

"That means you don't believe it was an accident." Mable folded her arms over her chest and fixed Graham with a pointed look. "If there's a killer out there, I want to know. I have a daughter to protect."

Graham shot me a quelling look. "Thank you for that."

"Hey, I didn't say anything."

"You've got a certain way about you. Whatever you're thinking appears on your face as if by magic. Don't ever play poker."

"I'll have you know that I'm an excellent poker player."

"Yeah, yeah." Graham waved off the statement and refocused on

Mable. "I don't know what to tell you. I'm waiting for toxicology results. It's up in the air right now. That said, I do have a few questions. Do you know who Honey was seeing these days?"

"What makes you think she was seeing anyone?" I asked.

"She was always seeing someone," Gunner replied for his father. "Sometimes she was seeing two someones at the same time."

I arched an eyebrow. "Is that why you and Honey broke up? Did she cheat on you?"

"That was never going to work out anyway. It doesn't matter."

"Who was she seeing?" Graham asked.

Mable looked annoyed at being put on the spot. "I've only heard of one recent person ... and you're not going to like it."

"Lay it on me anyway."

"Brandon Masters."

It was as if all the oxygen had been sucked out of the room. Brandon was Gunner's childhood best friend. Gunner still picked up hours at Brandon's lumberyard every week. They were close.

"You have to be kidding," Gunner sputtered. "Why would Brandon be dating Honey?"

Mable shrugged. "You'll have to ask him."

"But ... why wouldn't he tell me?" Gunner looked legitimately puzzled.

"Probably because all your time has been spent with this one." Graham jabbed a finger in my direction. "And probably because it was an uncomfortable situation, what with Honey being your ex-girlfriend."

Gunner's lips curved down. "That was years ago and I'm well over it. And he's my friend. He doesn't have to hide things from me."

"Well, that's good. I'm thinking we should question him after we eat. He might have some information that will be of use."

"And he should probably know that his girlfriend is dead," I added. "I mean ... that's the most important thing, right?"

Graham's expression clouded. "There is that. It's going to be a rough afternoon. Everybody better bulk up."

SIX

I felt out of place when we arrived at the lumberyard. Gunner's relationship with Brandon made me think what was to come should be a private moment, but I was part of the team and I wanted to hear what he had to say.

Graham took the lead, asking one of the workers where we could find Brandon. We were directed to the main office, a building I hadn't been in before. My previous visits included stops in the merchandise areas, so I spent the first few minutes after our arrival looking around. It was a homey environment, numerous photos lining Brandon's desk, which was empty.

We took seats across from his chair and waited, and we were rewarded with his presence within three minutes.

"Hey." He looked happy to see Gunner, which only made me feel even more guilty. In truth, Gunner had been spending the lion's share of his time with me the past few weeks, which probably meant Brandon was left out in the cold.

"Hey." Gunner shot his friend a wan smile. "How's it going?"

Brandon shrugged, noncommittal. "I can't complain."

"But you will."

The two friends shared an amused smile, and then Brandon sank into his chair. He looked paler than the last time I'd seen him and I wondered if he was feeling under the weather. If he wasn't before, he certainly would be feeling off his game once we finished with him.

"Why do I think this isn't a social visit?" Brandon asked after looking at all three of our faces. "You guys look serious." He focused on Graham. "And, no offense, but I can't remember the last time you decided to bring your father around."

"I remember," Graham countered. "It was when your father was still in charge and you and Gunner got in a fight at school. He punched you and I made him apologize."

Brandon smiled at the memory. "Ah, yes. Cindy Torkelson. We were arguing about who she should date. We probably should've just asked her, because she preferred Sarah Tomlinson and neither of us had a chance. Good times, huh?" He winked at Gunner, who couldn't even fake a smile.

"Okay, what's going on?" Brandon was serious. "Something has happened. It's not my mom, is it?"

Graham immediately started shaking his head. "No, it's not your mother. I'm sorry if you thought that. We have some ... bad news. The thing is, we're not even sure you're going to see it as bad news. Someone told us you might, but ... ."

I shot him a sidelong look. "How did you get to be chief of police when you're so bad at this?" I challenged.

He glared at me. "I'm doing the best that I can."

"How about you guys just tell me why you're here?" Brandon suggested. "I'm starting to freak out."

"Right." Graham sucked in a deep breath. "Okay, here it is ... we found a body behind the library this morning."

Brandon managed to keep his expression neutral, but the anxiety in the room kicked up a notch. "And you're here because you think I'm involved?"

Gunner jumped in. "Of course not! We know you're innocent."

"Actually, I do have some questions for you," Graham countered. "First, though ... it's my sad duty to report that sometime during the overnight hours Honey Martelle lost her life in the downtown area."

58

I watched Brandon closely for his reaction. Already pale, he lost every hint of color as the words seeped in, and his eyes clouded over.

"What?" Brandon's voice cracked. "I ... are you kidding?"

"That's not normally the type of joke I like to participate in," Graham replied quietly. "We're still trying to ascertain the details of her death, but ... someone in town mentioned that you and Honey were dating."

"Um ... yeah." Brandon rubbed his cheek, lost. My heart went out to him. He was clearly struggling to hold it together. "I don't understand. It can't be her."

"It's her," Graham countered. This part of the conversation was more comfortable for him, or at least he was used to it. Sure, Brandon had been a family friend for years, but Graham understood about moving the discussion along. "I made the identification myself. There's really no possibility of it being someone else."

"But ... ." Bewildered, Brandon shifted his eyes to Gunner. "He could've made a mistake, right?"

Gunner looked tortured as he shook his head. "I'm sorry, but ... no. I saw her, too. She's definitely dead."

"But ... no." Brandon was clearly in denial mode. "I just saw her last night."

"You did?" Graham leaned forward. "Can you tell me where?"

"We were out at the bar on the highway. We spent a few hours playing pool and talking, and then I had to go home because I had to work today. She was still there when I left."

"She didn't go with you?" Graham's expression told me that was an important point. "Was it normal for you to leave early when out on a date?"

"I ... ." Brandon worked his jaw. "I don't really know that I would call last night a date," he hedged. "I mean ... we were together, but it wasn't a formal thing. We were just hanging out."

"Oh, so you weren't dating?"

"We were." Brandon's gaze darted to Gunner, discomfort rolling off him in waves. "I'm sorry I didn't tell you. I just ... we haven't seen much of each other in the past few weeks and it just sort of happened."

"It's okay," Gunner reassured him quickly. "I'm not upset. I don't want you to think that. I dated Honey a million years ago and obviously there was nothing there, because it was easy to walk away. You were there. It wasn't exactly some great love."

"No. Still ... you don't date your buddy's ex. I mean, that's one of those unspoken rules we're supposed to follow. I didn't even realize I wanted to date her until we were hanging out together at the bar one night and got to talking. Even then I told myself it wasn't really a thing. I still went back to the bar the next night — even though that's not really my scene — and she was there and we talked again. Before I even realized what was happening, I was asking her out."

"Dude, I'm not angry," Gunner stressed. "I just wish I would've known. I feel like an idiot. This was an important life event for you and I didn't even know about it. Mable had to tell me."

Brandon's smile was more of a grimace. "I was afraid to tell you. I figured Mable would let it slip. Honey and I were at the farmer's market the other day and we ran into her. She seemed ... interested ... to see us together."

"Well, Mable is a gossip," Graham noted. "She's always interested when she sees people together. She can't help herself. How long had you two been dating?"

"Not long. I mean ... I guess we first met up at the bar about two weeks ago. It was a new thing. ... I really liked her." His voice cracked. "I can't believe she's gone."

Gunner smoothly got to his feet and moved behind the desk so he could rest his hand on his friend's shoulder. "I'm so sorry." His voice was low. "I don't know what to say to you. I just ... this is awful. I feel guilty because I didn't even know about it."

"Well, to be fair, I was trying to figure out the best way to tell you," Brandon admitted. "I knew you wouldn't care, but it still felt as if I was crossing a line or something."

"You weren't crossing a line. I know those rules exist for a reason, but ... I was basically a kid when I dated Honey. This isn't a very big area. There's going to be some overlap. Just don't try dating Scout or we'll have issues."

I understood he was trying to make a joke, but it fell flat.

Brandon slowly turned his eyes to me, and for the first time since he'd heard the news he almost looked amused. It was reflected as a brief glint in his eyes. "You guys have been spending so much time together that was another reason I didn't bring it up. I felt like an idiot talking about an ex-girlfriend when you obviously have a new one ... and you guys have been so wrapped up in each other that I've barely seen you."

"I'm sorry about that." Gunner was sincere. "I didn't mean to cut you out. I just ... we've been having a lot of fun together."

"And at the beginning of a relationship it's all about the other person," Brandon volunteered. "I get it. I was that way with Honey. You have nothing to feel guilty about."

One look at Gunner told me he didn't feel the same way. The fact that he didn't know an important life event about his best friend was likely to haunt him for a bit ... especially given the outcome.

"Well, I'm here for you now." Gunner's eyes found mine and there was an apology there.

Oh, well, great. Now he was going to feel guilty about abandoning me to take care of his friend. We really needed to work on his coping skills. They were lackluster, to say the least.

"I need you to run me through things," Graham prodded. "You say that you and Honey started talking at the bar on the highway about two weeks ago. Did she approach you? Did you approach her?"

Brandon looked taken aback by the question. "Does it matter?"

"I'm simply trying to get a picture," Graham replied. He was all business. "The thing is ... we're not exactly sure how she died. Her throat was a mess, but that doesn't necessarily mean we're looking for a human."

Brandon furrowed his brow. "I don't understand. What else could it have been? Other than a human, I mean."

"Well, it could've been an animal."

Brandon was silent for a beat. "Or a monster." He slid his eyes to

Gunner. "Do you think it could've been one of the things you hunt and kill?"

Gunner held out his hands, helpless. "I don't know, man. She had wounds around her throat, and it was a mess ... but we're not sure what we're dealing with."

I'd already told them what they were dealing with. I had no doubt it was a vampire. Like, none at all. Still, I wasn't aware of Brandon's relationship with the paranormal. I was fairly certain he was a normal human, but as Gunner's best friend he must've had some idea of the supernatural shenanigans plaguing Hawthorne Hollow. Of course, there was knowing and *knowing* ... and I doubted he was capable of seeing the full breadth of the situation.

"I don't know what I'm supposed to do with that information," Brandon admitted. "I just ... don't understand any of this. We were together last night. We were having a good time. How could she be gone?"

"I don't know," Graham replied, his sympathy for the young man he'd known for almost three decades written all over his face. "I need a rundown of last night. Why were you guys at the bar on the highway? That place is a little rough."

"It is, but Gunner is always at The Cauldron," Brandon explained. "Once we started officially dating, I didn't want to go anyplace where we could accidentally run into Gunner before I had a chance to talk to him.

"I mean ... I knew he was happy with Scout," he added hurriedly. "In fact, I knew there was something between them before he was even willing to admit it. That first day he brought her here, I could see how much he liked her."

For some reason I remembered that encounter differently. "He was giving me a hard time."

"Yeah, but that's how guys tell you they like you," Brandon replied. "We still revert to playground rules. If we like a girl, we pull her hair or punch her in the arm. We can't really get away with that as adults, so we have to do those things verbally."

He sounded so certain I could hardly argue with him. "Well, that's ... weird but interesting."

Gunner shot me a wink. "I told you that I was flirting with you from the start. You just didn't realize it."

"Yes, well, I stand corrected." I rolled my eyes. "What's the deal with this bar on the highway? I know I've only been in town a few weeks, but I've had at least four different people warn me away from that place. I don't understand why anyone would hang out there if the atmosphere is so toxic."

"There aren't many places to hang out," Graham explained. "If you want a drink, you're basically stuck with The Cauldron or the highway bar, which has changed names so many times I can't even remember what it's called now."

"The Bourbon Barn," Brandon supplied absently.

"Oh, that's just the worst name for a bar ever," Graham muttered. "That's not even remotely dignified."

His response would've made me laugh under different circumstances.

"Like I said, we kept going to the highway bar because I was afraid of running into Gunner before I had a chance to talk to him," Brandon explained. "I knew he was unlikely to care, but there's etiquette to these sorts of things."

"And what about last night?" Graham prodded. "Did anything out of the ordinary happen last night?"

Brandon took a moment to consider the question and then shook his head. "No. It was all the usual faces. We played pool. She was hanging out with a few of the other women there and wasn't ready to go. I had to get up early. She didn't. She should've been safe."

Gunner squeezed his friend's shoulder. "We're going to find out what happened to her. I promise you that."

"Yeah, well ... I think I need to go to the bathroom for a minute. I ... um ... just need to get myself together. I'm sorry."

"Take your time," Graham supplied. "We'll be waiting when you're ready. I'll need a list of the people at the bar last night."

"Absolutely. I understand. Just ... give me a few minutes."

"Take all the time that you need."

GUNNER WAS SHEEPISH WHEN HE FOUND me standing next to my bike in the parking lot an hour later. I'd made myself scarce for the rest of the conversation because I figured it was best for the men. There were things they might've needed to say to one another that didn't require an audience.

"Where did you go?" Gunner asked. "I was worried you took off without me."

I rolled my eyes. "Yes, because that sounds just like me," I drawled. "I often take off without telling you where I'm going."

"Actually, you do."

"Not since we started dating."

"Yeah, well ... I guess that's true." He rolled his neck until it cracked and studied the sky. "So ... um ... I promised Brandon I would hang out with him tonight. He's really upset about what happened to Honey. I think he needs a shoulder."

I waited for him to expound. When he didn't, I merely shook my head. "And you think I'll hold it against you because you want to be there for your friend?"

"No," he replied hurriedly, vehemently shaking his head. "Not in the least. I just ... I wasn't sure if we had plans."

He was amusing when he wanted to be. Heck, he was funny when he wasn't even trying. This was one of those times where he was inadvertently amusing. "Gunner, last time I checked we weren't physically sewn together. I'm not your keeper."

"No, but ... we've been together every night for the past few weeks."

"We have. We can miss a night."

"I don't want to miss a night," he offered quickly. "I like spending time with you. I just ... feel he needs me."

"He does need you," I agreed. "You don't have to worry about me. I am capable of taking care of myself. Our relationship won't fall apart because we miss a single night."

"I know. I just ... this is embarrassing to admit, but I'll miss you."

His earnest expression made me smile. "I'll miss you, too. Somehow I think I'll survive. Besides, your friend needs you. He looked sick before he even got the news. You should take care of him."

"I plan on it. We have time. He's sticking at work because he doesn't want to go home and do nothing. That gives us a chance to visit the bar on the highway."

I was instantly suspicious. "How did you know that's where I was heading?"

"I'm not an idiot."

"You don't have to go with me."

"Yes, I do. That place is a hole. And I know the regulars. It will be better if we go together."

"Are you saying that because we're co-workers who should have each other's backs or because you're an alpha male who believes women need to be protected?"

"I'm saying it because I want to get answers for my friend. They weren't together long, but he's obviously rocked. I want to give him some measure of peace, however small."

It was the best possible response. "Then we'll get him answers. Just for the record, though, I don't need to be protected."

"Oh, I know. You've proved that plenty."

"I just don't want you to forget."

"I could never."

SEVEN

"Okay, here's the situation — you need to let me do the talking once we're inside."

Gunner waited until we were in the parking lot of the Bourbon Barn to take control.

Instead of reacting with derision — which is what I felt — I reminded myself he was mired in guilt and there might be a legitimate reason for him to suggest such a thing. "And why is that?"

"Because the people who frequent this establishment are old school."

"I need more information than that."

He let loose a sigh, one that reminded me of his father when he was trying to get Gunner to see his way of thinking. It almost made me laugh. "I mean that the people who hang out at this place tend to hold to certain gender roles. They want them reinforced, not torn down."

I narrowed my eyes, causing him to shift his hips away from me.

"I knew I should've worn a cup for this conversation," he muttered.

I held it together, but it took monumental effort. "So, let me get this straight," I drawled. "You're saying the people inside are basically a bunch of inbred hicks who believe that women should cater to men. Do I have the gist of it?"

"I wouldn't put it so succinctly — and I'm sure not everyone who hangs out here feels the same way — but in a nutshell, yeah, that's it."

Oh, well, this visit was going to be more fun than I'd thought. "I appreciate the heads-up."

His expression was hard to read. "Does that mean you'll let me take the lead?"

"Oh, absolutely."

"See, your tone suggests you won't."

"I have no idea what you mean." I strode toward the door and then slowed my pace when something occurred to me. "Should I trail behind you, allowing you the dominant position?"

"I don't think it matters."

"Would it help if I bowed and washed your feet in front of them?"

"Ugh." He made a disgusted sound deep in his throat. "I just knew this was going to turn into a thing."

Oh, he had no idea how big of a thing this was going to turn into. Despite my agitation, I waited for him to catch up, and then allowed him to take the lead, bowing low and sweeping out my arm. "Your majesty."

"Oh, geez."

I had to swallow a laugh at his reaction. The smile I was smothering turned into an outright frown when I entered the bar and took a good look at my surroundings.

It was every movie's version of a dive bar. There was no other way to describe it. The floors had probably been shiny and nice at one point, but the wood had rotted in some places and was now uneven. The walls were plastered with every promotional beer sign they'd ever received from distributors and the bar itself looked like a neon nightmare floating in the middle of the room.

"Oh, well, this is nice," I drawled. "You should take me to more places like this."

Unfortunately for both of us, the music that had been rocking so hard it caused my ribs to vibrate ended right before I said it, so everybody heard. Thankfully there were only about eight people in the establishment, and clearly none of them had faces I particularly wanted to know.

"I really like what you've done with the place," I offered the burly dude behind the bar, flashing him a sarcastic thumbs-up. "Hepatitis has been on my 'must get' list for years. I think this visit will finally put me over the top."

The look Gunner shot me was one of disgust, but I thought I caught a hint of something else in his eyes. It might've been amusement, but that could've been wishful thinking. He cleared his throat and focused on the bartender. "Hank."

The ball of fur with a bald spot on the top of his head nodded. "Gunner." He inclined his head toward the end of the bar. "You and your friend want to take a seat?"

"That depends," I replied before Gunner had a chance to respond. "Are we going to stick to the seats? I don't think it will be worth it if we don't."

Gunner's hand was deft when it landed on the back of my neck. He squeezed, although not to the point it hurt. He was clearly sending a message. "We would love to sit down." He prodded me toward the open stools. "You'll have to excuse my friend here. She grew up in the city and her manners are lacking. She doesn't even realize it when she's being rude."

"Oh, I realize it."

He pretended he hadn't heard me. "Two Coronas please."

Hank nodded, his eyes trained on me. "Sure." He retrieved the beers, taking the time to open them and pop limes in the tops before sliding them in our direction. His expression was hard to read, but I had no doubt he was fixated on me rather than Gunner. "Who's your friend?"

"This is Scout Randall." Gunner squeezed the lime and then dropped it into the beer. "She's been working with me."

"With Rooster's group?"

Gunner nodded. "Yeah. She's the newest member of our team."

My curiosity was raging at this point. I wanted to know exactly what Hank — he of the hairy shoulders and tank top that didn't completely cover his beer gut — knew about our group. I knew that particular conversation could go somewhere dangerous though, so I managed to keep my mouth shut. It was a chore.

"People have seen the two of you around town together," Hank said after a beat. "People say you're involved."

"Last time I checked, people in this town say a lot of things," Gunner noted, his eyes drifting to me. For a second, I thought he was going to disavow our relationship and the notion left me bereft. "She's not so bad when you get to know her, but that mouth of hers runs wild. Still ... we're definitely involved."

Hank looked amused. "I like a mouthy woman ... under the right circumstances." His gaze was appraising when it landed on me. "Tell me about yourself, Scout."

I sipped my beer because it seemed to be the thing to do. I could feel multiple sets of eyes on me and knew I was the odd woman out. These people weren't going to talk to a stranger. They needed to think of me as one of them if they were going to open up. I probably should've listened to Gunner and let him do the talking as he'd requested. Unfortunately, that was out of my wheelhouse. I'd never met a tense situation I didn't want to make worse.

"What do you want to know?" I asked, tapping my fingernails on the bar and frowning when I realized how sticky the surface was. I considered asking for a rag but figured that would come off as needlessly aggressive.

"Gunner said you were from down south. Where at?"

"I've lived in several places throughout the state," I replied. "Most of my time was spent in Detroit or the suburbs."

"And what did you do in Detroit?"

That was a thorny question. "Pretty much the same thing I do here, though Gunner is a recent addition." I winked at him. "I didn't have one of him in Detroit."

"And she cried herself to sleep every night because it," Gunner teased.

"Yes, the pain was real."

Hank glanced between us for a few seconds and then shook his head. "You two are basically fornicating with words in the middle of my bar. I would say I don't like it, but in truth, I'm kind of turned on. Please continue."

His words had a dampening effect — which I'm sure he intended — and I frowned as I turned back to my beer.

Gunner chuckled at my reaction, casting a surreptitious look down the bar before turning back to Hank. "So ... I need to know about Honey Martelle."

Hank's expression never changed. "What about her?"

"My understanding is that she hangs out here pretty regularly."

"So what if she does?" Hank looked as if he was ready to start snarling. "Since when is that a crime?"

"I didn't say it was."

"No, but your daddy is the chief of police and we all know you tattle to him," a stacked brunette supplied from the end of the bar. She was tall, willowy even, and her hair had more height than I'd seen anywhere outside of a movie set in the 1980s. She wore jeans so tight I wondered how she managed to breathe, and because she was sitting they dipped low in the back, displaying a lacy thong. She wore one of those leather vests that I'd never seen outside of a catalog. It pushed her cleavage up to death-defying heights.

"Thank you, Rhonda," Gunner drawled. "I love it when you volunteer your opinion on important topics."

I had no idea who Rhonda was, but the look she shot Gunner promised mayhem.

"You didn't used to date her, too, did you?" I whispered. I was quiet enough that only Hank appeared to hear, and he looked amused.

"No, I didn't date her," Gunner shot back. "She's not my type. I already told you I like blondes."

"Honey is blonde," the man sitting on Rhonda's left noted. "Is that why you're asking about her? Are you going to trade up?" His brown eyes were keen as they surveyed me from top to bottom. "This one is mouthy, but she's kind of hot."

Next to me, Gunner tensed. I could tell he didn't like the way this guy was watching me. "Honey is dead."

I was surprised at the way he simply blurted it out.

"What?" Hank looked legitimately gobsmacked.

"She's dead," Gunner repeated. "She was found behind the library today. Her throat was ... injured. There are questions about how it happened. My father has to wait for the autopsy report to make a determination."

That was a bit of an exaggeration, but I didn't comment. This was now officially his show. I'd had my fun. It was time to let him do the heavy lifting.

"I don't understand." There wasn't a hint of a smile on Hank's face now. "She was just in here last night."

"I know. That's why we're here. My understanding is that she was in here quite often."

"I don't know that I would say that," Hank countered. "She was fairly regular. She came in once or twice a week."

"And recently she was with Brandon, right?"

Hank looked uncomfortable with the question. "Can't you ask him that?"

"I've already talked to him, and I will again later when he's had a chance to absorb the news. He was in shock when I was with him a little bit ago." He hesitated before continuing. "I didn't even know he was dating Honey."

"I bet that stuck in your craw, huh?" Rhonda chortled. "You dated her, right? Were you upset when you found out?"

Gunner pinned her with a dark look. "I was upset for my friend because he was clearly rocked by the news. As for Honey ... I can't even remember the last time I saw her. We dated when I was in my early twenties. That was a lifetime ago."

"And you've since moved on," Hank noted, his eyes back on me. He looked as if he wanted to ask me a question, but he remained on point instead. "Do you think Honey was murdered?"

Gunner raised his shoulders a fraction of an inch. "It's hard to know. My guess is she was killed, but my father says it could be an accident. The way her throat was mangled ... well ... they're saying it could have been an animal attack."

The guy next to Rhonda snorted. "An animal attack in the middle of town? What are the odds of that?"

"I don't know, Zed," Gunner replied. "I have trouble believing the story myself, but if you'd seen her throat ... . I don't know of any weapon that could do what was done to her."

"I have seen a few bears around," an old-timer with white hair hanging well past his shoulders volunteered from the far end of the bar. He'd been so still I wasn't even sure he was awake until he spoke. "There's one that's always hanging out by the ritual grounds on the north side of town."

"You mean Barney?" Gunner immediately started shaking his head. "Barney answers to Mama Moon. He's not responsible for this."

"How can you be sure?" Hank challenged. "I've seen that bear. While she seems to be able to order him around, he's still a wild animal. The tighter you try to hold on to a wild animal, the more likely you are to lose control and have to stand back and watch it go on a rampage."

I was familiar with Mama Moon, but I'd yet to see the famous bear. There was no way she would sit back and idly watch as an innocent woman's throat was torn out. That's not how she was built. Besides that, it was vampires. Even though Gunner felt the need to push and prod as he looked for answers, I already knew what sort of creature we were looking for. He simply refused to accept it.

"I understand that, but it wasn't Barney." Gunner was firm. "I'm not even sure it was an animal."

"You think she was murdered," Hank mused, rubbing his chin. He looked thoughtful. "That's why you're here. You want to know if she made any enemies recently. I know how this goes. You're looking at us."

"No." Gunner shook his head. "I need to know how she was acting. I didn't even know she was dating Brandon. The whole thing has me ... confused. No offense to you guys, but this isn't his normal stomping grounds. I'm assuming he was hanging out here because of Honey, but I'm still trying to wrap my head around it."

"They were an odd couple from the start," Zed volunteered. "In fact, when someone mentioned they were dating I thought they were having me on. I mean ... Brandon is an okay guy. I've dealt with him at the lumberyard numerous times and he's always been fair and reasonable. He's not judgmental either. You know how some people look at us like we're beneath them because we're not rich? Well, he never looked at us that way. I've always liked him."

"And yet you didn't think his relationship with Honey was a good thing," I surmised, speaking out loud even though I had initially planned to keep my mouth shut.

"I thought his relationship with Honey was ... odd," he corrected, pinning me with a pointed look. "I always liked her. I mean ... she wasn't perfect. Nobody is." The way he said it made me think he was trying to take me down a peg or two. It was completely unnecessary. While I definitely had attitude about the bar, there was no way I thought of myself as perfect. In fact, it was the exact opposite. "It's just ... she was different from him."

"Some say opposites attract," Gunner noted, sliding his eyes to me and grinning. "I mean, take Scout and me for example. I'm an intelligent, handsome, witty, and charming individual. She's the opposite, and yet things are working for us."

Rhonda snorted. "Oh, burn!" She snapped her fingers and practically did a little dance of glee.

"Right." I bobbed my head without missing a beat. "And on the flip side, I'm a sexual dynamo, I can go all night, and I'm a wonder with sarcasm. Gunner isn't, but it all evens out in the end."

He narrowed his eyes. "You'll pay for that one later."

I wasn't worried in the least. "How were Brandon and Honey different?"

"Well, she was a partier," Zed replied. "She was also kind of ... um ... free with the love."

I drew my eyebrows together. "Is that code for something?"

"Yeah," Rhonda replied. "She was a slut. She liked to sleep around.

There's nothing wrong with that if you own it, but she tended to lie about it. And she was a thief. You couldn't leave your purse at a table when going to the bathroom because she'd steal from you."

Gunner turned his eyes to Hank for confirmation and the bartender simply nodded.

"That's not all," Zed added. "She also liked her pharmaceuticals. She wasn't shooting up or anything, but she liked her oxy more than most people. I'm not saying there's anything wrong with that, but Brandon never showed signs of being okay with any of that."

"Definitely not," Gunner agreed. He looked troubled. "I don't understand how they were even together. Did he know these things about her?"

Rhonda shrugged. "It was one of those ... um ... what do you call it?" She looked to Zed for the right words.

"It was an open secret," Zed offered. "Everyone knew she couldn't be trusted. Everyone talked about it. She was okay to party with, but she was a mess."

"Do you know anyone who would've wanted her dead?" Gunner asked.

"Not really." Zed shook his head. "Like I said, people knew what to look out for when she was around, so she wasn't really an issue. Ten bucks here or there is hardly worth killing over anyway. I mean ... maybe she got in bad with whatever oxy dealer she was hanging with, but she didn't act worried."

"Yeah." Gunner sipped from his beer and flicked his eyes to me. "None of this makes sense."

EIGHT

"*I* don't understand any of this."

Gunner looked frustrated as we regrouped in the parking lot so I decided to give him a pass on the macho "boys rule and girls drool" crap he ran on me before we'd entered the establishment.

"Maybe you should talk to him," I suggested. "I mean ... if you can't understand, my guess is he's the only one who can make you understand."

"I can't do that." He looked scandalized. "I don't know if you realize this, but men don't talk about feelings. That's a chick thing."

And I was back to being agitated. "You talk about your feelings with me."

"No, I talk about my feelings regarding you ... and only in private. It's not as if I go to the bar with Brandon and tell him about the cute way you snore ... or how you curl your toes when you're stretching in the morning and how it makes me giddy. He would think I was nuts."

I stared at him, open-mouthed.

"What?" he said after a beat.

"I don't even know how to respond to that," I said finally. "It makes me want to punch you that you're such a dude about things. There's nothing wrong with talking about feelings. On the other hand, it kind of makes me want to drag you into those bushes and strip you naked for some fun it was so sweet."

He shot me a wolfish smile. "I vote for door number two."

"That's because the alpha male stuff is ingrained in you." I dragged a hand through my hair and sighed. "Here's the thing: Everyone has feelings. That goes for men and women. You have no problem talking to me about your feelings and you've known me two months. Brandon is your best friend and you're upset because he didn't tell you about his feelings. Maybe he feels the same way about you."

He didn't look convinced. "When was the last time you sat down and talked with someone about your feelings?"

Well, that was a low blow. "Um ... I talk about my feelings all the time."

"With who? And, before you answer, it doesn't count if you say me. If I can't use you for the same argument, then you can't use me."

Sadly, that seemed fair. "Well ... I talk to Bonnie sometimes."

He snorted. "You do not. At least not about anything serious."

"I do."

"Name one serious thing you've ever talked to her about."

I hated being put on the spot. "I told her I had feelings for you when she asked."

"Really? Be more specific."

"No, we're not playing that game." I wagged a finger. "The point is, I talk about my feelings."

"With who else besides Bonnie?"

"Um ... there's Merlin."

He made a face. "The cat doesn't count."

"Oh, and my Peeping Tim," I offered, referring to the perverted ghost that hangs around my cottage trying to get a gander at me naked. "I tell him all the time that I feel he shouldn't be trying to stare at me when I'm changing clothes."

The comment had the desired effect and Gunner barked out a laugh. "Is it any wonder I can't get enough of you?" He pulled me close and surprised me with a heartfelt hug rather than a playful kiss. He held tight for a moment, anchoring himself. "I feel as if I've somehow done Brandon wrong and I don't know how to fix it."

It was hard for him to admit. I recognized that, but I couldn't coddle him. He needed a dose of tough love. When I pulled back, I put a stern look on my face.

"Guilt is a useless emotion," I offered. "You can't benefit from those feelings. You have to try to salvage the good from the bad ... and guilt won't help you do that."

"I don't know what to say to him. I basically abandoned him the past few weeks."

"I don't think he's angry. He said so himself. At the start of a new relationship you tend to lose your head. You can't get enough of the other person. It's intoxicating. It's like pheromones are driving you and there's no way to control your impulses."

"You're so romantic," he teased, grinning as he poked my side. "You have hearts in your eyes when you look at me, don't you?"

"I'm just saying that it's normal to lose yourself in the beginning of a relationship. Or so I've been told. I've never wanted to lose myself with anybody but you."

Now he genuinely looked touched. "I think that's the nicest thing you've ever said to me."

"Yeah, well, don't get used to it. The important thing is to get over the guilt and be there for your friend. He needs you."

"What do you need?"

"Nothing right now."

"But ... what are you going to do without me tonight?"

"Are you asking if I'm going to curl into a ball and cry because you're not with me?"

He shrugged, his lips curving. "Would you think less of me if I said yes?"

"Most definitely."

"Then you shouldn't cry."

"I plan to take a long bath, shave my legs, watch some television ... and maybe conduct some research on that little fink at the house on the hill. I know you don't believe me, but I've met him before."

"It's not that I don't believe you."

"You said I was imagining things and getting him confused with some other short dude."

"That's not imagining things. That's getting things twisted around. There's nothing wrong with that."

Ugh. I was at my limit. It was probably a good thing that we weren't spending the evening together. "Don't worry about me. I have my cat to talk to and a randy ghost should I get really desperate. Focus on Brandon. He needs you."

"I'll still miss you."

He was too cute to shoot down. "I'll miss you, too. Just think how happy we'll be when we get a chance for another sleepover. Anticipation is half the fun."

"I'm only spending one night away from you. I don't care if it makes me look like a weenie."

That made me laugh. "Fair enough. Just get through tonight. We'll worry about tomorrow then."

"Okay, but I'm going to need a kiss to get me through this ... and maybe a little butt squeeze to hold me over."

I made a face. "I'm not letting you squeeze my butt in public."

"I was talking about you squeezing my butt."

"Oh, well, that I can do."

I DIDN'T TECHNICALLY LIE TO GUNNER. I had every intention of going home, taking a bath and hanging out with my cat. The odds of me trying to have a real conversation with Tim were slim, but he already knew that. Before I went home, though, I wanted to make a stop.

I found Honey's address online. Believe it or not, there was only one Honey Martelle in the area. She lived in a mobile home park on the outskirts of town. I watched the property for a long time. The units were practically on top of each other, and I didn't want to risk anyone seeing me break in. I could've waited until after dark to enter but I didn't have the patience. Instead, I parked my bike in a clump of trees at the back of the property and made myself invisible.

There wasn't much activity in the park. I would've expected more given the sheer number of homes and the time of year. It was summer, after all. I expected kids to be outside playing, riding their bikes, even throwing rocks at one another. That's what we did during school hiatuses when I was younger. I assumed the classics stuck over the long haul, but apparently I was wrong tonight.

I could've used magic to break into the mobile home, but I liked to go old school with some things, and opening a locked door was one of them. I had a kit to help me along the way. It was something I'd carried since I was a teenager, and in typical fashion I found opening doors people wanted kept shut was one of those skills that was hard to forget. Once inside, I donned a pair of latex gloves and hit the lights. Another problem with breaking and entering after dark was carrying a flashlight. It was always a dead giveaway if a neighbor saw the light bobbing about. With the sun still shining, odds were slim that anybody would even know I was inside.

It turned out that Honey was something of a slob. I wasn't the best housekeeper, so I could hardly throw stones when it came to other people's living situations, but Honey was a real pig.

Panties were strewn around the living room ... and bras ... and shorts ... and tops. It didn't look like a sex thing. I didn't for a second think she'd brought someone home — maybe even Brandon — and passion had overtaken them to the point they'd started ripping off clothes before they made it to the bedroom. No, this was a sloth thing. She was lazy and didn't like to pick up after herself.

I gave the panties on the floor a wide berth as I moved through the living room. The coffee table, which had seen better days, was littered with trashy magazines. Apparently Honey was very worried about the state of the royal marriage and whether or not Scientology was on the way out.

In the kitchen, I found a mountain of dishes. My stomach turned when I started doing the math. There were so many cereal bowls in the sink that she'd gone at least a week without washing anything. As if to prove my calculations correct, several flies buzzed around the dishes, going after the food still clinging to the plates.

"Gross," I muttered, my gaze falling on the purse resting on the kitchen table. I glanced around, as if expecting someone to come out of the woodwork and chastise me for considering going through a woman's bag. That was a line most people didn't cross. I, however, was not most people. I didn't even carry a purse. I didn't see the need. I had no qualms with going through Honey's bag.

I sat at the table, frowning when the chair tilted to the side. I allowed myself to get distracted by the fact that the chair wasn't level for a good two minutes before returning to her purse. The things I found inside were interesting, though mostly in a mundane way.

She had "Slut on a Hot Tin Roof" lipstick in a fiery shade of red that made me think of the *It* clown's hair. She had tampons, aspirin, small vials that were now empty but looked as if they had contained powder at one time. Her wallet held five credit cards and ten bucks. Tucked in the billfold section was a matchbook. Only one match had been removed. The business name advertised on the cover was one I'd never heard of: The Dirty Rooster.

A strip club maybe. Perhaps Honey was moonlighting. I shoved the matchbook into my pocket as a reminder to look up the establishment when I got home and continued rummaging.

She had condoms, several slips of paper containing names and phone numbers, and a Pez dispenser shaped like the blonde chick from *Frozen*. That was it. Nothing else.

"Find anything interesting?" a voice asked, causing me to jolt.

I whipped my head around to find Graham leaning against the door jamb, arms crossed, a dark look on his handsome features. I hadn't even heard him enter the house.

"Um ... not really," I replied, doing my best to pretend he hadn't taken me by surprise. "Just chick stuff."

"Really?" He arched an eyebrow. "What sort of chick stuff are we talking about?"

"Lipstick. Condoms. Tampons. There's some aspirin in here.

These, too." I held up the vials for him. "I'm not an expert, but I think these used to be filled with drugs."

"Oh, yeah? What sort of drugs?"

He was playing with me, trying to keep from yelling until he had his temper under control. I wasn't an expert on his moods as I was becoming with Gunner, but he was obviously angry. He would blow his stack soon. I was sure of it.

"I don't know. The people at the Bourbon Barn said she was on oxy." I held up the vials and studied them. "Grinding up oxy pills to snort is time consuming, but it does get you high quicker. You'll probably want to test the residue." I handed over the vials, which Graham took. "If you're going to yell at me you might as well get it over with. I can take it — and you look ready to burst."

"I haven't decided if I'm going to yell at you yet," he replied. "I'm still thinking about it. May I ask what you're doing here?"

"The same thing you are. You're not convinced an animal killed Honey so you want to see if you can find something that points to a potential murderer."

"That's why I'm here," he agreed. "Last time I checked, you're not a cop."

"No, but that doesn't mean I don't want answers." I thought about sharing the matchbook I'd discovered with him but ultimately decided against it. If pressed, I'd have no choice. For now, I didn't even know if it was a legitimate clue.

"Uh-huh." Graham stepped further into the room. "Is there a reason you're here alone? Where's my son?"

"He's helping Brandon tonight. He feels guilty about not being around the past few weeks."

"And it doesn't bother you that he's chosen to abandon you this evening in favor of hanging out with Brandon?"

"No. Why should it? We're not codependent."

"You've been spending a lot of time together."

"Let me guess ... you don't like it. You were fine when you thought it was just a fling. Now that it seems to be more, you don't think I'm good enough for him."

Graham's expression was unreadable. "On the contrary," he said finally. "I happen to like you a great deal. You're a little rough around the edges, but I think you're the sort of person Gunner needs.

"You don't put up with his crap — and, yes, he spouts a lot of crap — and you sit there and listen to his nonsense when he needs someone to hear him out," he continued. "I was never good at that. I think that's one of the reasons our relationship is so ... strained. I was always worried about other things and he paid the price."

I was surprised he was opening up to me. "I think you and Gunner have more than one issue keeping you at each other's throats. The biggest is that you're alike."

"We are not."

"Oh, you are so. The fact that you reacted the exact way he would if I said the same thing to him only proves it."

"Well, aren't you just a little ray of sunshine."

I smirked at his response. "I don't think you're half as bad a father as you seem to think. You feel guilty, and maybe you should because of what happened with his mother. He gets that guilt thing from you. He was feeling it from both sides today.

"On one hand, he felt as if he abandoned Brandon in favor of me," I continued. "On the other, he was afraid of abandoning me tonight in favor of Brandon. He's a bit of a martyr really. But he's loyal and handsome, so I can live with the martyr complex."

Graham snorted out a laugh. "You're something else, aren't you?"

"I have my own issues. I don't think there's a person alive who doesn't have issues. Honey definitely had some before she was taken out of this world."

Graham's smile slipped. "Do you think she was killed because of the drugs?"

That was a fair question. "I think that she was definitely killed. I don't care what your medical examiner says, she didn't die from some random animal attack."

"And you're still leaning toward vampires?"

"I am. I feel it in my bones."

"How will you prove it?"

"I don't know. Not yet anyway. I'll figure it out, though."

"How do you know that?"

"Because I always do." I sent him a small smile as I stood. "I should probably get going. I don't think there's much left here to discover."

He watched me cross the room, not saying anything until I'd moved past him and was in the living room.

"Scout," he called out, causing me to still. "I think you're really good for my son. I mean ... *really* good. You're definitely good enough for him. I believe it. He believes it. You need to believe it. I get that your life hasn't always been easy and you probably have self-esteem issues after being abandoned, but you're more than worthy."

The sentiment made me feel better. "Thank you."

"Also, if you break into another crime scene I'll have no qualms about arresting you," he added. "It will give me great joy to call my son and tell him he has to bail out his girlfriend."

I cast a rueful smile over my shoulder. "That seems fair."

"It's the truth. Don't break into victims' homes again. I don't like it."

"Fair enough." I kept moving toward the door. "Have a good night."

"You, too. Try not to cry because you miss my son so much."

I frowned. Yeah, they were definitely alike.

NINE

*T*here was no listing for The Dirty Rooster on the internet. I looked on every search engine I could think of. Nothing.

After leaving Honey's place, I returned to town long enough to get a coffee and consider my options. I had every intention of going home and chilling with the cat until I found the matchbook. Now that I couldn't find a business to go with it, I was slowly becoming obsessed.

On a whim, I cast a spell. I used my magic to see if the place really existed. I was gratified when a magical line appeared and directed me out of town. I hopped on my bike and followed it ... to the middle of the freaking woods.

No joke. I rode my bike down a rutted and uneven two-track that was more than a little dangerous. When I reached the end of the line I found a magical fence, for lack of a better word. There was nothing else.

"Well, this is interesting," I muttered, scuffing my boots against the ground as I surveyed the barrier. It was a wall of some sort. I'd seen magic like this before. It was sort of like my invisibility spell, although not as good. Others couldn't see the magic when I used it. This was sloppy ... though relatively strong.

It needed to come down. There was something important behind it and I was determined to learn what that something was.

I took a moment to study my surroundings. Behind me, there were only trees and bushes. I didn't sense danger. On the other side of the barrier, however, there was magic. I had no idea what I would find, but I was salivating at the prospect of discovering what I assumed was a breeding ground for the paranormal nexus.

I was wrong.

I pulsed my magic at the barrier, testing it. After a few minutes, I found several weak spots. It took only a few seconds to break the force field. It shattered like glass when I slammed my magic against one of the weak spots.

As it fell, my eyes went wide ... and I found myself looking at another world.

"Well, well, well." Mama Moon sat at a table sipping what looked to be moonshine from a glass jar. Several of her acolytes sat with her, and they all looked to be having a good time. "Look what the cat dragged in. I should've known you'd find this place eventually."

I pursed my lips and slowly lowered my hands.

There was no bar. Well, not really. There was a bar top sitting in the middle of a clearing and an older man and a younger woman working behind it. Tables were spread across the clearing, a bevy of faces I didn't recognize loitering at them. Above our heads, dainty twinkle lights cast a magical umbrella glow over the clearing.

It smelled like power. I wasn't sure how many of the faces I saw boasted it, but at least some of them did ... and we're talking a lot of power.

"You're fixing that," the man behind the counter announced, his hands on his hips. He was a big guy, tall, and wore a silk shirt unbuttoned to his navel. His hair, which was longer in the back than it was on the top, was streaked with green.

"Um ... fixing what?" I said finally, finding my voice.

"The barrier, stupid," a woman with streaked purple hair replied. She sat at a nearby table with two other women, and when she moved her hand I saw glittering scales retract. "It's what keeps us protected. There's a reason random people can't simply stumble across us."

"Oh." I turned back to the fallen barrier. "You know, whoever did that particular piece of magic did a poor job. It was uneven and there were tons of weak spots. You need a uniform approach." As if to prove that, I raised my hands and unleashed my magic.

It didn't take long to rebuild the wall. It wasn't a terribly difficult spell. When I finished, I flashed a smile at the bartender. "Better?"

He studied the new protective field and merely shrugged. "I don't even know what to say."

Because I knew Mama Moon, I turned my attention to her. "Are these people about to smite me or what?"

She chuckled in response, seemingly genuinely amused. "I think you're okay," she replied, patting the open spot next to her. "You should come over here just to be on the safe side, though. We need to talk."

Even though I'd been warned about her, I happened to like Mama Moon. Did I trust her? To a certain extent. I had no doubt that in a tight spot she would sacrifice me to save herself. That was human nature, though. Most people would react the same way. She was knowledgeable and funny. That's what I cared about most.

"I don't understand why this place is in the middle of nowhere," I offered as I sat next to her. "It's not exactly convenient to get to."

"That's by design," Mama Moon noted, sipping her drink. Her expression was thoughtful. "How did you find this place?" She flashed a smile for the bartender's benefit as he deposited a glass in front of me. "It's supposed to be unplottable."

"It's a long story." I tipped the glass to the side and studied the contents. "Is this moonshine?"

"Magical moonshine," the green-haired man replied.

"It's not going to kill me, is it?"

Mama Moon chuckled as the man wrinkled his nose. "You'll have to excuse her," she said. "She's a pain in the ass when she wants to be. She can't help herself."

"That's not true," I countered. "I can help myself. I choose to be a pain in the ass ... and I'm not sorry about it."

Instead of being offended by the statement, the man smirked. "She's exactly like you said she was, Moonie." He grinned and shook his head. "She's got a mouth on her, but I kind of like her all the same."

"I told you she was something," Mama Moon enthused. "She's going to fit right in out here."

I cast her a sidelong look. "I'm not even sure what this is supposed to be. Why hasn't anyone mentioned this place before?"

"It's a secret," she replied. "It's not much fun to have a secret meeting place if it doesn't stay secret, is it?"

She had a point, but still ... . "Why don't the others know about this place?"

"The others?" Green Hair asked, a serious expression on his face. "Who is she talking about?"

"The Spells Angels." Mama Moon was grim. "Nobody wants Big Brother watching over their shoulder when it comes time to cut loose. There's a reason the Spells Angels aren't wanted here."

"Yeah." Green Hair bobbed his head. "They rat ... and they'll kill certain members of my clientele if they know where to find them."

That sounded unlikely. "I know I've only been here for a few months, but I haven't found that to be true. I've never seen them kill anyone."

"Really?" Green Hair folded his arms over his chest, clearly dubious. "Didn't you kill Lancelot yesterday?"

Wow. There was so much in that short statement I wanted to unpack that I didn't know where to start. "I'm pretty sure I didn't kill Lancelot. Didn't he die because he was messing around with Guinevere? Maybe I'm remembering the story wrong."

Green Hair scowled. "Lancelot was the dude who lived in the Myers Swamp. Well ... he did up until two days ago, when you apparently blew him up."

That made more sense. "You're talking about the bog monster."

"Lancelot." Green Hair narrowed his eyes. "He wasn't just a monster. He was a friend."

"Well, your friend was terrorizing people in the woods, showing them horrible things, and a few went missing. It's obvious they're dead."

"Yes, well, he had a few issues." His eyes flashed with annoyance. "That didn't mean he had to die."

"If you're going to lure unsuspecting people into the woods and eat them — and I know darned well that's what happened so don't bother denying it — then you're going to get some pushback. All he had to do to save himself was not eat people. He couldn't manage that so he had to take a ... sabbatical."

Mama Moon snorted as Green Hair glared at me. "I told you, Cedric. She's got a mind of her own. She's not going to play the game the way you want her to."

Cedric. I didn't recognize the name. The look he shot me now was filled with malice.

"I'm going to miss that little idiot," Cedric insisted. "I liked him. He was funny."

"He also had an open tab," Mama Moon pointed out. "You're more upset you'll never see that money. Admit it."

"I don't think I want to admit it," Cedric countered. "It makes me look shallow ... and nobody likes shallow."

"That's true." Mama Moon sipped her drink and inclined her head toward mine. "You'll be fine if you drink that. I promise it's not poisoned."

It seemed rude to decline — and I was already on at least one list for killing a member of the clientele — so I sipped the moonshine. I expected to be grossed out by a liquid so strong it could strip my insides, but it was surprisingly smooth. "Oh, this is good."

Cedric arched an eyebrow and shook his head. "You have to work on your manners if you want to hang out with us."

"I'm not sure I want to hang out with you," I admitted. "Knowing Rooster, I'm probably breaking ten rules I haven't even thought about, so I might have to make my visits infrequent."

"I like Rooster, but he's a real tight-ass sometimes," the purple-haired woman announced. She was playing solitaire with tarot cards that glowed and she seemed transfixed. "You should do what you want to do ... but I have a feeling that's never been a problem for you."

"Are you a seer?" I queried, genuinely curious.

"I am ... many things." Her eyes fixed on me. "My name is Tempest. That's what my friends call me. I haven't decided if we're going to be friends."

She was blunt. I liked that. "Okay, well, let me know when you decide."

"You're a child of the stars," she said. "I was taught to be leery of your people."

I froze. That wasn't the first time I'd heard that term. I had no knowledge of my actual origins so I was always agitated when someone else seemed to know more about me than I did. Two weeks ago a wolf shifter named Drake, a man with a shady past, claimed to have information about me. He promised to supply answers ... just as soon as his sister was back on her feet. She'd been held, essentially tortured by the world's worst wolf, and he was focusing on her. I couldn't blame him, but I wasn't exactly the patient sort. I was desperate for whatever information he could provide, but I couldn't push him.

At least not yet. Eventually, though, I would be forced to go after him if he didn't volunteer the information I needed.

"And how do you know that?" I asked finally.

"You have a pink aura." Her expression was thoughtful. "You're powerful, too. Children of the stars are rare these days. You're ... unique ... even for them."

"Does that mean you know who I am?"

The question seemed to confuse her. "Don't you know who you are?"

I rose, every intention of walking over to the table and shaking her until she started volunteering information propelling me, but Mama Moon grabbed my wrist before I could go on a rampage.

"You'll want to think long and hard about this," she warned, her eyes somber. "I know that you grapple with a past you can't remember, but she can't help you."

I wasn't convinced. "She knows what I am."

"That doesn't mean she knows who you are. There are children of the stars everywhere. Your specific tribe is a mystery and you can't change that at the moment. Starting a fight won't help anyone, including you." She tapped the side of my mason jar. "Drink that ... and loosen up. You can't go starting fights your first night here. That's a surefire way to get yourself banned."

I'd yet to decide if I wanted to stay so I wasn't particularly worried about that. Still, there was a reason for my visit. "How long have you guys been in operation?"

"Does it matter?" Cedric made a face. "I'm more curious how you found us without an invitation. We're very careful to leave the Spells Angels off the list ... and yet here you are."

"The Spells Angels are paranormal, so that doesn't make much sense. I guess that's your prerogative, though. I'm here because I found this." I held up the matchbook. "Why was Honey Martelle hanging out here?"

Mama Moon snapped her eyes in my direction. "What do you know about Honey?"

That was an interesting reaction. "What do you know about Honey?" I shot back.

"I know that she's been banned from this place." Mama Moon was suddenly alert. "You didn't bring her with you, did you?"

Her reaction caught me off guard. "No. I don't think you have to worry about her ever coming back. She's dead."

A low murmur went through the crowd and Cedric straightened.

"What do you mean?" he asked after a beat. "Do you mean literally or figuratively?"

"I mean literally. Her throat was ripped out and her body was dumped behind the library." I tapped my fingers on the tabletop. "You guys didn't know?"

"No," Mama Moon confirmed, finding her voice, "and I'm not sure what to do with the news. Honey was causing problems in the paranormal community. While I'm never thrilled with the prospect of murder, it's a relief to know she won't show back up here and try to get in."

"I need more information than that," I argued. "I'm trying to figure out what happened to her and, so far at least, I'm running into brick walls. The matchbook was a fluke ... but I'm confused." I glanced around again to confirm my suspicions. "Everyone here has some sort of paranormal ability. To my knowledge, that wasn't true of Honey. Why was she hanging out here?"

Cedric and Mama Moon exchanged a weighted look. When the green-haired bartender started speaking again, it was in measured tones.

"Honey aligned herself with a certain faction."

"Is that faction here right now?"

"No, and I don't know if they're coming back." Cedric looked pained. "Look, I don't know how to say this without coming off as callous. The thing is, Honey was not a good person. She was a thief ... and she was always open to selling private information. She jumped from man to man in an effort to find someone to fund her drug habit. She was just all over the place."

"You mustn't think that we wished her ill," Mama Moon reassured me hurriedly. "That's actually the opposite of how we felt. We wanted to help her, break her of the addiction that was causing her to spiral, but she wouldn't let us help. Instead, she stole from us ... lied to us ... and caused problems. We had to ban her."

That was interesting information, but I was still left with gaping holes to fill. "Why was she out here? She wasn't paranormal, right?"

"Not exactly." Mama Moon shifted on her chair, clearly uncom-fortable. "There are some new players in town ... and they're not exactly playing nice with others. Honey aligned herself with them."

We were finally getting somewhere. "And what players are we talking about?"

As if on cue, the barrier began to flicker, causing me to jerk my head in the opposite direction. "What's that? Is my magic failing? I ... that's weird." I was on my feet and ready to fix whatever I'd broken when a door opened at the far side of the barrier.

"That was the doorbell," Cedric replied grimly, his attention on the opening. "And, funnily enough, I think you're about to get an answer to your question. The new players we were talking about are here ... and nobody is going to be happy to see them."

I focused on the three blondes sliding through the door. All females, thin and striking. I recognized one of them. "Melody Summers," I muttered.

Mama Moon slid me a keen look. "Do you know her?"

"I met her this morning. She lives in the house on the bluff ... with that little ferret who likes to hide in the bushes and attack people."

"I don't know what that means, but it sounds intriguing." Amusement flitted across her face. "You know what they are, don't you?"

I didn't, but I had an idea. "They're half-vampires."

"Very good." She beamed. "I wasn't sure you'd figured that out."

"I didn't. Not until right now." As if sensing me watching, Melody slowly lifted her head and scanned the crowd until she found me staring. "Well, this is going to be an amusing night after all. I think we're going to have a lot to talk about."

"Just don't destroy my place," Cedric ordered. "I have it looking exactly how I want it now. If you make a mess, you're picking it up."

That seemed more than fair.

TEN

*H*alf-vampires.

I knew a little about them. In the city, they were used to procure meals — human sacrifices — under the promise of immortality. Those promises were rarely kept. Three of them here meant a master was close ... and I was fairly certain where it was living.

"What are you going to do?" Mama Moon asked, her face lined with concern.

"I haven't decided yet." I took another sip of the moonshine and frowned. "Is there alcohol in this?"

She shook her head. "It's a magic booster. It's supposed to balance you metaphysically."

Oh, well, that sounded lame. "Great. At least I won't have to worry about driving home."

Mama Moon smirked. "You look intense, as if you're trying to figure something out. I find you entertaining ... even when I'm certain you're about to do something stupid."

"You don't have to worry about me." I flashed a smile for her benefit. "I'm a survivor. I never do anything truly stupid."

"I've spent a total of six hours with you and I've witnessed you do at least eight stupid things."

She had to be exaggerating. At best she'd witnessed me do three stupid things.

As if sensing me watching her, Melody slowly shifted her eyes across the bar, not stopping until her searching gaze found me. Her face registered shock for a moment, and then she politely shuttered it behind a smile that was more feral than welcoming.

"Well, we meet again," she drawled.

Her friends followed her gaze. Their expressions were harder to read.

"It was only a matter of time," I said as I debated exactly how I wanted to approach this. Finesse was clearly warranted. It would be a battle of wits. "So, you guys are half-vampires, huh?"

Yeah. Screw a battle of wits. I've always preferred laying all of my cards on the table.

Melody's eyebrows hopped. "I see someone has been talking out of turn." Her gaze was dark when it landed on Mama Moon. "I guess I should've expected that."

"Don't blame her. I would've figured it out eventually. Your little buddy up at the house was hanging out with a vampire last time I saw him. It's not a leap to figure out what you are."

"What buddy?" Mama Moon asked, clearly intrigued.

"This little guy with bad coats," I replied. "I met him when I was a teenager. He hid in the bushes and tried to jump me."

"I believe you have Bixby confused with someone else," Melody argued. "It happens occasionally. You should be careful about the accusations you throw around."

"I actually believe the opposite. For example, if I throw around the accusation that you — or perhaps your boss — killed Honey Martelle, I'm reasonably assured that I'm right. I'm also sure there's not a thing you can do about it."

"I wouldn't get too full of yourself," one of the other women seethed. She was shorter than Melody, though she had legs that went on for miles. "I don't think you realize who you're dealing with."

"That's where you're wrong. I have no doubt who I'm dealing with. Dracula wannabes. They're fairly normal in the city ... though the ridicule there seems to be at a higher level. None of these people are making fun of you, which is a true disappointment."

"Dracula?" The woman's voice was high as she trilled out a laugh. "That is absurd. I've never heard nonsense like that in my life."

"Ignore her," Melody admonished. "She's simply looking for attention. Don't reward her for bad behavior."

They wanted to play games so I decided to indulge them. "Yeah. All of you fang-bangers are fans of Dracula. It's like goth kids quoting *The Raven* ... or the way annoying teenagers quote the Kardashians ... or annoying adults still quote *South Park*. I'm over it because it's so pathetic."

"You listen here ... !" The unnamed half-vampire took a menacing step in my direction. I remained in my seat. Technically it was a position of weakness but I didn't want them thinking they'd gotten to me.

"Stop it!" Melody hissed, grabbing the other woman's arm and tugging hard. "You're playing right into her hands. You need to stop."

I kept my eyes defiant as the woman glared. This was too easy, even though I wasn't exactly getting anywhere. Pushing all their buttons was well and good, but there was more to accomplish. "I guess you guys aren't all that new to the area if you've already established yourselves as regulars here, huh?" My mind was busy. "What are you hiding up at the house? Is that where your master lives?"

"We don't have a master," Melody shot back, her eyes flashing. "You don't know what you're talking about. You should really stop speaking."

"Oh, if that was the rule, I would never open my mouth," I drawled. "I'm sure that there are plenty of people who would prefer that, but I don't roll that way."

"No, you like sticking your foot in your mouth at every turn," Mama Moon agreed.

"I'm good that way," I agreed readily. "So, Melody, you haven't introduced me to your friends. I find that a little rude, but I'm willing to overlook it."

"You don't need to know them," Melody shot back. "We're here to unwind after a hard day. There's no need for you to even interact with us." She inclined her head toward a table all the way across the clearing. "Now, if you'll excuse us."

I'd almost forgotten Cedric was there until he cleared his throat. This time when Melody turned back it was with a hint of agitation. "What do you want?" she barked.

"You can't stay here." Cedric was matter of fact. "We talked about this last time ... when I told you that you couldn't visit again. This place is off limits to you."

"I thought you were joking." Melody turned haughty. "It seems to me that a guy who sets up shop in the middle of nowhere needs all the bodies he can get."

"You might think that," he agreed. "But you'd be wrong."

"But ... we want to stay," the third woman said. She'd been silent since entering. Unlike the other two, she didn't seem big on posturing and was clearly more thoughtful. She was the one I was most interested in, though I was certain I could push Melody to the point of no return if I wanted.

"Well, I don't really care what you want," Cedric countered. "This is my bar. You're not allowed. I warned you what would happen if you didn't behave."

"And how did we misbehave?" Melody was suddenly the picture of innocence, batting her eyelashes. "I think you have us confused with someone else."

Cedric wasn't the type to be swayed by a pretty face. "No, I don't. You need to go."

Melody's demeanor switched in an instant. "Do you really want to make enemies of us?"

"I don't care in the least."

"Well ... then I guess that's a mistake you're going to regret." Melody turned, sweeping out her arms. "We should go, ladies. We don't want to hang out here anyway. These people are zero fun."

"But ... ." The third woman looked as if she wanted to argue, but Melody pinned her with a quelling look.

"We're leaving," she ordered.

I watched them go with a mixture of amusement and curiosity.

When they reached the door, Melody turned long enough to stare directly at me. If she thought she was intimidating, she was wrong.

"What do you think?" Mama Moon asked, her gaze intent on me as I downed the rest of my drink.

"I think I'm going to follow them," I said as I stood. "I know where they're going, but I'm dying to see who's hanging out with them at that house on the hill. I'm wondering if I already know him, too."

"Like you know this minion?"

I stilled. "I've never heard that word used in normal conversation, but I like it. That guy is clearly a minion ... and he's a pervert to boot. I should've ended him back then, but I didn't know what I was dealing with. His friend was powerful enough to give me pause ... and I had other things on my mind at the time."

"Do you think you're dealing with the same vampire?"

That was a good question. "I guess I'm about to find out."

IT WASN'T DIFFICULT TO FOLLOW THE HALF-VAMPIRES. They returned to the house, as I knew they would, and were mired in full-on persecution complexes by the time they landed at the remote property.

I secreted myself behind some trees so I could listen, fighting the urge to laugh at the whiny complaints flying fast and furious.

"That place isn't worth our time," Melody assured the other two. "It's lame. I mean ... it's in the middle of the woods."

"I liked it." The third woman was morose as she sank into one of the metal chairs in the middle of the garden. She looked sad, as if she were trapped in a life she didn't particularly appreciate. She was definitely the one I wanted to isolate.

"Well, then you're even dumber than I initially thought," Melody snapped. "That place is stupid."

The sound of footsteps on the cobblestones caught my attention. I didn't see Bixby until he was clear of the bushes. He looked surprised to find the women in front of the house. "That was quick. I didn't expect to see you until right before dawn." He sounded imperious, which is exactly how I remembered him. Well, that and perverted. I didn't care what anybody said, the guy clearly had issues.

"We changed our mind about staying," Melody replied. "It was the same group as always, and they can't help us."

"Not exactly the same group," the quiet woman argued. "There was a new face there, and she seemed to recognize you."

"Yes. Scout. She stopped by with her boyfriend earlier. He's interesting. He's a shifter, but I think we can use him. Her, however ... ."

"I would be careful about her," Bixby cautioned. "She's strong. You can feel the power emanating from her. She's not to be trifled with."

Melody made a disdainful sound. "Oh, please. She's a witch, nothing more. We've handled witches before."

"She's more than that," Bixby persisted. "She's a child of the stars."

Silence greeted his proclamation as I shifted from one foot to the other, anxious. I had no idea how people kept pegging me with that moniker. I'd yet to find someone who could fully explain what it meant. Only weeks before I'd discovered that a blood relative of mine was in Hawthorne Hollow. I never interacted with him and he died before I could ask the obvious questions. I was still reeling from the fallout.

I didn't like to look weak in front of others, but it was daunting to have no idea where I came from. I'm filled to the brim with magic, have been for as long as I can remember, but there was never anyone to teach me to use it. I was self-taught, abandoned as a small child. There had to be a reason ... other than neglect. I refused to believe I was simply unlovable, although in my darkest moments that was the doubt that threatened to bring me to my knees.

"I don't know what that means," Melody said finally. "Does that make her somehow special?"

Bixby hesitated before answering. "She's different," he said finally. "There are many children of the stars who grow to be absolutely nothing. Some of them, though, turn into powerful beings who can ... wipe out ... all of us."

The quiet blonde sat up straighter. "What does that mean? Can she destroy us?"

"If she wants, I have no doubt that she can at least put up a fierce battle. As for the amount of destruction she's capable of, I believe that's entirely up to her."

"Well, I'm not afraid of her," Melody shot back. "I don't like her, but I'm not afraid of her. She's all posturing and no substance."

"People could say the same of you," Bixby pointed out.

"Not if they want to live to tell the tale."

"Go ahead, be as petulant as you want," he chided. "That won't help you with the woman. Your job is to keep up appearances and serve him. You haven't been doing much of that lately."

For the first time since I'd crossed paths with her, Melody looked uncomfortable. "Has he mentioned being upset with my job performance?"

"You know as well as I do that he doesn't talk about such things. He won't mention it. He'll simply end you if he becomes unhappy. If I were you, I would focus on your duties and less on the woman. Stay away from her."

Well, that was interesting. What "he" were they referring to? I lifted my eyes and scanned the house for hints of movement. There was nothing.

That didn't mean that something evil wasn't dwelling within the bowels of the house. Even as I wondered, my skin began crawling. This place was evil, and the occupants were definitely up to something.

I had to find out what.

GUNNER'S BIKE WAS PARKED IN FRONT of the cabin when I pulled up. It was almost midnight, and I was surprised to find him sitting on the porch, Merlin on his lap. He arched an eyebrow as I dismounted and deposited my helmet on the bench by the front door.

"A less trusting man might be curious about what his girlfriend was doing out so late," he supplied as he looked me up and down. "Especially since she said she was going home to watch television and hang out with her cat."

"I also said I might talk to the perverted ghost," I reminded him as I sank into the open chair to his left. "Don't forget that."

"How could I ever forget that?" His expression was unreadable. "I know you're not about running around with other guys, so I'm guessing you were sticking your nose into the business of others."

I watched him a moment, conflicted, and then something occurred to me. "Your father called and ratted me out, didn't he?"

Gunner's face split with a wide grin. "My father does like to tattle. He said you were in Honey's house. He almost sounded proud that you had the gumption to break in and go through her things."

"He didn't seem proud. He seemed annoyed."

"That's why I said he almost seemed proud." He waited a beat, his fingers stroking the cat into a coma. "Did you find anything?"

"As a matter of fact, I did. Were you aware that there's a supernatural speakeasy in the middle of the woods? It's called The Dirty Rooster. I thought it might be a strip club at first, but it turns out it's just a clearing in the forest. It's protected by a magical barrier, which I broke and had to fix. Mama Moon hangs out there."

He arched an eyebrow. "Are you messing with me?"

"Not even a little."

"Well, tell me more."

He was being so amiable I did just that. When I finished, he was thoughtful.

"I know Cedric," he said after a moment. "I've always liked him. He's a bit persnickety, but when you're in this business that's to be expected. I had no idea about the bar, though. I wonder why he kept that secret."

"Oh, I know exactly why he kept it secret. They don't want us in there. They think we're all law and order over fun ... and they're mostly right. They were upset about the bog monster. Apparently his name was Lancelot and he had an open tab."

That was enough to make Gunner laugh. "Well, that sucks for Cedric." He dragged his hand through his hair. "I guess I can't blame them for wanting a place of their own."

"They didn't really give me too much grief ... other than for breaking their barrier. I built a better one for them. They were more agitated by the half-vampires."

"I don't believe I've ever dealt with half-vampires. What should we do about them?"

"I don't know. I don't think they're the real threat, but Melody wants us to believe they are. She's got a big ego ... and she's decided to focus on you. She thinks you'll be of use to her."

"Well, she's not going to get what she wants on that front. You have nothing to worry about ... although I find it cute that you're jealous."

I slid him a dubious glare. "I don't get jealous."

"Green is a good color on you."

I rolled my eyes. "Not that I'm not happy to see you, but I thought you were hanging with Brandon tonight."

"I did that. I listened to him cry. He got drunk, passed out, and I was stuck there alone thinking about you. It turns out I missed you even more than I thought I would."

Even though I was loath to admit it, his words made me go gooey all over. "Well, I guess it's good you found me then, huh?"

"That's what I was thinking." He tilted his head toward the cabin. "You look tired and I'm dead on my feet. How about we turn in for the night and formulate a plan on how to deal with the half-vampires tomorrow?"

"You read my mind."

Somewhere from the trees to the east, I heard a voice. "Leave the curtains open if you're going to do something dirty."

I made a face. "Go away, Tim."

"It was just a request."

ELEVEN

*G*unner was awake before me the next morning, still tucked in at my side. He had a lazy smile on his face as he brushed my hair from my forehead.

"Good morning."

To me, there was nothing good about a morning. Sure, I liked getting up as early as my body clock would allow, but that didn't mean I was happy about it. "Go back to sleep," I whispered.

He smirked. "Why? We're both up. I was thinking we could converse."

"Converse, huh? Is that what they're calling it these days? We can do that in an hour. It's quiet time."

He pursed his lips but said nothing as my eyes drifted shut. His fingers were light as they brushed against my back, rubbing soothing circles. He didn't say anything. He didn't move. Other than his hand, he was still.

"Fine." I wrenched open my eyes. "Be an animal."

He snorted, seemingly genuinely amused. "Believe it or not, when I suggested conversing I meant just that. I've been thinking about what happened last night."

"Before or after we left the porch?"

"Before you came home. I'm thinking about the half-vampires. What can you tell me about them?"

"Oh, so this is a business conversation. You should've told me so we could've gone to Mable's Table and written the meal off on our taxes." I rolled to my back and stretched my arms over my head, groaning as a few joints popped. "What do you want to know?"

"I don't think I've ever seen a half-vampire. I don't even know what they are."

"I forget how isolated you are up here. It's basically all shifters and bog monsters all the time."

"We have mummies and spriggans, too."

"Good point."

"If we're going to have to fight these things, then I want to know their weaknesses."

"They're only half-vampires," I reminded him. "They're also half human."

"Meaning?"

"Meaning they can be turned back. They're not lost causes yet."

His brow wrinkled. "How did they become half-vampires?"

"Vampires are either born or made. The strongest ones are born, but that only occurs when you have two born vampires willing to procreate with one another. Their numbers have thinned over the years. They didn't even realize it was happening until recently."

"That seems like impractical planning."

"I don't disagree. The born vampires are trying to shore up their lines, but it's an uphill battle. There are a lot of groups out there like us and very few vampires who are willing to play by the rules. They're being wiped out faster than they can procreate."

"Which brings us to the second type of vampires," he mused.

I nodded. "To save themselves, the vampires started creating others. These are weaker. They don't possess the same mind magic as their born counterparts. While they're stronger than humans, their weaknesses are more pronounced."

"Can born vampires walk in the sun?"

"No. No vampire has managed that. Well, I take that back. There's an urban legend about a vampire who was gifted with the ability to walk in the sun by a mage. I think that's a load of bunk, though."

"Why do you think that? I've never crossed paths with a mage, but they're supposed to be powerful."

"Yeah, but this is beyond even a mage. It would have to be a special mage. Supposedly it happened right here in Michigan."

"Well ... that's interesting. You don't think that's the vampire we're dealing with, do you?"

"Absolutely not. I don't know much, but I guarantee this vampire can't go out in the sun. That's why he has half-vampires protecting him. They're the barrier between him and the outside world."

"Because they can walk around in daylight?"

I nodded. "That little booger he's got as a minion probably helps, too. I can't wait to rip that guy's head off."

"And you still think you've met him before."

"I know it." My temper got the better of me and I started to roll away from him, but his arm snaked out and snagged me around the waist.

"Fine. I believe you've seen him before. I won't bring it up again."

His expression told me otherwise, that he was just saying that because he hadn't ruled out rolling around and getting sweaty before hopping in the shower. I let it go all the same. I was warm and comfortable. There was no need to ruin that.

"Go back to the half-vampires," he prodded. "You still haven't told me how they were created."

"It's not a big mystery. To turn humans, a vampire has to drain them to the point of death and then force them to drink his or her blood. In this particular case, a healthy human is either forced or willingly drinks vampire blood. No drinking on the other end is required."

"Huh." He wrinkled his nose. "That's kind of gross. Do you think many humans would willingly drink blood?"

"It depends on what they're offered."

"For example?"

"Immortality. On paper, vampires live forever. Many of them have shorter lives than they would've if they'd stayed human because they're wiped out by hunting parties, but the humans who are desperate to stave off death don't think that far ahead.

"In some instances it's humans who have found out they're terminally ill," I continued. "Death is so frightening for some that they'll do anything to make sure it doesn't happen, even surrendering their souls. In other cases, it's hubris. Some people think they're better than others and have the right to live forever because the world will somehow be worse without them."

"I take it you're not interested in living forever."

"No. Who would want that?"

"I might." He brushed his thumb over my bottom lip, his expression thoughtful. "I mean ... I kind of like the idea of spending eternity with someone, traveling the world and seeing how things change with time. If you're a vampire, things like global warming and nuclear war are nothing to fear. I'm not saying it's something I would really do, but it's interesting to dream about."

I studied his angular features for a long time and then sighed. "You're looking at it through romantic eyes instead of realistic ones."

"Oh, really?" His lips quirked. "Well, tell me the reality of it, wise one."

"What happens when all the people and animals die? How do the vampires feed? What happens if all the humans are tainted, including the blood? What happens if the night somehow dies and there's no way to go out because of endless sun? Also, just because the vampires won't die in a nuclear attack doesn't mean they won't be disfigured. Their flesh will be subject to the same issues as human flesh."

He made a face. "Well, if you're going to be a downer about it."

I couldn't stop myself from laughing at his hangdog expression. "I prefer to focus on this life, on making it the best it can possibly be, and not dreaming about something else. Besides, you lose your soul if you become a vampire. They say the born ones have souls, but I've yet to see that proven. The made ones definitely don't have souls."

"Yeah. That would suck." He rubbed his chin.

"You can't love without a soul," I reminded him. "Television and movies might want to argue that point, but that's one of the few things I believe with my whole heart."

"Well, then I definitely want to keep my soul." He dipped his head in and gave me a soft kiss. When he pulled back, he looked resigned. "I'm guessing you've already got our morning planned. We should probably get moving."

The shift threw me off. "What do you mean?"

"Oh, don't pretend you're not returning to the house on the bluff to mess with them. I might not have known you that long, but I'm getting familiar with how your mind works, and there's no way you'll pass up that opportunity."

He wasn't wrong. "We have time for breakfast at Mable's first. It is on the way."

"Sold. But you're buying." He gave me another kiss before rolling out of bed and jerking his head toward the bathroom. "We might yet be able to do the conversing you were talking about earlier if you get it in gear. You'll have to be quick. I'm hungry."

I watched him go for a moment, an emotion I wasn't entirely familiar with washing over me. Was it love? It felt too soon for that. It wasn't lust, because there was genuine emotion associated with the feeling. I wasn't sure what to deem it, but adoration came pretty close.

He was smart, handsome, and always took my feelings into consideration. Nobody was perfect, but I was starting to think he was darned close. I didn't like putting my feelings out there for others to see, but I was fairly certain I wouldn't have a choice with him.

We were bonding, and in a way that made me think it would last forever.

How's that for a scary thought?

MY BELLY FULL OF EGGS AND HASH BROWNS, I was riding high on warm and cuddly emotions when we returned to the house on the hil. The feeling didn't last long, because I immediately crashed into a barrier when I tried to cross onto the property.

"Son of a ... !"

I was too late to warn Gunner, who kept walking and immediately bounced off the wall of magic, flying backward and landing on his perfect behind. "Ow!" He rubbed the spot where he'd landed and flicked his eyes to me. "What is that?"

"Wards. At least I think." I raised my hands, calling magic to my fingertips, and tried to push through the barrier. That was a mistake, because the magic came flying back at me twofold and I barely missed being scorched. I had to dive to the side and almost eat a mouthful of dirt thanks to the way I landed.

Laughter from the second floor of the house assailed my ears when I regained my senses. I rolled and searched the windows until I found the one I was looking for. There, Melody sat and gaily waved. She was clearly having a good time.

"Good morning, lovebirds," she called out. "How are you feeling this fine summer day?"

"Like I want to rip your head off your shoulders," Gunner muttered as he recovered.

I slid my eyes to him, assuring myself that he wasn't seriously injured before focusing on the individual who was quickly becoming my new nemesis. Well, her or the perverted little dude. He was still on my list.

"What's with the barrier?" I decided to get to the heart of matters. "Someone might think you're afraid or something. You can't be afraid, right? You're strong ... and brave ... and totally a natural blonde even though your eyebrows are dark."

It was hard to make out Melody's expression, but I could practically feel the hatred wafting off of her from fifty feet away, so I knew my insult hit the mark.

"We like to think of it as a home protection system," she explained. "You can never tell when people who don't have your best interests at heart might show up. I mean ... it's possible for people to hide in the trees at night and eavesdrop even when it's none of their freaking business what's going on."

Oh, well, that answered that question. She obviously knew I'd followed them last night. She wasn't aware at the time, though, which meant someone had informed her after the fact. But who? I decided to play a hunch.

"I'm guessing your master picked up my scent. You're already in trouble with him because you're lazy. That's why he suggested the wards. That was probably a good idea, but if I was a betting witch I'd put everything on you being in the doghouse. Is he threatening to take your immortality?"

Melody sounded a feral growl. "You don't know what you're talking about. Why do you keep flapping your lips when it's obvious you're a moron and have no idea what's happening? I mean ... what is wrong with you?"

Gunner moved to my side to help me up. "I don't think we should stay here," he said in a low voice. "The longer we sit and engage in her game, the more control she has. We need to take it away from her."

I knew he had a point, but there was nothing I loved more than a verbal hair-pulling contest. And, while Melody struck me as a moron, she was good with the insults.

"And what's your deal?" Melody pressed, her full attention on Gunner. "Why are you with her? You could do so much better. Do you know she was out at the bar without you last night? She was picking up men and everything. She's a total whore."

"Hey!" I jabbed a finger in her direction. "You can't lie when playing the insult game."

"Says who?"

"Says anyone who has ever mastered it. You know what? I'm not playing with you today. Until you follow the rules, you're cut off." As if to prove I was just as immature as her, I flipped my hair a little as I turned on my heel and stalked back toward my bike. "I mean ... there's only one rule to the game. Lies aren't allowed."

Melody called to my back: "You're just upset because your boyfriend is hot for me. Oh, yeah. I saw the way he was looking at me yesterday. He totally wants to upgrade. Don't you worry, baby. We're going to get you into the fold before it's all said and done. You've got my word on that." She blew him a kiss as he rolled his eyes and followed me to the bikes.

"You have a wonderful way with people," he deadpanned as he mounted his ride. "Has anyone ever told you that?"

"I can't decide if I want to kill her or the minion first. I'm genuinely torn."

He shook his head. "You are going to give me an ulcer before this is all said and done."

I WAS STILL POUTING AN HOUR LATER when Doc, the newest member of our Spells Angels tribe, hit pay dirt on a computer search. He wasn't magical — at least not that I was aware of — but his technological abilities were through the roof.

"I found your woman," he announced, drawing my attention from my iced tea.

Only Rooster, Gunner, Doc, and I were in the bar — the others were actually working — and it had been a quiet morning — other than my constant grousing, of course.

"Which woman?" Rooster, a pool cue in his hand, asked. He and Gunner were shooting a game of eight-ball. They promised to keep an eye on the bar while Whistler ran to the bank, but it wasn't as if anybody would come in before noon.

"The woman you mentioned when you first came in," Doc replied blankly. He wasn't high on the social graces meter, but he was accidentally mildly entertaining regularly.

"He's talking about Melody," Gunner volunteered. "I included her name on the list of people we needed background checks run on, along with that Bixby guy."

"Him I haven't been able to find so far," Doc volunteered. "I'm guessing that's not his real name or he's somehow managed to hide his identity. I haven't given up finding him yet, but it's going to take some time. Melody Summers is another story. I found her with a simple Google search."

Rooster abandoned the game and moved closer to the booth where Doc sat. "What did you find?"

"She's missing."

That was the most absurd thing I'd ever heard. "She's not missing. We know exactly where she is. In fact, she's probably still sitting in that window taunting our shadows. Oh, and telling lies. She cheats at the insult game and lies."

Gunner rolled his eyes and shook his head. "Let it go. It's not as if I believed her."

"That doesn't matter. You can't cheat at the insult game. I mean ... if the rules of that game go out the window what can we rely on in this day and age?"

Rooster's expression reflected bafflement. "Do I want to know what she's talking about?"

"No." Gunner was firm. "She's lost her head. I think Melody bewitched her or something. I've never heard her rave like this."

"It could be PMS," Doc volunteered. "I've heard that makes women irrational."

I was close to showing him exactly how irrational a woman could get when I realized that he had no idea that what he'd said was insulting. He was a blank slate when it came to social niceties, which wasn't necessarily his fault.

"How is she missing?" I gritted out as I fought to control my temper. When I risked a glance at Gunner, I found him watching me with overt amusement. It made me want to smack him ... or at least pull his hair. Okay, I kind of wanted to kiss him, too. Seriously, what is wrong with me?

"She's not from this area," Doc replied, all business. "She lives in a suburb of Detroit. Some place called Birmingham. I thought that was in Alabama."

"I think every state has a Birmingham," I shot back, my voice sparking with temper. "I know the place. It's one of the richer cities in the state."

"I guess that's why her husband is offering a million-dollar reward for her safe return," he mused.

I was officially dumbfounded. "Wait ... she's married?"

"Yeah. He's been all over the news down there. She disappeared six months ago. He thinks sex traffickers took her or something. He's desperate to find her."

Well, that was a new wrinkle.

TWELVE

*I*t was a lot to think about. When I have deep thinking to do, I like to pace, so that's what I did for the following thirty minutes.

"I think she might've blown a gasket," Rooster noted. He'd gone back to his pool game with Gunner and they were talking in hushed tones.

"She gets like that." Gunner sounded more amused than worried. "She has tunnel vision. You should see her do laundry. Everything has to be folded a specific way."

"You two are getting close."

"Do you have a problem with that?"

"No. Just remember, I don't like relationship drama playing out on my team. If you guys are going to be immature and break up or something, do it away from everybody else."

"I don't think you have to worry about that."

Rooster snorted. "Those are bold words from a guy who refused to go out with a woman a second time because she remembered to shave one leg and not the other."

"Hey. That was a legitimate concern. I mean ... how did she not notice? I'm a wolf. I would've been fine with two hairy legs. Two

112

shaved legs would've been fine. One of each is creepy."

"I can't really argue with that."

Finally, after a few moments I was certain my brain might actually start smoking, I moved back to Doc. "Can you bring up the photos with the articles?"

He nodded, hitting a few buttons and turning his screen to me. Sure enough, Melody stared back at me. She looked somehow more pleasant in the photos.

"Any kids?" I asked.

"Not that I can find mention of."

"Then there aren't any kids. The news media would trot out little kids to snag the attention of the public in an effort to find her. I just ... I wonder what they think happened to her."

"Okay, you need to come over here and talk to us." Gunner took me by surprise when he grabbed my elbow and directed me toward the pool table. "You just ignored a perfectly good conversation that mentioned a woman having one shaved leg and one hairy. You didn't comment. Are you sick?" He pressed his hand to my forehead.

Annoyance rolled over me and I slapped his hand away. "I'm not sick. Stop it."

"Whew. You are in there." He stared directly into my eyes and smiled. "I wasn't sure. I was starting to worry that your body had been taken over by aliens."

"Why must you always assume it'll be aliens taking over bodies when the time comes?" I challenged. "It's far more likely to be parasitic worms. They go in through the ear canal — like that really old *Star Trek* movie — and then a master controls the worms."

Gunner worked his jaw. "I am never going to forgive you for putting that image in my head. Now I'm going to think there are worms crawling into my ears whenever your hair brushes against me in sleep." As if to prove it, he stuck his index finger into his ear canal and jostled it. "You're mean when you want to be."

That was enough to get me to smile. "I'm sorry. I can build a spell to keep the worms out if you want."

"Really?" Hope etched his features. "That would be great."

"If you two are done verbally copulating, I think we should focus on the problem at hand," Rooster challenged. "How did this woman end up here if she went missing in the southeastern portion of the state?"

"Obviously the vampire enticed her," I replied. "Immortality is hard to say no to." I gave Gunner a pointed look. "Even people who know better think it's a great idea."

"Oh, don't give me that," he complained. "I didn't say that the notion was without problems. I simply said it could be romantic to be with the same person for eternity. You're the one who brought up nuclear war facial growths and starving to death."

"It sounds like you two are having some deep conversations," Rooster muttered, shaking his head. "I'm guessing you told her the romantic thing because you were hoping to get some."

Gunner pinned our boss with a dark look. "That's not very respectful. As her boyfriend, I feel the need to pound you. As your employee, I'm guessing that won't go over well."

Rooster snickered. "I'll try to be more respectful." He turned to me. "As for you, it would be helpful if I knew what you were thinking. You're all over the place. What do you believe we're dealing with here?"

"A vampire."

He gave me a "Well, duh" look. "I never would've considered that, what with the half-vampires and everything. Of course we're dealing with a vampire. There has to be more to it than that."

"Okay. Chill out." I held up my hand and made a face. "There's no reason to get excited."

"Obviously there is," he argued. "That woman you've been fighting with either voluntarily left her husband and ended up in our neck of the woods or somebody took her. I'm of a mind that she left on her own ... but that's still going to rain down a tsunami of crap if anyone figures out who she is."

"She's using her real name," Gunner pointed out. "It's only a matter of time before someone tracks her down. She claimed to own the house on the bluff. That's easy enough to check, right?" He turned to Doc for an answer.

"I'm on it," the computer genius offered perfunctorily. "Just give me a second."

"What we really need is the inside scoop on her disappearance," I supplied. "Maybe there's a backstory nobody knows about ... like the husband was abusive or he's a suspect in her death. There's always more than what's printed in the newspaper."

"How do you suggest we get that information?" Rooster asked.

I hesitated before answering, which gave Gunner the time he needed to figure it out ... and groan. "Oh, man. You're going to call that cop who is hot for you?"

"He's our best shot," I replied reasonably. "And ... he's not hot for me. He flirts with everybody."

Gunner muttered something under his breath that sounded suspiciously like "I'll show him hot when I set him on fire" but I couldn't be one hundred percent certain.

"I think it's worth a try," Rooster volunteered. "Any information we can get at this point is welcome."

MIKE FOLEY WAS A FRIENDLY GUY. We'd gotten to know one another during my stint with the Detroit branch of the Spells Angels. He was one of the few cops I didn't avoid like tetanus. There were some members of the department who were aware of the paranormal issue and others who were in the dark. Thankfully, Mike was aware. He suffered post-traumatic stress issues from a previous incident and chose to seclude himself away in a dark office and work via computer all day so he rarely had to deal with people.

I didn't like to judge, but his self-isolation seemed a waste because he was one of the good ones.

"Scout Randall, as I live and breathe," he said as he picked up the video call.

I flashed him a smile. He wore a loud shirt that said something about bytes, and he seemed relatively relaxed ... at least for him. He was one of the few people I could say without hesitation was always glad to see me. "Hey, Mike. How's it going?"

"It could be worse. I've been thinking about starting online dating now that you're gone and I have no hope of enticing you. I was looking at the offerings last night. They're ... not good."

It took everything I had not to laugh. "Well ... you need to be patient. I'm sure there's someone out there just looking for a guy who spends all of his time looking at porn on the internet."

"Ha, ha, ha." He shook his head. "What's going on with you? Do you need something?"

I only contacted him when I needed something, which was enough to make me feel guilty ... even as I barreled forward to get more information. "I need information on Melody Summers."

He sat there a moment and blinked. "That name sounds familiar."

"She went missing out of Birmingham six months ago."

"Ah." He bobbed his head. "Now I remember. Housewife. Husband is loaded. She disappeared after he left for work one day and absolutely nobody has any idea what happened to her. There are whispers the husband might've done it."

That was exactly the sort of information I was looking for. "Who is spreading the whispers about the husband?"

"The usual suspects." Mike shrugged and popped a berry into his mouth. "Listen, you know as well as anybody that the husband is always the primary suspect. These two had been married for a few years — three or four I think — and most everyone in their circle said they had a good marriage. But friends always say that until evidence starts stacking up, and then they start changing their tune."

"Yeah, well, she's not dead."

He stilled. "How do you know that?"

"I met her yesterday."

"One second." Gunner interjected, lifting a finger. He'd been sitting next to me, off screen, and made a series of faces whenever Mike made an attempt at flirting. He wasn't a fan of our relationship, even though I'd admonished him several times that he had nothing to worry about. He hit the mute button on the computer so Mike couldn't hear us. "Do you think it's a good idea to tell a cop that a missing person is up here?"

"Why not?"

"We could end up with a contingent of Birmingham police detectives on our doorstep, and that'll make taking down your vampire difficult. They'll be watching the house."

He had a point. "It will be fine." I reached around his hand and unmuted the computer. "There's absolutely nothing to worry about. Mike doesn't care about the missing woman. She's not in his jurisdiction."

"That's true." Mike flashed a smile and focused on Gunner. "I see you're still around."

Gunner's expression was dark. "Yes, and I'm not going anywhere."

"Oh, geez," Rooster groused, moving in at my other side. "Why do you turn into a posturing moron whenever this guy is on the screen? It's ridiculous. Grow up."

"Yeah." Mike winked at me as Gunner growled.

"You grow up, too," Rooster warned, wagging a finger at Mike. "We need information on this woman. She's definitely up here and we're unsure how to proceed."

"Well, I don't know what to tell you." Mike turned serious as he started tapping on his keyboard. "All I know is what's in the official file. I can try to sniff around with the Birmingham detectives, but I won't lie, Scout. You remember what Birmingham people are like. You haven't been gone that long."

Rooster focused on me. "What is that supposed to mean?"

"They're hoity-toity," I explained. "Most of them are rich. The entire town is a bit ... affected. It's affluent. The kids are entitled jerks. The parents all drive expensive SUVs and BMWs. There's nothing gritty about the city, which means the cops are just as entitled as the residents. We definitely don't want them coming here."

"Can we dig for information without risking that?"

"I don't know." I tapped my bottom lip and regarded Mike. "Just give me the basics on Melody, whatever is in that file you've got there. That's at least something."

"Sure." Mike turned back to his screen. "Okay, for starters, she's smoking hot."

My lips twisted. "She's not that hot."

He ignored me. "She graduated from Michigan State University with a degree in women's history."

"Of course she did," I muttered.

"What does that mean?" Rooster looked legitimately confused.

"That she went to college to snag a husband," I answered.

"Which she did," Mike said. "According to this, they met junior year, were engaged a month after graduation, and married a year later. Their wedding was covered by the *Detroit Free Press* because his father is some international banking bigwig."

"So he has money," I mused.

"He's the king of money. There are photos of their house — it's a mansion. It's worth, like, two million if the property records are correct, and I have no reason to think they're not."

"Anything else about her?"

"Um ... the husband has various notations next to his name. They've been hunting for a mistress and have come up empty so far. Now they're focusing on him being gay. They figure that's the reason they can't find a mistress."

"They're determined that he's the culprit," I said. "They're not really looking for her."

"That would be my guess."

"That could be why her name didn't pop on the property records," Gunner mused. "They weren't really trying to find her because they have tunnel vision on the husband."

I agreed. "What about the property records up here, Mike?"

"They check out. But she didn't inherit the house. She bought it from the bank four weeks ago. She got it cheap."

"That's because it's falling apart."

"Yeah, but the photos seem to indicate it will be awesome when she finishes restoration."

"Yeah, that's never going to happen." I rolled my neck as I considered my options. "Anything else?"

"No, but I can keep digging. The cops really are focused on the husband, who has lawyered up but keeps holding weekly news conferences. Because he is who he is, the media keeps showing up, but the wife is no longer at the top of the news cycle."

"They must believe she's dead," Rooster said. "They're not looking for a missing woman. They're looking for a dead body."

"Yeah." I rubbed my cheek. "Okay, keep digging. Don't let it slip that she's up here until we know what she's doing."

"That seems cruel to the husband," Mike noted.

"Yeah, but it could get a lot crueler if we don't play this right."

"You're the boss." Mike hesitated before disconnecting. "You really should dump that guy and come back home. It's boring here without you."

Gunner scowled. "She is home." He switched off the call and glared at me. "I hate that you encourage him."

"I hardly think I was encouraging him," I countered. "You need to chill out."

"I agree." Rooster sank into one of the chairs across from me. "Do you think Melody voluntarily went missing?"

"Yes. She's far too into what's happening here. If she was taken against her will she would be more reticent. Her access to money explains why the master was interested in her, but the other two are still a mystery."

I tapped my fingers on the tabletop, lost in thought. My reverie was disturbed when the door flew open and Raisin stalked in. It wasn't even noon, so the fact that she wasn't in school was a giveaway that something had happened.

"I need help!" She wailed in dramatic teenager fashion.

I arched an eyebrow. "Aren't you supposed to be in school?"

"Yes, she is." Rooster looked furious. "What are you doing skipping school, young lady? I promised your grandmother that you hanging around with us wouldn't turn into a negative. Now, here you are in the middle of the day, hanging out at a bar and skipping classes. I just ... are you trying to kill me?"

I had to fight off a smile as Raisin pinned him with an exasperated look.

"Oh, don't be annoying," she drawled, the arrogance that only youth could muster on full display. "It's my free hour, and I just got this." She held up what looked to be a frilly dress, something from a different era. "Do you know what this is?"

"Ugly?" Gunner volunteered helpfully.

The glare she shot him was withering. "This is my costume for the play, and you know what? It doesn't fit. They say there's nothing they can do about it because they don't have the money."

Oh, well, this sounded dire. "What do you mean it doesn't fit?"

"It. Doesn't. Fit." Her tone was sarcastic. "I mean ... how many different ways am I supposed to say it?"

I held onto my temper, but only because she was kind of cute in the midst of her meltdown. "I mean is it too small or big?"

"Big." She jutted out her lower lip. "The top has loads of room up here." She held her hands in front of her chest and indicated breasts by flexing her fingers. "I'll never have enough to fill it out."

The fact that Rooster and Gunner looked decidedly uncomfortable with the direction the conversation had taken only served to further amuse me.

"Well, I have good news for you." I stood, the problems of the day forgotten ... at least temporarily. "I can fix your dress."

"You can?" Raisin looked suspicious.

She wasn't the only one. "Yeah, you can?" Gunner's eyebrows drew together doubtfully. "How?"

"If you go out to my motorcycle and find a blue fabric box in the storage container, I'll show you."

Gunner slowly got to his feet. "Are you telling me you can sew?"

"Yes."

"But ... ."

"Just get me the box." I was at the end of my rope. "It won't take long to fix the costume and then we can get Raisin back to school ... hopefully with no one being the wiser that she was gone."

"That would be nice," Rooster acknowledged. "I just ... can you really sew?"

Ugh. All these doubts were making me want to punch all three of them. "I guess there's only one way to find out, huh?"

THIRTEEN

"Omigod! It's perfect!"

Raisin was absolutely thrilled an hour later when she twirled in the middle of the bar to show off her costume to Gunner and Rooster. Whistler had returned by this point and was equally amused by her reaction.

"You look good," I encouraged. "The big debut is tonight, right?"

She nodded, chewing her bottom lip. "Um ... you guys are still coming, right? Nothing has happened to drag you away, has it?"

"Of course not," Rooster reassured her. "We will be there. You, however, need to get out of here. If someone catches you ... ."

"Yeah, yeah, yeah." Raisin imperiously waved off his concerns. "I've got it." Her eyes were filled with an emotion I didn't recognize when she turned to me. "Thank you."

The gratitude was so heartfelt it threw me for a loop. "It's not a big deal." My cheeks burned when I felt the others focus on me. "You'll be great. I'm looking forward to seeing you steal the show tonight."

"I'm kind of nervous," Raisin admitted. "I've never done anything like this."

"But you were so excited a few minutes ago," Gunner protested. "What happened to change that between now and then?"

Raisin didn't immediately answer. Oddly enough, even though I wasn't keen on standing up in front of people and acting for the masses, I understood what was bothering her.

"It's normal to be nervous," I told her. "Some of the most famous actors in the world say that their first theater performance was nerve-wracking. They also say that the moment they took the stage all those doubts went away and they knew exactly what to do."

Raisin's expression was so suspicious it almost made me laugh out loud. "Oh, yeah? What actors?"

"George Clooney." It was the first name that came to mind. I had no idea if he actually did theater, but I figured it didn't matter.

"Who?"

I frowned. "How can you not know George Clooney?"

"He was Batman in a very bad movie," Gunner volunteered.

Raisin tilted her head to the side, considering, and then shook her head. "No. That was Christian Bale ... and Ben Affleck, although Affleck should've never put on the suit."

"Before them," I said.

"Um ... I don't think Batman was a thing before them."

Wow, did I feel old.

Gunner slid his eyes to me and I could tell he was thinking the same thing.

"What about *Ocean's 11?*"

She shook her head.

"*Three Kings?*"

"Nope."

I was starting to get desperate. "*Gravity?*"

"Yeah, I don't think I saw that."

It was time to change tactics. "I believe Julia Roberts said the same thing."

"Emma Roberts' aunt? I think I've heard of her."

Yup, I was officially done. "You should be heading back to school."

"You should," Rooster agreed. "Change back into your regular clothes and then we're leaving. I'm taking you back to school to make sure you go."

Raisin looked resigned. "For a biker gang, you guys are awfully annoying about following the rules."

"Yes, well, we're more than one thing."

Once Raisin left, I did my best to ignore Gunner, who I could feel staring at me. Finally, I couldn't take it a second longer and practically exploded. "What?"

"Nothing." His lips curved. "You're just a constant surprise. I can't believe you can sew. That's so ... domestic."

"You try living on three hundred bucks a month at eighteen," I suggested. "You'll learn how to fix your own clothes really quickly, too. Otherwise you'll go naked, and that's not a good thing if you spend a lot of time in rough neighborhoods."

His smile faded. "I really wish you wouldn't say things like that. It makes me feel angry ... and a little entitled."

"Well, then you should be careful who you tease."

"Fair enough."

I DRESSED IN SIMPLE BLACK PANTS AND A NICE top for Raisin's debut. Gunner picked me up in his truck because we figured it would be easier. He let loose a low wolf whistle when he saw me, which I proceeded to ignore as I fastened my seatbelt.

"What?" I was feeling on display today, and I didn't like it.

"You look nice."

I waited for him to add something to the statement, like an ill-timed joke. When he didn't, my cheeks started burning. "Oh, well, thanks."

His amusement was obvious as he leaned forward to kiss my cheek. "Sometimes a compliment is just a compliment," he whispered, sending chills up my spine.

"I know. I ... am still getting used to it."

"Well, try a little harder. You're beautiful." He studied me for a moment and then put the truck in gear. "You remind me of Raisin a little bit. You're both nervous about ridiculous things."

"I get where she's coming from," I argued. "It's difficult to let down the protective wall and let others in. It's not easy to make yourself vulnerable, and that's exactly what she's doing tonight."

"Yeah, but if you make yourself vulnerable — and I'm doing it, too, with you, so it's not as if you're the only one — you open yourself to great things happening. How can that not be good?"

He had a point, which was annoying. "I'm just saying that it's an adjustment."

"Well, you're doing a fairly good job adjusting, so I guess I'll let it go for today." He extended his hand over the console and twined his fingers with mine. "Are you looking forward to high school theater?"

The question was posed with such good humor that I could do nothing but laugh. "I think we'll survive, or maybe that's just wishful thinking."

"I think it's going to be a fun night, and Raisin really needs it. She's lived a hard life. Things are going better for her now, but she still needs reassurance."

"She does, but she also needs to learn boundaries. Whistler could get in real trouble if some undercover investigator from the state drops in during one of her impromptu visits."

"We've told her. She doesn't understand the gravity of the situation."

"Well, she needs to."

"Do you have any suggestions on how to make that happen?"

"No, but I'll give it some serious thought."

"Sounds like a plan. For tonight, however, I would appreciate if you saved all your serious thoughts for me. I have some plans for you after our trip to the theater, and they don't include frowning and fretting."

My lips curved, unbidden. "One thing I have to give you, somehow you always manage to have plans no matter the circumstances."

"I'm good that way."

"You're ... something."

HIGH SCHOOL THEATER IS ONE OF THOSE things you either

love or hate. To love it, you need to have a child performing on the stage, someone you love beyond reason. To tolerate it, you have to find the laughter in the production.

That's what I did.

Raisin's take on *Little Red Riding Hood* was something straight out of a web soap opera. For those curious, a web-only soap opera is even cornier than regular soap operas, which I happened to like because one of my foster mothers was addicted to *General Hospital* and she taught me all about the genre.

To be fair, Raisin warned us it was an updated take. So, instead of Red Riding Hood skipping through the forest to visit her grandmother, this version had Red slink around the mean streets of Detroit looking for a drug dealer. No joke. It was an extremely gritty take, or would've been if the dialogue wasn't so laughable.

"I'm confused," Gunner hedged as he sat next to me, my fingers linked with his. He was focused on the stage, but his expression was one of complete bafflement.

"What confuses you?" I asked in a whisper. "Is it the fact that the Big Bad Wolf is actually a biker guy with a bad wig or the fact that Raisin keeps talking about Red Riding Hood moonlighting as a prostitute?"

"Both." Gunner looked anything but thrilled. "This is a school production. It's supposed to be clean ... and she's mentioned getting paid for sex three times."

It took everything I had not to burst out laughing. "They're teenagers."

"That's not an excuse."

"Do you remember what it was like to be a teenager?"

"I don't remember having plays like this. We stuck to the boring stuff, like Shakespeare and ... what's that play with the four little women?"

"*Little Women.*"

"That's what I said."

I rolled my eyes, opting to change tactics. "I think you're missing the point. Raisin said the kids wrote the play themselves. That means they got to put their spin on it. Kids today are exposed to a lot of news stories and bad reality television — and that's on top of those Kardashians, who I swear are rotting the brains of people everywhere."

His lips quirked. "I get all of that. I still don't understand why some adult didn't come in and stop this before it happened."

"You mean censor it."

"I mean ... fine. I don't particularly like the word, but this is awful."

"It's fine. Just ... suck it up and keep your smile in place. No matter what happens, Raisin needs to believe that you're enjoying yourself."

"Right." He squeezed my hand tighter. "I'm going to need some very vigorous bedtime stories to wash this thing out of my head later."

"You and me both."

NINETY MINUTES LATER, I WASN'T SURE what I felt. Numb might've been the best word. The production only got weirder, with Red Riding Hood essentially blowing off the wolf's head after trying to put a diamond-studded collar on him. Technically the play ended on a high note, with Red Riding Hood surviving ... and going back to her life as a prostitute. It didn't leave me with a happy feeling, though.

"I want to wash my eyes out with lye soap," Gunner hissed as he stood with me at the back of the gymnasium. "I mean ... that was horrible."

I glanced around to make sure nobody had overheard him. Thankfully most of the guests had fled the second the final curtain dropped. It was a mass exodus of epic proportions. We weren't the only ones freaked out by the play. The other attendees clearly couldn't wait to escape.

"You need to be careful what you say," I warned, pinning him with a serious look. "This is important to Raisin. The play may have been a little ... peculiar ... but she was still great in it."

Instead of agreeing, he snorted. "Peculiar? That was a toxic dump of ... I don't even know what."

"Gunner ... ."

"Scout." He mimicked my tone and gave me a wide smile. "You don't have to worry about me saying anything to hurt her feelings. I'm not an idiot. You have to admit that was a terrible play, though."

"It was ... unique."

He folded his arms over his chest and waited. "I'm not going to get naked for you tonight until you admit it was crap."

"Um ... that's not an appropriate threat for a woman. I can go without sex longer than you."

"Oh, please. We both know that's not true. You're hot for me."

He was a little too cute to argue with, so I decided to change the topic. "Just tell her she was good. After what happened with her father ... ." I trailed off. The memory of her bruised and battered face would haunt me for a long time. Her father was an abusive jerk who not only hurt her but also threatened to take her life. We taught him a valuable lesson before making sure Raisin was in a safe environment with her grandmother. I knew she was better off. Still, certain things about that night haunted me.

"Hey." Gunner's voice was gentle as he nudged my arm. "It's okay. I was just teasing. I won't say anything to upset Raisin. I'm not an idiot. I know how this is done."

I mustered a smile. "Yeah, well ... you're better at it than I give you credit for."

He slid his arm over my shoulders and tugged me to his side, pressing a kiss to my temple. When we swiveled to face the sound of pounding feet — I had no doubt it was Raisin coming to claim her accolades — I found Marissa watching us with annoyed eyes.

"What?" Gunner asked when he realized we were being observed. "Do I have something on my face?"

Marissa replied after a beat, shaking her head. She didn't look angry as much as resigned. "Don't worry about it."

Raisin picked that moment to burst into the gymnasium. She was back in her street clothes, her eyes lit with excitement. "What did you think?"

"You stole the show," Rooster automatically answered.

"You were a total star," Bonnie enthused.

"I didn't get the part about her being a prostitute," Doc fretted.

"You were magnificent," Whistler volunteered. "I think that's the best play I ever saw."

"You didn't suck even a little," Marissa offered.

Raisin's expectant eyes landed on Gunner and me. "Well?"

Gunner offered up a wide grin. "You were mesmerizing. I couldn't look away from you. I can't believe how powerful your performance was."

Raisin preened under the compliment and wiggled her hips. "Thank you." When she turned to me, I was ready.

"I think you had a hand in writing some of that dialogue," I supplied. "I heard traces of you in there, and it was brilliant. You're an excellent writer as well as an actress. It's amazing how you can do so many things."

"You really heard me in the script?" She looked delighted. "I ... wow! I wasn't sure anyone would pick up on that."

"It was absolutely wonderful."

"Oh, thank you." She impulsively threw her arms around my neck, causing me to stagger back. I wasn't expecting the embrace, so I stood there like a moron for a full two seconds before returning the hug.

Gunner's expression reflected amusement over Raisin's shoulder. He was clearly enjoying himself.

Rooster cleared his throat to interrupt the moment, for which I was profoundly thankful. "How about we get some celebratory ice cream and then I'll take you home? I already cleared it with your grandmother. I invited her, but she was so overwhelmed by your performance she wanted to absorb it for a bit before discussing it with you."

I'd seen Raisin's grandmother afterward and overwhelmed was the right word. That woman looked positively shocked. I had no doubt there would be a discussion of sorts when Raisin returned home.

"Oh, yay!" Raisin clapped her hands. "I'm getting a hot fudge sundae."

We walked to the parking lot as a group. Rooster and Gunner both drove trucks, but everyone else was on bikes. The lot was almost deserted as we started to cut across the pavement, the night silent.

Then the hair on the back of my neck stood on end.

"Everybody stop!" I ordered, raising my hands and igniting my fingertips. Something very bad was about to happen. I could feel it.

"What's wrong?" Gunner was instantly alert, taking up a pugilistic stance. He was ready for a fight.

Rooster, Whistler, and Bonnie followed suit, while Doc and Marissa remained rooted to their spots, clearly confused.

"Hello, witch," a voice called from the trees. "How are you this fine, moonlit evening?"

I recognized the voice right away. Melody.

"You really shouldn't have come here," I called out, my temper getting the best of me when I saw the frightened look on Raisin's face as she cowered between Rooster and Whistler. This was her big night and it was being ruined by vampires. "Now I'm pissed off."

"Oh, well, that's terrifying," Melody mocked from somewhere beyond the tree line. I was positive she was slightly to my left. The problem was, I could feel someone — multiple someones, actually — moving in the shadows to my right ... and behind me ... and even on top of the school. I felt as if we were surrounded.

"We should go in and get her," Marissa suggested. "She's alone. It won't take much to handle her."

I jerked out a glowing hand to stop her before she could take off. "She's very far from alone," I countered.

Gunner slid his eyes to me. "What do you mean?"

"She means that I have an army at my disposal," Melody called out, laughing delightedly. "She means that she's just realized her fatal mistake."

"Fatal?" Raisin's voice was shaky. "W–what's going to happen?"

"It's going to be fine," I promised her. "You have nothing to worry about."

"Yes, it's going to be fine," Melody mimicked. "Just as soon as we rip your arms from your body and drink until you're dry."

"Rooster?" Raisin looked to him for comfort at the same moment I stepped forward and unleashed my magic.

"*Deflagro*," I hissed as I clapped my hands together, my hair blowing back as a wave of magic so powerful it heated the air we breathed moved out in a circle.

I heard voices crying out in surprise. It was already too late for some of them. I watched as at least six spots in the woods sparked, flames flaring up before dying. Then things fell silent.

"What was that?" Gunner asked.

"Death," I replied, focusing on the spot I believed Melody was hiding. It hadn't sprouted flames, which meant she was most likely alive. "Do you want another round?" I called out.

I heard murmuring again, this time from a greater distance. The vampires were retreating. "You don't want to mess with me," I warned. "Bixby told you it was a mistake last night. You should've listened."

Melody found her voice. "You'll want to stay away from us. A line has been drawn. You stay on your side of it and we'll stay on our side."

That wasn't going to happen. For tonight, though, I would take it. "Don't come back here," I called out. "I'll do worse next time."

"Don't come back to the house," she shot back. "I'll burn your world to the ground."

She talked big, but I knew better. There was something else behind her words: fear.

Life was about to get very interesting.

FOURTEEN

"We have a problem."

I waited until I was certain the vampires had gone to speak.

"Oh, really?" Marissa said, her tone withering. "What was your first clue?"

I refused to be baited into a fight, especially when I was certain that at least a few sets of eyes had remained behind to watch us interact from a distance.

"It's a nest," I said, my gaze on Rooster. "You know what that means?"

He hesitated as he ran his hand over Raisin's back in a soothing motion. "I'm not sure."

"I thought it was one master, one minion, and three half-vampires. I thought the half-vampires were protecting the master during the day. That's not what's going on."

"Would you like to expound for the class?" Gunner queried.

"I'm not sure how many we're dealing with, but it has to be at least twenty."

"And you think they're all living in one rundown house together?" Rooster asked. "How does that work?"

"I don't know if they're all living in that house. I don't know if there's one born vampire leading them or five. I just ... don't know. We're definitely dealing with a bigger problem than I thought."

"Well ... then we'll figure it out." Rooster was resolute. "I'm sure the problem isn't so big that we can't solve it together. That was a nice bit of magic you threw in their direction. You killed some of them, right?"

I nodded. "At least five or six. That was the fire you saw. I can't just toss out that spell willy-nilly, though. If an innocent gets in the way, he or she could go up in flames, too."

"Still, it's good to have in our arsenal." He flashed a smile for Raisin's benefit. "You're okay, kid. You don't have to worry about anything. The vampires aren't interested in you."

Raisin didn't look convinced. "If they're after all of you, then they're after me, too."

Gunner chuckled. "Loyal to the end, huh? That's just what I like in a woman." He slung an arm over her shoulders in a friendly manner and met my gaze. He didn't say anything, but I knew what he was thinking. We were in trouble, and it was going to take all of us working together to get out of it.

"You know what I think?" Raisin said after a moment's contemplation.

"What?" Gunner asked kindly.

"I think it will be easier to talk strategy over ice cream."

Everyone laughed, the pall that had been hanging over us at least temporarily forgotten. I had to admire her rebound rate. She was one of those kids who refused to let the world break her spirit. She was the reason we did what we did, why we fought the evil.

"Great idea." I grinned at her. "I'm definitely in the mood for hot fudge."

"Who isn't?" Rooster winked at Raisin, but I could see the worry lurking in the depths of his eyes. We'd been caught unaware tonight. We couldn't let it happen again.

"YOU DIDN'T SAY MUCH AT THE ICE CREAM shop," Gunner

noted as he navigated the winding road that led to the cabin. "Everyone else was throwing out ideas about killing vampires, but you were quiet."

"I know how to kill vampires."

"Yeah, but ... it's obvious you're upset."

Upset didn't seem to be the right word. "I'm ... just thinking."

"I like a smart woman, but it would be helpful if you told me what you were thinking about."

"I'm not sure."

"Or you could keep it to yourself and wedge a wall between us."

I slid my eyes to him, frowning, and made a face when I realized he was smirking. "You're kind of a pain sometimes," I noted.

"Yes, well, that's how my father raised me." He reached over and snagged my hand, causing my heart to stutter when he pulled the palm to his lips and pressed a kiss there. "I'm serious. You're obviously struggling with what happened tonight. I didn't see anything. I sensed danger, but only after you'd already picked up on it. I need to know what's going on."

"That's just it. I don't know what's going on." And, truthfully, that's what bothered me most. "I should've realized it was a nest."

"I don't understand. What's the big deal about it being a nest?"

"Nests are dangerous."

"I figured that out from the way you reacted. You think there were twenty vampires in the trees gearing up to attack. That part I understand. The thing is, you scared them all off with one little burst of magic."

He tried so hard, but he didn't always grasp the severity of complex paranormal issues. His experience was limited. "That's not what happened. I used a spell that I shouldn't have access to. I knew when I was using it that it could've gone wrong. I mean ... we were in a high school parking lot, for crying out loud. What if some of the kids were hiding in the trees smoking pot or something? Do you realize that I could've taken out any number of innocents with what I did?"

It was obvious that he didn't grasp that. "I ... ."

"I don't think I did. In fact, I'm positive I didn't." And that was the only reason I wasn't freaking out. "There were six ignition points. Those were the vampires I fried. It wasn't kids."

"Then why are you so upset? You can't always control what could be. It's important to focus on what is."

"And thank you so much for that, oh wise one," I muttered.

"Hey." He squeezed my hand until I looked at him. "I'm trying to understand. I get that you think I'm somehow ... lacking ... when it comes to this stuff. I'm doing my best."

And that made me realize I was being an ass. "I'm sorry." Briefly, I pressed my eyes shut and forced myself to get it together. "This is not your fault. It's mine. I just ... I don't like vampires."

He pulled into my driveway and immediately killed the lights, keeping the engine running before unfastening his seatbelt and turning to face me. "Something happened," he surmised. "You've fought vampires before."

I nodded. "Oh, so many times."

"Yeah, but something bad happened."

That was an understatement. "I don't really want to talk about it."

"Try. We both agreed that we weren't the best at communicating but it was necessary for this to work. I still want this to work."

He was backing me into a corner. "And you don't think I do."

"I think you are haunted by something and what happened tonight is bringing it back," he clarified. "I want to help. I ... care about you a great deal, but you need to meet me halfway. That's the only way this will work."

In my head, I knew he was speaking the truth. My heart wanted me to be a coward, though. I hated opening old wounds. "I don't know where to begin."

"How about you just nutshell it for me? You're clearly not ready to get into the nitty-gritty. Just give me the basics and we'll cover the rest after a good night's sleep."

He said it in such a reasonable tone that I figured I had no choice but to acquiesce. "I wasn't always a loner in Detroit. Eventually I worked mostly on my own. I would occasionally partner with people for big jobs, but for the little jobs I insisted on being alone. That was one of the reasons Rooster wasn't sure I would be a good fit here. All the people in your group work together."

"Our group," he corrected. "It's not just my group. It's our group."

His reaction was enough to make me smile. "Our group."

"I take it you had a partner before you went all solo cowboy."

"Pretty much. Evan. He was the closest thing I had to a friend."

Gunner looked pained at the admission. "I know you had friends. I've seen you and Mike. You guys clearly hung out."

"Yeah, but it was in a lazy way. Evan and I were partnered up after I finished training. I did my best not to like him from the start because I didn't want to get attached — that was always the rule in foster care because you never knew how long you would be staying in one place — but he was impossible to shut out."

Gunner stiffened slightly next me. "You were involved."

I shook my head. "Not like you're insinuating. He was gay, which I think is how we managed to bond the way we did. I don't mean that in a discriminatory way," I added hurriedly. "It's just ... I was always leery of people wanting to take advantage of me sexually. That's one of the things they beat into your head when dealing with state counselors."

Gunner's fingers were gentle as they brushed my hair from my face. "I'm not going to lie. All this talk about your time in foster care — even though it doesn't sound terrible — hurts my stomach. Like ... big time. I wish I could go back and make it better for you."

"Then I wouldn't be who I am, and I happen to like this me."

He smiled. "I like this you, too. It's still difficult to hear."

"From your point of view, I can see that. For me ... I try not to think about Evan."

"You obviously lost him," Gunner noted. "How did it happen?"

"Part of me wants to say it was my fault, but that's not really true." I shifted my eyes to the window. "I just didn't know."

"Of course it's not your fault."

I fought a small smile ... and lost. "How do you know it's not my fault? I haven't even told you the story."

"Because I know you." He kept hold of my hand. "You don't have to tell me if you're not ready."

"It's not that. It's just ... I don't like thinking about it. Basically we were sent out to this neighborhood in Detroit. Prostitutes were going missing. The cops apparently didn't care. That's what they told us, but I have no idea if it's true. We were assigned to figure out if what was happening was paranormal.

"At that time, we'd been on a few jobs together and we'd started hanging out and having drinks on weekends," I continued, losing myself in the story. "We were feeling cocky because we took out a trio of sirens who were dropping bodies in the Detroit River a few days earlier. We didn't know it was vampires we were after ... and we were out later than we should've been."

I swallowed hard before finishing up. "We were caught unaware. There were ten of them. We were outnumbered and I didn't know that nifty little trick I showed off tonight. They took him ... and drained him right in front of me. They were going to do the same thing to me, but I managed to draw some elemental fire, enough to burn the two holding me, and I jumped out a window to escape.

"I dislocated my shoulder and broke two fingers. And I left Evan's body behind because it was the only way for me to escape."

"Oh, geez." Gunner pulled me to him for a hug. "I'm so sorry."

"It wasn't really my fault."

"No, it wasn't."

"But if I hadn't been so cocky it wouldn't have happened."

"Baby, everyone makes mistakes like that."

"Yeah, but this mistake cost Evan his life. After regrouping, we went back to the area with a huge group and annihilated them all. I used my new magic trick, something I picked up from this dark witch we were holding, and burned them where they stood."

"Did you get to bury Evan?"

"I never did find out what they did with his body. The Detroit River is notorious for dragging bodies under. Most are never found."

"I'm sorry."

"Yeah, well ... ." I pursed my lips as I focused out the window. "I think this nest is bigger than that one. We need to be careful. You ... need to be careful."

"Because you don't want to lose another partner."

"Because I don't want to lose you." It was the simplest answer ... and absolutely the truth. "We need to come up with a plan."

"We will."

"Before they do something to hurt one of us. That's what they're going to do. You heard Melody tonight. That was psychological warfare. She's going to try to isolate one of us, maybe even arrange for that person to be turned. We can't allow that to happen."

"We won't." He stared hard into my eyes, as if searching for something. "I swear it's going to be okay. We're not novices. While we haven't dealt with many vampires, we'll handle it. I promise you don't have to worry."

That was easier said than done, but I knew better than to push the matter further. That would only make both of us unhappy. "I'm really tired. I think I need some sleep."

"We both do. But I'm terrified that Raisin's play is going to haunt me forever."

"Yeah. You and me both."

He gave me a quick kiss and then released me. I had no doubt he would do better once we were inside. He waited in front of the truck for me, something I found quite cute, and when I joined him I was about to suggest another activity to ensure we would sleep well.

Then I sensed another presence. When I snapped my head toward the porch, I saw movement. "Who ... ?"

Gunner tensed and shoved me behind him, growling as he prepared for battle. His macho showing aside, I was more interested in who would dare approach the cabin alone in the middle of the night ... until my mind brushed against something familiar.

"It's Brandon," I offered, wrapping my fingers around Gunner's wrist to still him. "He must've come here looking for you. He probably needs a friend to talk with."

Gunner relaxed, though only marginally. "Well ... I'm not leaving. The vampires are out there and I'm not leaving you alone."

"They can't get inside the cabin," I reminded him. "I'll be perfectly safe. If you need to go with Brandon ... ."

"No. I don't want to leave." Gunner relaxed his stance and forced a smile for his friend, who was still meandering through the shadows to get to us. "Hey, bud. I didn't realize you were coming out here. You should've called. We were at Raisin's play. I was going to check on you tomorrow."

"Sure. Sure. Sure."

There was something odd about Brandon's voice. He almost sounded drunk, giddy even. There was a happy tone to his words.

"Where's your truck?" Gunner glanced around, confusion lining his forehead. "How did you get out here?"

Before Brandon could answer, I heard whispering in the back of my head. My inner danger alarm was dinging.

"Get out of the way!"

I don't know what made me do it. Perhaps it was talking about Evan. Maybe worry for Gunner's safety took me over. Either way, I raised my hands and pulsed out a burst of magic before Brandon even managed to get close enough for us to see his face. The instant the magic left my fingertips his face became illuminated ... and the red tinge of his eyes was obvious.

"Brandon?" Gunner took a step toward his friend at the same moment the magic collided with him. "Brandon!"

The formerly amiable lumberyard owner's body made a sickening thud when he hit the ground. Gunner was immediately next to him, checking his vitals. I remained standing, my gaze keen as I surveyed the hills and trees surrounding the cabin.

"Why did you do that?" Gunner snapped, his voice ragged as he checked his friend. "Why did you attack?"

"That's not Brandon," I said after deciding that we were alone. "He's different now."

"Different how?"

I moved closer, using my phone as a flashlight and holding it over the man's waxy features. Gunner had his fingers pressed to Brandon's pulse point and he looked relieved.

"He's not dead."

"He's not," I agreed. "I never had any intention of killing him." I crouched down, lifting the phone until it illuminated his neck. There I found the marks. It was hardly a surprise. "He's been taken over."

Dumbfounded disbelief washed over Gunner's handsome features. "What does that mean? Is he ... going to be one of them?"

I shook my head. "No. He's going to be a half-vampire like the others. I'm guessing they gave him a double dose of blood to better control him. That's why I sensed he was different. It usually takes me longer with half-vampires because they can pass for human. He was practically feral."

"But ... what do we do?" Gunner looked lost as he pressed his hand to his friend's forehead. "He's cold and clammy. Should we take him to the hospital?"

"There's nothing they can do for us. We have to find a place to strap him down. The second he wakes up he'll come after us again."

Gunner balked. "No. We can't do that. I ... we have to help him."

"We're going to help him. First we have to make sure he doesn't hurt us. We need to find a place to tie him up, and it has to be some-place the other vampires can't get to him. That means a private residence."

Gunner's eyes immediately moved to the cabin. "You want to tie him up in there?"

"That's our easiest option."

"And then what?"

That was the question. "I don't know. Let's take it one step at a time. We need to secure him ... and I'm going to need magic to do it to make sure he can't escape and attack. We can't protect him if he threatens our lives."

Gunner didn't look convinced, but he didn't mount an argument. "Okay, but we need to fix this. He's ... my friend."

Now it was my turn to comfort him. "He's not gone yet. We can still save him. Everything will work out. I promise."

He looked comforted by the words. Now I just had to make sure they were true, because I was way out of my depth here.

FIFTEEN

y intention was to tie up Brandon, magically enchant his bindings, and go to bed. My mind was weary and there was a lot to think about. I figured if we warded and gagged him we would be okay.

Gunner apparently had other ideas.

"Why is Rooster on my front porch?" I demanded as I exited the bathroom.

Gunner was already on his way to the front door. "Why do you think?"

"But … ." I looked down at my sleep outfit and frowned. I didn't go for fancy nighties or the like, but I also preferred not sleeping in a bra. I crossed my arms over my chest and frowned as Gunner swept open the door. "You could've warned me."

The look he shot me was odd. "You didn't think we were going to leave him tied to a chair while we were sleeping, did you?"

"Um … yeah. I thought I would try to free him tomorrow."

"Well, you can still try to free him, but we can't keep him here. The cabin is too small and … it's weird to have him out here while we're sleeping."

I was instantly suspicious. "You just don't want him listening in case you decide to get romantic."

"There is that." Gunner winked as he pulled open the door. It was his attempt at lightheartedness, but it was a lame effort. He was obviously worried about his friend.

Rooster wasn't exactly happy when he strolled through the door. "Can't you guys go to bed like normal people at least one night a week?" he groused.

"Hey, this isn't our fault," Gunner countered. "We were coming back to crash when ... well, I'm not sure what happened." He nodded to me. "Scout took him out."

"Wait ... he's dead?" Rooster lifted his hand to still us. "I thought he was still alive."

"Oh, he's still alive," I replied. I felt on display in my tiny sleep outfit. "He's a half-vampire. We have to keep him restrained until we can cure him."

"Uh-huh." Rooster didn't look convinced. "And have you ever done that?"

I shook my head. "No, but how hard can it be?"

Rooster muttered something that sounded like "famous last words." It was late and he was obviously wiped but because the day had decided to throw another curve at us, he had no choice but to deal. "Where is he?"

"Scout tied him to a chair in the kitchen," Gunner replied. "She warded the ropes so he can't move."

"Well, that's something."

"He's kind of mad," Gunner added.

"Hey, he'll live." I was in no mood to feel sorry for the guy who had come to kill us. Whether Gunner had gotten far enough to put that together, I couldn't say. I had no doubt that was Brandon's intention. The vampire had found him sometime after dark and decided to enlist him as a weapon ... or maybe he'd been grooming him from the start. He was already pale the day we tracked him down to inform him of Honey's death. There was only one reason to fixate on Brandon, and we were it.

"Well, hey." Rooster's smile was amiable enough as he crossed into the kitchen and studied Brandon. The half-vampire was struggling against his ropes and sputtering what I assumed were vile threats behind his gag. His eyes were wild as he yanked on bindings that would never give. "You don't look so good, Brandon." Rooster hunkered down so he could be at eye level with the demented lumberyard owner. "Are his eyes supposed to be red like this?"

When I realized the question was directed at me, I shrugged. "How should I know? It's not as if I've ever had a half-vampire for a pet."

Rooster feigned patience, although he didn't put much effort into it. "Yes, but you're more familiar with this phenomenon. I've never seen a half-vampire. They're not common up here."

"Yeah, I've been thinking about that."

"For right now, I need you to focus on him." Rooster extended a finger toward Brandon's face. "Is he supposed to look like that? I mean ... with the blood tears and everything?"

He was asking a question I couldn't answer. "I'm sure he's fine."

"Except you're not sure."

"I ... well, no. It's an assumption."

Rooster grunted as he straightened. "I think we need a second opinion."

"And who should that come from?" Gunner asked. "Like you said, we're not exactly experts. This is shifter territory."

"There is one person I know who took out a nest of vampires back in the day. I don't know if she's an expert, but she's the closest thing we have."

Gunner turned grim. "Mama Moon?"

"Can you think of anyone else?"

"No."

"Then Mama Moon it is."

IT TOOK MAMA MOON A FULL HOUR TO MAKE it to my place, and she was grumpy to the point of belligerence when she arrived.

"This had better be good," she growled when I answered the door.

While we waited for her, I'd excused myself long enough to throw one of Gunner's T-shirts over my head to hide my lack of bra. Mama Moon hadn't bothered. She was dressed in a tank top (sans bra) and a pair of sleep leggings that were so tight I had to force myself to look the other way so as not to appear rude.

"They're in the kitchen," I grumbled, wrinkling my nose as I took in the plastic things she'd stuck in her hair. "What are those?"

"What?" Mama Moon made a face as she glanced around and then chuckled when she realized what I meant. "Oh, these are curlers."

That didn't mean anything to me. "No. I've seen curling irons before. I don't use them because I don't see the point, but I've seen them. That's not what those are."

"No, these are different," Mama Moon agreed. "You put these in your wet hair at night. Then, you unroll them in the morning and you have a new, fresh hairdo."

"But ... why?"

"Because it's a look some people like."

"But why?"

"Oh, geez." She rolled her eyes and gave me a little shove to get me to move. "I can tell already that you're going to be a pain tonight. I'm not in the mood. Show me the ... whatever it is."

I gestured toward the kitchen, following as she stalked in that direction. I almost careened into her back as she pulled up short on the other side of the door. Apparently the sight of Brandon magically warded to a chair was enough to throw her.

"I don't ... understand." Her eyes were turbulent as she looked over the struggling half-vampire. "What's going on?"

"It's a long story," Rooster hedged.

"You have five minutes to tell me," Mama Moon countered. "No embellishments. I just want the facts and nothing more."

"Fair enough." Rooster launched into the tale, glossing over a few things but getting the gist of it out. When he finished, Mama Moon seemed perplexed — and maybe a little angry.

"I see." Her tone was clipped as she began to circle Brandon. She didn't look happy. "So, this is why you were so interested in the half-vampires in the woods the other night." Her eyes briefly flicked to me. "You should've told me what was going on."

"And then what?" I challenged. It was late and I was exhausted. I was ready for this night to be over. "What good would that have done? You couldn't have smoothed over the situation. You didn't have any additional information to help matters that night."

"You don't know that," Mama Moon challenged. It was obvious she wasn't used to being questioned, and my attitude was known to have a chafing effect, which she clearly hated. "I thought you were playing games last night. I didn't realize you had a genuine beef with the half-vampires. If I had, I would've warned you."

"You would've warned her about what?" Rooster asked.

"I would've warned her that the area was suddenly crawling with vampires. I mean ... I assumed she had noticed, but that doesn't appear to be the case."

Oh, now she was just messing with me. "Are you saying you knew that we were dealing with a nest last night? Why didn't you say something?"

"Actually, I would like to hear the answer to that, too," Rooster supplied. "Why wouldn't you share that sort of information? I know that we're not always on the same team — we can't be by virtue of what happened — but I thought we were on the same page for the big stuff."

"You slow your roll, Rooster," Mama Moon ordered. She curled her lips and poked her finger into Brandon's cheek. Even though he was tied to the chair, his mouth gagged, Brandon turned in her direction and jerked his head as if he was ready to attack. "This is interesting. He's not even trying to pass for normal."

"I think that's on purpose," I volunteered. Actually, I'd given it a lot of thought while we were waiting for her, and I had a few ideas. "They want to rattle me, throw me off my game. They think turning Brandon into a monster will distract me."

"But why?" Rooster's face was blank. "You barely know Brandon."

"No, but I know Gunner ... and he loves Brandon."

"Ah." Realization dawned on Mama Moon's face and she bobbed her head. "I get it. They're trying to distract you. But why you?"

I tracked my eyes to her, confused. "What do you mean?"

"Why you?" she repeated. "There's an entire contingent of Spells Angels in the area to deal with. They're fixated on you. There has to be a reason for that."

"I would guess I'm on their radar because they saw me the night I took out the bog monster. I didn't realize it at the time — and that was probably a mistake — but that makes the most sense."

Gunner stirred. "It's not just the bog monster," he argued. "You sensed something about that house from the start. I believe they were trying to fly under the radar — at least as far as we're concerned — but Scout pushed the issue because she sensed something about the house."

"What did you sense?" Mama Moon asked.

"It wasn't the house necessarily," I hedged. "It was more that I could feel eyes on me. When Marissa and I got back to our bikes, I felt ... off. I sensed that someone had been near our bikes but I had no proof so I let it go. Marissa was complaining nonstop because I blew up the bog monster. I didn't want to listen any longer, so we left."

"But you thought people were watching you," Gunner persisted. "That's one of the first things you mentioned to me. That's why we headed out there after breakfast the next morning."

"And that could've been the trigger," Rooster mused. "It makes sense. They thought they were relatively safe until two Spells Angels representatives showed up on their front porch. What did they do when they saw you?"

"Well, it was weird." Gunner took on a far-off expression, as if losing himself in the memory of the moment. "There was this little guy— we're talking like five feet tall — and he came out to give us grief. He wasn't exactly welcoming and it was obvious he was trying to get rid of us. Bixby. That was his name."

"He's a minion," I muttered. "He's not a half-vampire. He's a minion ... and he's different."

Gunner slid his eyes to me, thoughtful. "And you thought you recognized him from the start."

I wanted to explode. "I did recognize him. You don't believe me, but ... I totally have met that dude before. You think I'm crazy, hormonal or something, but I swear I've interacted with him."

"Hold up." Rooster extended his hands and stepped between us, perhaps worried we might fight. "This is the first I'm hearing about this. Where do you think you know this guy from?"

I was fairly certain I'd brought up Bixby in front of Rooster before and I wanted to point out that the men who refused to listen were the problem, but I knew it was a wasted effort. We had other things to worry about, and the biggest was tied to a chair in my kitchen.

"I met him when I was a kid," I explained. "I was late and hurrying home. Well, I mean ... it was a group home. The guy who ran it was fairly lenient with me because I lived there so long and really didn't cause much trouble, but there were rules. The doors locked at a certain time. They were on a timer. If I didn't make it, I would be forced to sleep on the street. I didn't want to risk that, so I was in a hurry ... and that's when I saw him."

"Wait a second." Gunner's eyes flashed with something I couldn't immediately identify. "Are you telling me that a state-sanctioned group home locked you out and forced you to sleep on the streets of Detroit if you were late?"

I shrugged. "Yeah. All the homes were like that. I remember I was only a few weeks from getting booted from this one because I was graduating from high school. I had a lot on my mind when I ran into this Bixby freak."

"I hate hearing these stories," Gunner muttered.

"That's because you have a kind heart." Rooster patted his shoulder. "You also have a hero complex and want to go back in time and save her from the horrible things that happened. That's impossible, so you need to focus on the here and now."

"Oh, thanks so much for that," Gunner said dryly. "I never would've figured that out myself."

"Knock it off." Mama Moon, who was anxious to hear the rest of my story, focused on me. "I want to hear the story. You met this minion you say is hanging out at the house on the bluff before? Did he remember you?"

"He acts like I'm confused, but I know it's him. He's wearing the same jacket ... and there have been a few times when he's looked at me when he thinks nobody is watching and I see the recognition there. He's annoyed that he didn't kill me then."

"And what happened that night?" Mama Moon folded her arms over her chest and waited. "Did he try to put his hands on you?"

I allowed my memory to wander to the night in question. "He was hiding in the bushes. I sensed him and called him out."

Gunner's hand automatically moved to my back, as if he expected me to say something terrible. "Did he try to hurt you?"

"No. Well, he might've, but I wasn't a ... normal teenager." I flashed a smile that was just evil enough to cause Mama Moon to chuckle. "I called him out, threw in a few choice names, and then took off. Another guy showed up at some point. He was really dark ... and tall ... and he suggested I would see him again. He also said I was safe for the night and to go. On any other night I might've pushed the issue, told him he wasn't safe, but I didn't want to sleep on the street, so I took off."

Mama Moon's eyebrows drew together. "You think that was the master vampire?"

"I don't know." That was the truth. "I didn't realize we were dealing with a nest until earlier tonight when they approached us outside the high school. I thought it was simply a master and three half-vampires. This is different. It's ... more dangerous."

"It certainly is," Mama Moon agreed. "We need to get ahead of it ... especially if they're turning locals into half-vampires. That's never good."

I turned back to Brandon and eyed him speculatively. "Well, if it's any consolation, I don't think they plan to turn multiple people. They went after Brandon because of his ties to us."

"But we can turn him back, right?" Gunner almost begged. He

looked almost desperate at the thought. "He won't stay like this, will he?"

"We can turn him back as long as we get the master," Mama Moon confirmed. "Until then, we need to keep Brandon locked up. It's not wise to confine him here, because they're likely to come looking for him."

"We'll take him to The Cauldron," Rooster interjected. "There's a storeroom. We've used it as a cell more than a few times. He'll be comfortable. Most importantly, he won't be able to get out. It's warded."

"That's a good idea." Mama Moon bobbed her head. "As for this nest, I don't know what to tell you. I've sensed them for a few days. I haven't seen them. They've been careful. If they've stopped being careful ... ." She trailed off, letting the sentence hang.

"They didn't really show themselves tonight," Gunner argued. "Scout sensed them and put on a magic display that killed at least three of them. We didn't see how many we were dealing with."

"Which is troublesome," Mama Moon mused. "I'm not sure what we're dealing with, but it can't be good. We might have to work together on this one."

"Then we'll work together." Rooster declared. "This is now officially more than a distraction. This is our primary concern. We can't let these vampires get a foothold in our territory. They have to be eradicated — and we're the only ones who can do it."

SIXTEEN

$\mathcal{M}$oving Brandon was difficult. He put up a terrific fight when I started untying him, backhanding me hard enough that I flew into the wall next to the table.

"Don't touch me! You're a witch!"

I rubbed my cheek as I regarded him. "Thanks for the news flash."

"What happened?" Gunner asked, scurrying into the room. He looked frazzled. "I heard a thump."

"Your friend and I were just bonding," I replied dryly, still rubbing my cheek as I watched Brandon try to untie his dominant right hand with his clumsy left. "It's going swimmingly."

Gunner couldn't hide the confusion clouding his features. "Did he ... hit you?"

"It's fine." I forced my hand down and pasted what I hoped was a comforting smile on my face. "Don't worry about it."

Unfortunately, that was beyond Gunner's acceptance level. "Did you hit her?" He was incredulous as he turned on Brandon, his hands clenched into fists at his sides.

Brandon stopped what he was doing long enough to meet Gunner's accusatory gaze. "I don't know what you're talking about." He adopted an air of innocence. "She's lying. I didn't touch her."

"She didn't say that you did." Loyalty is a funny thing. Gunner obviously cared about Brandon a great deal, considered him a friend. But right now he looked as if he wanted to murder him. "What is wrong with you?"

Brandon was taken aback. "Excuse me? I'm tied to a chair in your girlfriend's house. I don't think the question is what's wrong with me. It's what's wrong with you. She knocked me out with her magic."

"You were attacking us."

"No." Brandon vehemently shook his head. One of his wrists was still lashed to the chair. He diligently worked to free it, but his eyes were focused on Gunner. "I was trying to talk to you. I wasn't attacking. I don't know why you would think that. Of course, you attacked before I could even explain why I was here."

Gunner's eyes slowly tracked to me. "Is that possible?"

He was asking me to tell him his friend was okay. That was something I couldn't do.

"Look at his neck, Gunner." I kept my voice low. "Remember his eyes when he attacked. He's not himself."

"Don't listen to her," Brandon snapped. "She's trying to make you doubt me, turn you against me. Don't let her win."

"And why would she want me to turn against you?" Gunner's expression was hard to read, but he remained calm.

"Because she's trying to isolate you from the group. She wants you in a vulnerable position so she can turn you."

"Turn me into what?"

"You know ... one of her."

"I don't know." Gunner's tone was perfectly reasonable, but I could practically see him seething under the surface. "What is she?"

"She's evil, man." Brandon's expression was imploring. "Why can't you see that? She's trying to turn you against me. It's not fair. It's not right."

"But she hasn't turned me against you. In fact, she encouraged me to spend time with you following Honey's death. She thought you needed me."

"That's part of the act."

"Uh-huh." Gunner looked up as Mama Moon and Rooster entered the room. He didn't have to say anything for me to know that he was in great pain. He blamed himself for what had happened to Brandon. I could sense the emotions rolling off him. It wasn't reasonable or right, but it was crawling beneath his skin.

"Why is he untied?" Mama Moon asked.

"Because I was getting ready to transport him," I replied. "We got a little distracted before we could finish the job."

"So I see." She narrowed her eyes and studied my cheek. Her nearness made me uncomfortable. "We should get moving. The faster we lock him up in his new digs, the faster we can get some sleep ... and I desperately need sleep."

"That makes two of us," I agreed.

"That's because you use the cover of darkness to seduce my friend and turn him evil," Brandon hissed, his eyes glittering slits as he practically spit on me. "You're a seductress, a heathen. You'll meet a fiery fate soon enough."

"Looking forward to it," I said with faux brightness, pushing myself away from the wall. "I love fiery fates. I think they're pretty ... and warm ... and who doesn't love s'mores?" I looked to Gunner, hoping to find a ghost of a smile on his face as I attempted to lighten the mood. Instead, he moved closer to me. Gently, he brushed his fingers over my cheek. I could see the turmoil churning in his eyes and struggled to find a way to make this better.

"I'll fix him," I said after a beat. "I promise. This is my fault. I should've seen it coming."

His forehead wrinkled. "Do you think I blame you for this?"

"I think you blame yourself ... and I'm part of that by extension."

"How do you figure that?"

"He was obviously attacked after you left last night. You said he was drunk. That probably means he didn't even put up a fight. It was easy for them to take him over. If you'd been there it might not have happened."

"Probably not," he agreed. "That doesn't mean I blame myself. He's a big boy. He got involved with Honey on his own. She was obviously part of this. They didn't just pluck him randomly from the whole town."

"You wanted to check on me last night. That's why you left. If it wasn't for me ... ."

"Don't." There was no anger emanating from him, only sadness. "I came here because I wanted to be with you. As for Brandon ... ." He looked frustrated as he eyed his best friend, who was back to messing with the rope. "You said it yourself. Nothing that's been done to him is permanent. We can fix this."

"Oh, geez." Mama Moon rolled her eyes and shook her head. I'd forgotten she was present ... which isn't easy because she has one of those larger-than-life personalities that can swallow an entire room. "Are they always like this?"

The question was directed at Rooster, who shrugged. "They're ... a work in progress," he replied after a moment. "They're both a little ... I guess the word would be slow ... when it comes to relationships. Usually I find it funny. This is a little tragic."

"This is a lot tragic," Mama Moon countered, although there was a twinkle in her eye. "I guess they're kind of cute."

"I can think of a few other words." Rooster moved closer to Brandon, who immediately stopped trying to untie the rope and tried to pretend he was innocent of every possible charge we could throw at him. "What do we think the best way to transport him is?"

"I think you should untie me and I'll sit in the seat like a good boy," Brandon offered. "I really have nothing against you. I want to cooperate." He was silent for a moment and then glanced at me. "Well ... I have nothing against most of you."

"I don't understand why he's acting like this," Gunner offered, frustration evident. "I mean ... why is he directing all his anger at Scout? Why is she at the center of all this for him?"

"Because whoever enslaved him made her the focus," Mama Moon replied calmly, her voice soft. "Scout was obviously pegged as the biggest threat before they went after him."

"That would make sense if they set this plan in motion tonight,"

Gunner argued, "but it's obvious they didn't. This was something they put together before this happened."

"Yes, well ... ." Mama Moon pursed her lips and turned her full attention to me. "You mentioned that you interacted with the minion before. You didn't get into too many specifics. You said you were late, in a hurry to get home, and you crossed paths with him. Did he jump you? Did he try to haul you into the bushes and feed you to a vampire? How exactly did you two meet?"

"It's not like we were introduced," I countered. "I was walking down the sidewalk. I sensed danger. I called out to him, which seemed to surprise him, and I kept going. Then another guy showed up, this one younger and hotter, and started lambasting him. It wasn't much of an exchange."

"Did you get a good look at the other man?"

"The hot one," Gunner grumbled, eliciting a genuine smile from me.

"I was a teenager. It's not as if he was Taylor Lautner or something."

"Taylor Lautner?" Horror washed through the room as Gunner looked to Rooster and then back to me. "Please tell me you didn't like that guy."

"Hey, when I was seventeen, he was one of the 'it' guys. At least he was tan and buff. The other guy was pasty and white. They had to paint fake abs on him. It's not my fault there were no good teen heart-throbs when I was of a certain age."

"I can't even look at you right now." Gunner held up his hand and turned back to Brandon, who was tugging so hard on the rope I was surprised he hadn't drawn blood. "You need to stop doing that, Brandon. You're going to hurt yourself."

Brandon immediately stopped fidgeting. "I'm not doing anything. Why do you think I'm doing something? It's because of her, isn't it?" The look he shot me was straight out of a misogynistic movie from the 1980s. "Seriously, all our problems started with her. You need to get rid of her."

"Yeah, that's not going to happen." Gunner reached for the rope.

"I'm going to untie you. If you try to run I'll be forced to knock you out. If you touch Scout again I might have to kill you. I know that's difficult to hear because you're my best friend, but it's the truth." He lowered his voice and stared directly into Brandon's eyes. "Don't ever touch her again."

I wasn't big on the macho stuff, but the threat was effective ... and caused my heart to flutter, which was an absolutely disgusting reaction that I refused to admit to anyone, including Gunner.

"You'll need my help to untie that rope," I said after I watched him fumble with the knot for a full thirty seconds. "It's magically tethered to the chair."

He shot me a dirty look. "You could've told me before I screwed around so long I looked like an idiot."

"What fun would that be?" I sent him a small smile, one meant solely for him, and then reached for the ropes. "Brandon," I called out, trying to draw the man's attention to me.

He refused to look in my direction.

I tried again. "Brandon," I said, more softly this time.

When he turned to look at me there was abject hatred reflecting back. I had to remind myself that the real Brandon didn't feel that way. This was being forced upon him.

"I'm going to fix this and make it so you can go back to your life," I promised him.

"I don't care what you say. I don't believe you."

"Well, believe this." I was firm. "If you try anything while we're transporting you I'll curse you with an itching spell that will make you want to scratch your private parts until they fall off. It will be so bad that you won't be able to use them for a full year. And, before you convince yourself that I'm bluffing, you might want to think about the stories I'm certain Gunner told you about the wolves who were in town a few weeks ago. I'm more than capable of doing it."

Brandon swallowed hard. "I ... ." He darted his eyes in Gunner's direction.

"Behave yourself," Gunner ordered. "She's serious. She gets off on casting karma spells, and you have some really crappy karma right now. Behave yourself ... at least for a little while."

THE BACK ROOM AT THE CAULDRON WAS surprisingly posh. It featured a cot with a blanket and pillow, a small television and even a bookshelf, though the selection looked to run to the classics, and therefore dry, rather than anything hot and steamy.

"I take it this isn't the first time you've locked someone in here," I said as I glanced around.

Whistler, who had been roused from sleep by Rooster, shook his head. He looked half asleep, though he didn't utter a word of complaint. "Nope. This room was built as a cell. There's no way he can get out. Nobody ever has."

"You can't leave me in here," Brandon insisted as he glanced around. "There's no window. What if there's a fire? You can't lock me in a room with no window."

"If there's a fire, we'll get you out," Gunner promised him. "Don't worry."

"That's easy for you to say," Brandon grumbled. "You're not the one being locked in a cage."

"It's a nice cage," I offered helpfully. Only hatred was reflected back at me when I tried to make eye contact with him.

"I know what you are," he hissed. "I know what you're trying to do. You're a child of the stars. Your time has passed. You don't belong here."

I was sick of hearing that term tossed at me. I wanted Drake to get it together and provide the information he promised. I had sympathy for his plight, but only to a certain extent. I needed answers. Of course, this was the absolute worst time to get them. I had other things to worry about, which is why I refocused on the present.

I refused to let Brandon upset me. I shook my head. "Everyone knows about the children of the stars but me. I have no idea if it's good or bad ... or how I fit into that world. I'm guessing I don't, because they abandoned me to this one. Either way, you can't use it as a weapon against me because I have no idea what it means."

Gunner's hand landed on my shoulder and he squeezed. "You're in the world you're supposed to be in. You're with me."

"Aw." Rooster and Mama Moon cocked their heads to the side and made twin expressions of delight.

"Shut up," Gunner growled, causing me to smile. "Brandon, I'll be back tomorrow to check on you. Try to get some sleep."

"I can't sleep here." Brandon had run the gamut of emotions since appearing at my cabin. He was angry ... then sly ... then manipulative ... then sad. Now he was desperate. "You can't leave me here." He turned quickly and grabbed Gunner by the front of the shirt, his neck wound on full display as he begged his friend to help him. "I'll die if you leave me here. Die!"

"You'll be fine," Gunner promised. "I won't let anything happen to you. You have my word."

"Like you gave your word to Rain?" Brandon's demeanor suddenly shifted and he was aggressive, to the point of threatening. "You tried to lock her in here, too, didn't you? How did that work out? Not so well."

I was taken aback. Rain was the woman who had held my position (and lived in my cabin) with Spells Angels before I arrived. Something had happened to her. I was assuming that something was dark, but no one wanted to talk about it. I'd heard tidbits here and there and recognized that Rain's end was bad enough that it haunted all of them.

Gunner wasn't fazed. "The situations are ... different."

"Really? They don't feel different. I remember sitting with you after she died. You felt guilty, thought you failed her. Do you want to feel that way again?"

"I won't fail you." Gunner sounded certain of himself, but I sensed a bit of hesitation. He was questioning his resolve.

"He won't," I agreed, moving closer to him. "None of us will fail you. We'll fix this, Brandon. I'm not sure how, but we will."

"Oh, shut up." Brandon's lips curved into an evil smirk. "I don't trust you. I know what you are. Stop trying to convince me you're on my side. You're evil!" He lashed out to strike me again, but Gunner caught his wrist.

"Stop." His tone was icy as he glared at the thing wearing his friend's face. "I warned you what would happen if you touched her again."

Brandon shrank back in the face of Gunner's fury. "I ... she's evil."

"No, you're confused ... and I've had enough of you." Gunner gave Brandon a terrific shove, one so hard that the lumberyard owner tripped over the cot and smacked against the wall. Gunner was grave as he turned and gestured toward the door. "Everybody out. We're locking this up tight."

Arguing would've been an ugly business, so I did as he asked, watching as he and Whistler locked the door once we were safely outside.

"It's secure," Whistler announced. "He's locked in there tight. We'll need to figure out shifts for meals in case he decides to get violent, but for now we're okay."

"I'll do that first thing in the morning," Rooster offered. "I'll make sure somebody is always here."

"Then I guess that's it for tonight." Whistler doled out pointed looks for each of us. "That's your cue to get out so I can sleep."

Under different circumstances I might've laughed at his reaction. Tonight, I was too tired. "I'll check in with you in the morning. I might have a few ideas for modifying his mood."

Whistler nodded. "Don't show up too early. I need my beauty rest."

"You don't have to worry about that. I need mine, too." I switched my attention to Gunner, who was staring at the closed door with something akin to despair. "Come on." I reached out and snagged his fingers, giving them a little tug. "We'll come back tomorrow. I promise we'll fix this."

His eyes were glassy when he turned and I was stunned by the thought that he might cry. I had no problem with it. I'm not one of those people who think men shouldn't cry. It was a humbling emotion, though, and I wanted nothing more than to take him in my arms and tell him everything was going to be okay.

That would have to wait until we were back at the cabin. It wasn't something that either of us felt comfortable displaying in front of a larger audience.

"It's going to be okay." I kept my voice low as I gripped his hand tighter. "Have faith in me. I will fix this. I promise."

"I know you will." Briefly, he dropped his forehead against mine and closed his eyes. "I just have never seen anything like that. He was like a different person."

"He is a different person. But we'll get your friend back. I swear it."

SEVENTEEN

"You're quiet," Gunner noted when we returned to the cabin. It was almost two in the morning, which meant we had only a few hours before we had to get up. Every muscle in my body screamed for rest even as my mind churned.

"I'm just ... thinking."

"Yeah. There's a lot of that going around."

I was too tired to worry about pajamas, so I stripped down to my underwear and climbed into bed. Gunner followed suit, hitting the lights before letting loose a long sigh. It was pitch black in the room. I wasn't worried about visitors sliding through the trees and approaching us. I'd warded the cabin. On top of that, I had a perverted ghost hanging around. He would warn us if trouble approached.

"Good night," I murmured, closing my eyes.

"Good night."

Absolute silence followed for a moment, and then he slid his arm under my waist and tugged me until I rolled against him, my cheek resting on his shoulder. "You have questions about Rain."

The simple statement caused my eyes to snap open.

"I do," I confirmed. "Ever since I arrived nobody has wanted to answer those questions. I don't foresee tonight being any different."

"It's a little different ... thanks to Brandon. You're allowed to be curious."

I hesitated.

"Ask whatever you want," he prodded.

Well, that was an opening I couldn't very well ignore. "Okay." I licked my lips. "Were you together?"

"No." He immediately started shaking his head. "We worked together, had a few drinks together now and then, but we were never romantically involved."

"And yet you're tortured by her death."

"I'm ... bothered by what happened," he corrected. "Rain was, let's just say she was a wild child. She liked to throw herself headlong into whatever investigation we had going at any given moment. She was headstrong ... and belligerent ... and brave. She was also petulant and pouty. She wasn't the easiest person to deal with."

"And at some point you locked her in that cage."

"She was acting out of sorts. We were convinced she was possessed." He opened his mouth for a second and I was certain he was going to say something important. Instead, he pressed his lips against my forehead before continuing. "I'm starting to wonder if the same thing happened to her that has happened to Brandon."

"Seriously?" I pulled back. The strong lines of his face were visible despite the limited moonlight, but I couldn't ascertain what he was feeling. "Do you really think that's true?"

He shrugged as he pulled me tighter against him. It was as if he needed the contact. "She was running around at the time, dating someone she didn't want us to know about. I didn't think much of it. She was always jumping from dude to dude."

"And you're certain you never dated her?"

He chuckled. "I'm certain. Before you, I was convinced that dating people in our group was a bad idea."

"Given what happened to Brandon, I'm not sure that it's not," I muttered.

He stiffened next to me. "What are you saying?"

"Don't worry." I rested my hand on his chest. "It doesn't matter if it's a good or bad idea at this point. It's done. It's not as if you and I are going to be able to stay away from one another. Even if we decided after the fact that it was a mistake we're already both goners."

His lips curved against my forehead. "That's true."

"I guess I just assumed you guys were involved given the way Brandon was reacting."

"No." Gunner sobered. "Brandon knew I was upset about how things went down. Obviously whatever has taken him over knew to use that memory against me. What I don't understand is why he's so fixated on you."

That was easy enough to answer. "They've pegged me as a threat. I think it has to do with the fact that I remember Bixby and what I'm assuming was the master from Detroit all those years ago. That's the one thing that sticks out to me."

"What if you're wrong?"

"Then I'm wrong. But it doesn't feel wrong."

"Well ... I guess you would know best." He snuggled down deeper into the covers. "Do you want to hear about Rain?"

Did I? It didn't seem that I had much choice. "Yeah."

"She'd become secretive toward the end. She was hanging out with people we didn't know. She was acting furtive, shirking her duties. Still, that wasn't enough to force us to turn on her. We assumed she would get it together and return to the way she was."

"But something happened."

He nodded. "Yeah. Something happened. We caught her breaking into Rooster's office and going through his files. When questioned on it, she tried to deny what she was doing. It was obvious she was lying. Then she lashed out and threatened to kill us all. She actually pulled a knife on Marissa."

I was taken aback. "And she didn't stab her? That shows restraint."

He poked my side, amused. "You're a funny girl."

"I should have my own stand-up special."

"This is not a funny situation."

"No," I agreed. "Not remotely funny."

"We locked her up, promised we would figure out what was happening, and then observed her for three days."

"And?"

"And nothing. We don't know what happened to her. We don't know why she was acting the way she was. We only know that she escaped."

Ah. We were finally getting somewhere. "How did she escape?"

"Raisin. She heard Rain cursing a blue streak. She assumed Rain had accidently locked herself in the storage room."

"Raisin is probably lucky that Rain didn't hurt her."

"Very lucky," Gunner agreed. "We think it's because she heard Whistler. He came in right after Raisin and gave her a good talking to about being in the bar. Because she didn't realize anything had happened, Raisin didn't admit to being the one who'd let Rain out. By then ... it was too late.

"We didn't want Raisin to blame herself for what happened, so we played it off," he continued. "We went out to her cabin — your cabin now — but she'd already packed her things and cleared out. We thought she was going to run, but during the next few days we heard reports about her being seen in the area."

"Who was she hanging out with?"

"We don't know."

"How is that possible? What happened to her?"

"Whatever force took her over compelled her to kill herself," he replied softly. "You know that cliff that overlooks the lake where we went hiking about two weeks ago?"

I nodded. "The day after Drake took off to take care of his sister and I was melting down because I wanted information? Yeah."

"We finally found her one day, had her closed off. We were determined to help. She saw us, probably figured out our intentions, and took off racing. That road is treacherous up there. She knew it, but she didn't slow down. She took every curve as if she didn't care if she would fly off the road. When she hit the top and realized we were still in pursuit she purposely kept going ... right over the edge."

I was horrified on his behalf. The picture he painted was heartbreaking. "I'm really sorry. I just ... don't understand. Someone had to be controlling her, changing her personality. You said before you were wondering if it was like now. Something must've made you consider that."

He cleared his throat. "Brandon. He's acting out of sorts, just like Rain. I saw the realization on Rooster's face earlier. He thinks the same thing." Gunner shifted so he was lower in the bed, his arm still around me as we faced each other. "What if these vampires were here back then and nobody knew it? What if they were using Rain as a smokescreen? What if we could have ended this months ago but none of us figured it out? That means Honey died for nothing ... and now Brandon is in danger."

I worked my jaw. He was a melancholy pain when he wanted to be. "You can't go back in time. We might never know what happened with Rain. All we can do is move forward ... and that's what we'll do. We'll figure it out ... and save Brandon. I promise I won't let anything happen to him."

"You can't promise that. I know you mean well, but you're not omnipotent. You can't control everything."

"No, but I can control this. I won't let you lose him."

He held me tighter. "This can't be all about me. You're involved in this, too. I want you safe."

"I don't think I'm in the right line of work for that. But it doesn't matter. We'll figure it out because it's necessary."

"Yeah." He closed his eyes and kissed my cheek. "I'm sorry he hit you. That's not like him. I need you to know that. He's not the type of guy who hurts women."

"I know. You wouldn't surround yourself with people like that. I'm not upset."

"I am."

"I can tell." On impulse, I repeated the gesture and kissed his cheek. "Go to sleep. We have a long day ahead of us tomorrow."

"Right now, right here with you, I know that everything will be okay. I can't think otherwise. I might be more of a Debbie Downer tomorrow. I can't promise anything."

"Fair enough. Just get some sleep."

I WOKE TO POUNDING ON THE DOOR loud enough to disorient me.

"What the ... ?" Gunner swore viciously under his breath as he extricated himself from the embrace we'd fallen into the previous evening. Neither of us had moved, which seemed to indicate that we were exhausted. "I'm going to kill whoever that is."

I remained where I was, my morning-muddled mind refusing to fire on all cylinders, and only managed to rouse myself when I heard angry voices in the living room. When I made my way there, I found Graham and Gunner facing off.

"It's barely even light out," Gunner complained, hands on hips. He made quite the morning spectacle, what with his chiseled chest and the cute boxers with little dogs on them.

"Yes, well, some of us start the day early," Graham fired back, his eyes drifting to me. "Nice hair."

It took me a moment to realize what he was talking about, and I reached up to smooth away my bedhead.

"Your hair is fine," Gunner shot back, grabbing my hand before I could make a fuss. "He's just being a pain in the behind."

"Yes, that's the only reason I'm here," Graham drawled. "Would someone like to make me some coffee?"

When Gunner didn't immediately respond with a snarky comeback, I realized the question was directed at me ... which didn't make me happy.

"You're only asking because I have ovaries, right?"

Graham looked horrified by the question. "What?"

"Serving coffee is apparently work for women in your world." I was in no mood to play nice. "That means I'm the one who has to get your caffeine."

"To be fair, I *was* expecting you to get my coffee," Graham admitted. "It's not because you're a woman, it's because you're the hostess. Most hostesses would've already offered."

"Oh." I chewed my bottom lip, the righteous indignation I was gearing up to embrace evaporating. "I guess that makes sense." I didn't miss the amused looks Gunner and his father shared as they followed me to the kitchen. I'd forgotten that I wasn't wearing sleep shorts until I felt a cool breeze lift the T-shirt I was wearing. That only served to make my mortification complete. "Um ... I should probably put some pants on." I wrestled the T-shirt lower. "It will just take me a second."

Gunner took pity on me and nodded. "I'll handle the coffee this morning, even if you are the hostess and it's your job."

"Yeah, yeah, yeah."

By the time I came back, Gunner and Graham were seated at the table, mugs of coffee in front of them. There was an air of defiance floating around Gunner. He refused to put a shirt on and seemed to be daring his father to comment on it. Graham silently sipped his coffee and returned the stare. It was something of a standoff, and I couldn't help but wonder if I would ever understand men.

"You guys are acting like children," I pointed out as I shuffled toward the counter. I'd taken time to run a brush through my hair, but now I regretted it because I was feeling defiant, too.

"We know," Gunner replied, breaking off the staring contest with his father and turning his face to me. "I made yours how you like it and put it in your 'witch, please' mug." His lips quirked, forcing me to stare anywhere but his mouth for fear I would lose it ... or kiss him in front of his father. Neither option seemed a good way to go. He pulled out the chair next to him so I could sit, giving me a long once-over and then smiling. "I wish you would've left the hair like it was. Now I know you're not going back to bed."

"If your father is here before the crack of dawn I don't think I'm going back to bed regardless."

"Which is another reason he sucks," Gunner lamented, his hand moving to the back of my neck as he glared at his father. "Well, out with it. You said you couldn't tell me what was going on until Scout was here because you didn't want to explain it twice. She's here ... and I'm ready for the big news."

Instead of immediately responding, Graham grinned at his offspring. "You guys are kind of cute. I mean ... domestic. Do you sit on the couch at night and share popcorn while watching romantic comedies?"

"Out with it," Gunner growled. "We had a late night. Things ... took a turn."

Graham sobered. "I heard about Brandon. I'm sorry."

I was taken aback. "How did you hear? There was only a small group of us dealing with the problem and I'm pretty sure everyone else is still in bed."

"I ran into Mama Moon while out and about last night. She told me."

Where was Graham hanging out with Mama Moon in the middle of the night? The supernatural speakeasy in the woods was my first thought, but if they didn't want the Spells Angels hanging around, they certainly wouldn't want the chief of police there.

"Are you dating Mama Moon or something?" I asked out of the blue.

Graham looked horrified by the thought. "Why would you think that?"

"Because she was with us until almost two ... and you look like the sort of guy who goes to bed at ten o'clock on the dot. I just thought that maybe you guys were ... you know."

Graham's expression was dark. "First, young lady, my personal life is none of your business. Second, I'm a night owl, so you're wrong about the ten o'clock thing."

"That's true," Gunner volunteered. "He's up until at least eleven o'clock ... unless he falls asleep in his recliner."

Graham ignored his son. "Third, Mama Moon and I have a ... complicated ... past. It does not involve romance. I respect her, but she's a wild card and I don't like my women wild."

Gunner smirked. "He only likes prim and proper ladies. Ones who wear little bonnets and ankle-length skirts."

I glanced between them for a beat, absorbing the tension going wild between them, and then shook my head. "Why are you here again?"

"Brandon losing his mind isn't the only thing that happened last night," Graham replied grimly, turning serious. "There's no easy way to say this, so I'm just going to lay it out for you. Honey Martelle is gone."

I blinked several times in rapid succession and drank my coffee, confused. "Did you think she was just faking it or something?"

The sigh Graham let loose was a sign of extreme exasperation. "I mean her body is gone. From the morgue."

"But ... how?"

"We're not sure. The medical examiner hasn't even completed her autopsy. There was a fire two towns over and that was given precedence because three people died and arson is suspected.

"The back door was open, which means that someone either managed to get in through it and claim the body or ... ." He didn't finish. He didn't have to.

"Or she was turned after all and got up on her own," I mused, rubbing my chin. "Does the building have security cameras? That might help."

"It does, but none of them were operational last night."

"That seems ... convenient."

"It does," he agreed. "I thought you guys should know. You might have another enemy out there."

"Or someone who simply wants us to think we have another enemy," I countered, my mind busy. "It's weird that it happened the same night that Brandon went off the rails."

Gunner jerked his eyes to me. "What are you thinking?"

I took a big gulp of coffee and then stood. "I think we need to talk to your buddy. If he won't talk to me — which doesn't seem likely — you'll have to question him. Once word gets out that Honey's body is missing from the morgue we're going to have issues."

"Yeah, I'm worried about that, too," Graham agreed. "This thing could blow up in our faces — and fast — if we're not careful. We need to figure out what's going on."

EIGHTEEN

*B*randon didn't have the best night. He was a ranting lunatic when we checked on him.

"This is all her fault," he spat as he jabbed his finger at me. He looked as if he was considering rushing me, perhaps trying to wrap his fingers around my throat. That wouldn't work, but he appeared deranged enough to attempt it. "She's the devil."

"Brandon ... ." Gunner shook his head. It was apparent his temper was dangerously close to exploding.

"It's okay," I volunteered, sending him a reassuring smile. "It's not him. And I don't exactly suffer from delicate feelings."

"That's because she's the devil," Brandon explained. "Only the devil doesn't care what others think about her."

The statement was so absurd it almost made me laugh. "Since when is the devil a woman? I'm pretty sure that he's a man ... that's why high heels are a thing."

Brandon rolled his eyes. "Stop talking to me, demon," he hissed, tapping the side of his head. "I'm wise to your games. You cannot control me. I'm too powerful."

I narrowed one eye as I regarded him, something occurring to me.

"You're too powerful, huh?" I pulsed out a bolt of energy strong enough to pin him to the wall and moved closer, ignoring the way he flailed. "Did they give you this power?" I studied the wound on his neck. "We should probably put an ointment on this. It looks like it hurts."

"Let me go, you devil!" Brandon was howling now. He strained against the invisible ropes I'd restrained him with. "It burns! It hurts! She's killing me!" He was obviously going for sympathy, but Gunner didn't fall for it.

"Stop it!" Gunner's eyes blazed. "Just ... stop."

I slid my gaze to him. Seeing his friend like this was almost more than he could bear. I was convinced he was the only one who might be able to penetrate the haze overwhelming Brandon's mind, but I wasn't certain it was worth the pain he would have to go through to do it. I was just about to suggest letting Marissa take over babysitting duty — if anyone deserved the punishment, she did — when I was distracted by the appearance of Rooster.

"How are things?" he asked as he studied the situation.

"Is that a serious question?" Gunner looked pained. "Look at him. He's out of his mind."

Rooster was a calming presence and he exerted that power on Gunner as he rested his hand on his shoulder. "You need to calm down. We're going to fix this, but it's not going to happen overnight. It's something we have to figure out. You need to be patient."

"I'm not sure I can be patient." Gunner sank onto the cot. "I'm afraid we've already lost him."

I wasn't certain if coddling him or tough love was the way to approach his defeatist attitude. Tough love came naturally, so that's what I went with. "Suck it up," I ordered, refusing to cringe when his annoyed eyes landed on me. "You're no good to us if you've already given up. Brandon needs you to fight for him. You're his friend. That's your duty."

"I ... ." He worked his jaw and I was convinced he was about to argue. Instead, he slowly nodded. "You're right. I'm not helping matters."

"You need to stay here and talk to him," I insisted. "You're closest to him. You need to try to break through whatever barrier they've erected in his mind. And you have to be patient when you do it.

"Remember, this isn't his fault," I continued. "We'll get him back. He's only fixated on me because the vampires want to cause trouble. Don't let them win."

He nodded. "Okay. What are you going to do?"

"I'm heading back out to the house on the bluff."

His eyebrows practically hopped off his forehead. "Excuse me? How is that the smart play? You're vastly outnumbered."

"Yes, but vampires can't go out during the day," I reminded him. "I'll be perfectly safe. There's nothing to worry about."

"There are at least three women in that house who can walk around during the day."

"They're not a concern. I can easily take them. All I expect from them is more taunts from inside."

"What about the minion?" Rooster asked. "He might be more powerful."

"Maybe," I conceded. "The only time he ever tried to move on me was when I was a kid, and that was before he realized how powerful I was. I don't think he's stupid enough to try anything."

"Okay." Rooster was using his reasonable tone, which told me he was about to mount some sort of argument I wasn't going to like. "What are you going to do up there? I thought there was a barrier. It's not as if you can get inside the house."

"It's a magical barrier. I'm certain I can tear it down if I figure out the right spell."

"And that's your plan?" Rooster folded his arms over his chest. "I'm not sure how smart that is. What if you do pull the barrier down? Are you going to run headlong into danger and take out all the vampires while they're sleeping?"

"Do you have a problem with that plan?"

Gunner snapped up his head. "Um ... I have a problem with that plan." He raised his hand as if in a classroom. "I don't think you should go up there alone. If you do get into a fight, you'll be on your own.

They could attack when your back is turned. You don't seem to think they're a threat, but I don't want to risk it."

I tugged on my limited patience. "How many times do I have to tell you that I can take care of myself?"

"How many times do I have to tell you that you're no longer a one-woman team? You're part of my team, and I don't want anything to happen to you."

"Just because we're dating doesn't mean that I'm going to cede my independence."

"I haven't asked you to. You're still not going up there alone."

He stated it as fact, which made my temper flare. "When were you declared the boss of me?"

"I'm not your boss. When you do stupid things, though, I'm going to call you on it ... and protect you. If you insist on going up there, I'm going with you."

"You have to stay here and deal with Brandon."

"We don't know that's going to work. I do know that I can watch your back. Sometimes you have to pick one priority over another. You're my priority."

"Well, you're not invited."

"It's a free world."

Rooster cleared his throat and glared. "This, this right here, is exactly why you shouldn't crap where you work. You two are ... there are no words." He tugged on his hair and made a disgusted sound as he shook his head. "Okay, this is what's going to happen.

"I'm the boss," he continued, not missing a beat. "I say what goes. No more relationship drama in public. If you two want to verbally stab one another in private, that's on you. But you can't do it on the job. I'm putting my foot down."

The way he declared it almost made me laugh. "You're putting your foot down?"

"That's right." He nodded. "Gunner is right, Scout. It's not safe for you to go up there alone."

My stomach twisted as Gunner shot me a triumphant look.

"Scout is also right, Gunner," Rooster added. "The barrier they've erected needs to be tested. She's the strongest warrior we've got. If anyone can bring it down, she can."

Gunner's smile faltered. "But ... ."

"No." Rooster refused to back down. "She's going up there and you're staying here. You are our best option for reaching Brandon. Because I agree it's stupid for her to tackle this alone, she will have backup in the form of Bonnie. I'll text her and have her meet Scout up there. That should be enough to placate you."

Gunner didn't look as if he agreed in the least. "I think I should go with her," he persisted. "I'm familiar with the players. Bonnie hasn't interacted with them at all."

"You have another duty here." Rooster lifted his chin, practically daring Gunner to further the argument. "I've made my decision. Bonnie's going with Scout. If you don't like that ... well ... I don't really care what you do. I'm the boss, right? I make the decisions."

Rather than waiting for us to continue arguing, he turned on his heel and stalked out the door as Brandon started cackling like a maniac.

"Oh, he told you," Brandon chortled.

I pursed my lips as I slid my eyes to Gunner. "I hate it when he pulls rank on us."

Despite the tense cloud hanging over us, Gunner snickered. "It's definitely annoying." His gaze was somber as it locked with mine. "Promise me you'll be careful."

The earnestness of his words was enough to eradicate the anger that had been building. "I promise. You have absolutely nothing to worry about."

"I wish I could believe that."

I BEAT BONNIE TO THE HOUSE, BUT ONLY by a few minutes. She didn't appear agitated about being forced into babysitting duty, instead greeting me with a friendly smile before turning her attention to the house.

"I bet it was pretty back in the day," she noted as I knelt next to the magical barrier and studied the way it glimmered at the junction where it touched the ground. "I bet it was a real showplace. It's kind of sad how it looks now."

"Yes, it's heartbreaking," I drawled. "The vampires are living in a rundown house. I don't know how I'll ever get over the heartache."

Her expression was hard to read as she turned back to me. "You seem ... agitated."

"I am royally ticked off," I countered.

"Do you want to talk about it?"

"No."

"Fair enough." She held up her hands in a placating manner and focused on the barrier. "This is a nifty piece of magic." She extended her fingertips until they intersected with the magic and then jerked back her hand. "Um ... ow."

Despite myself, her reaction amused me. "I wouldn't suggest touching it."

"You could've warned me."

"I thought it was a given." I focused on the edge of the barrier and pulsed out a burst of magic, quickly moving to the side when it ricocheted back at me.

"Oh, that's interesting." Bonnie forgot about her singed fingers and moved closer to me. "It's a rebound barrier. Anything we throw at it fires back at us."

"Pretty much." I was grim as I planted myself on the ground and sighed. "I need to think."

"Is there a way to get around the rebound thing?"

"I don't know." I shifted my gaze to the house. I hadn't seen a hint of movement. That didn't mean there weren't people inside watching us. In fact, I could feel eyes on me. "Can I ask you something?"

Bonnie nodded. "Of course."

"What's the deal with Rain? Gunner told me a little about her situation last night, but I'm still confused. I didn't want to push him too hard because he's dealing with the Brandon situation, but there are a few holes in the story."

All traces of good humor fled Bonnie's pleasing features. "How much did he tell you?"

I shrugged. Her leeriness said I needed to tread carefully. "I think he just hit the basics. It was late ... and the only reason I knew to ask was because Brandon used the incident as a weapon."

"That's ... unfortunate." She made a tsking sound and shook her head. "What happened to Rain was a tragedy. We all learned a little something from it, including the fact that we need to watch out for one another instead of sitting back and letting things play out."

I couldn't help but believe that was a pointed dig. "I'm guessing Rooster told you that Gunner and I were arguing about me coming up here alone."

"That he did." She smiled at me. "He said he felt like he was trapped in a room with hormonal teenagers."

"I don't believe that's an accurate assessment."

"He also said you were more emotional than Raisin."

"That's definitely not accurate."

She laughed, the sound low and throaty. "Oh you're funny. I'm so glad you joined this team. We're overrun by testosterone sometimes ... and it's not exactly as if I want to bond with Marissa. You're a good fit, even if you do have attitude problems."

I opted to let the comment go. I had other things on my mind. "Gunner said that given the change in Rain's demeanor before things went south, he thinks it's possible she was being controlled by a vampire. What do you think?"

Bonnie looked taken aback. "I don't know. I hadn't considered it."

"I think the only reason Gunner considered it is because of Brandon. He's been ... unsettled ... with the way Brandon is reacting to me. He's upset because if it was anyone else he would be throwing punches. Brandon isn't in control of his mouth, so Gunner can't really protect my honor."

"I can see where that would be an issue with Gunner," she hedged, her eyes serious. "As for Rain ... that situation was harder on Gunner than he probably lets on. I'm not sure how much I should tell you, but you're in a relationship with him — and I happen to think you're good for him — so I'm just going to go for it."

Oh, well, this sounded promising. "I wholeheartedly concur that's a good idea."

She snorted. "Of course you do. Anyway, Rain had a crush on Gunner. That's probably not all that surprising. He has a certain presence that drives women wild. You've seen Marissa. She's way too old for him and yet can't stop herself from panting."

"I can't decide if she really likes him or it's an ego thing," I admitted. "I try not to spend too much time thinking about it because it will give me a migraine."

"That's probably best." She smiled. "Rain convinced herself she had deep feelings for Gunner even though he was gentle and tried to let her down easy. He told her that he couldn't date anyone he worked with, and I thought he actually meant it until I saw him with you. Then I realized he was just shining her on."

"I think it's more likely that he was being sensitive," I countered.

"I'm not saying he was trying to be mean," she said hurriedly. "He was convincing when he said he couldn't date someone he worked with. Rain was upset about it but seemed to accept the statement as fact. It wasn't until you came along that I realized he didn't believe what he'd said."

"Oh, I think he meant it." I smiled to myself as I extended magical feelers to test the barrier. "I don't think either of us had any intention of dating anyone in the organization. Sometimes ... well, sometimes things just happen."

"I think sometimes things are destined to happen," she said, grinning. "I'm pretty sure you guys are one of those things."

"Oh, geez. Let's not get schmaltzy."

She snickered and shook her head. "As for Rain, once Gunner made it clear that nothing would ever happen between them, she started acting out. She partied a lot, hung out with people at that terrible bar on the highway, and disappeared for long stretches when she was supposed to be working.

"Rooster made noise about firing her, but he never followed through on it," she continued. "I think he was convinced that she would come out of her funk on her own and he didn't want to cripple her future if he didn't have to. Rain was gone before we realized how serious things were."

"And you're certain she's dead?" That was the one part of the story I couldn't get out of my head. "Gunner said she went over the cliff but her body was never found."

"That area is extremely hard to get to. Gunner tried to climb down the embankment but only made it so far. He said he scented a body down there and was convinced it was her. That was good enough for us because nobody else was reported missing."

That made sense, and still ... . "If these vampires have been hanging in this area for longer than we realized, it's possible they tried to recruit Rain as their inside person. It's unlikely she could survive a fall off a cliff like that, but Brandon said something interesting today. He intimated that he was more powerful than he used to be. If that's true and the vampires somehow fortified Rain, she could still be out there."

Bonnie turned thoughtful. "Are you suggesting they turned her into a full-fledged vampire? I don't think that's possible. She was out during the day. She was definitely human when she went over that cliff."

I hadn't considered that. "Well ... then I guess she's stuck out there because her body can't be recovered. It's too bad. Finding her might serve as some much-needed closure for you guys."

"I agree, but it's not worth someone else risking his or her life to try to find her. The Rain we knew before the change wouldn't have wanted that."

"Yeah." I exhaled heavily and rubbed my neck, my skin prickling as I felt a set of eyes land on me. When I turned my attention to the house, all the windows were empty. That didn't mean someone wasn't inside spying on us. Of course, we weren't doing anything but fruitlessly testing the barrier. "I don't know what to do with this wall. I need to do some research."

"Any idea on where we should start?"

"No. I'm at a loss."

"Me, too. It's interesting, though."

I wished I could be as excited about the clinical aspect as she was. I was more frustrated than anything else. There had to be a way around the barrier.

NINETEEN

I like to win.

I've been that way for as long as I can remember. There was no trophy to claim at the bluff house. That didn't mean that someone wouldn't come out victorious.

"You look crabby," Gunner noted as we settled into a booth at Mable's Table for lunch.

"Thanks," I replied dryly. "That's just what every woman wants to hear."

He smirked. "I didn't say it was a bad thing."

"Yeah, well ... ." I shifted on my seat and extended my legs, my feet brushing against his. Rather than moving them, I kept them there. The brief contact was exactly what I needed.

"Do you want to play footsies with me?" he teased.

"Maybe." I pressed the bottoms of my feet against his as he settled into the game. "Can I ask you something?"

"You can ask me anything."

"Why didn't you tell me how extensive Rain's feelings were for you?"

He stilled, his feet ceasing to push against mine. The expression on his face was hard to read, but I sensed a flash of annoyance. "I take it Bonnie has been talking out of turn," he groused.

Rather than pushing him on the subject, I waited.

"I was not in a relationship with Rain," he stressed.

"I didn't say you were." I refused to get mired in an argument that would offer neither of us a solid outlet for our fiery emotions. "I'm not accusing you of anything. I just want to know why you didn't tell me about her one-sided feelings and the way she tried to push herself on you."

"I don't see how it's important."

"You don't see how the fact that the woman who lived in my cabin before me had strong feelings for you is important? You made it sound like a simple friendship when it was so much more than that."

He scowled, his eyes flashing. "See? That's why I didn't tell you about it." He jabbed a finger in my direction. "That right there is exactly why."

I refused to let him derail the conversation and drag me into an unnecessary argument to avoid a real talk. "I thought we were supposed to discuss things," I pressed. "That's what you've been saying to me for days now. Weeks really. You said this relationship was never going to work if I didn't open up to you. I guess that was a one-way street, huh?"

His eyes flashed with something I didn't recognize. "Why do you have to push this?" he complained. "It was a long time ago."

"Months," I corrected. "She's been gone for only a few months. That means whatever you're feeling is still close to the surface."

"What makes you think I'm feeling anything?"

"You can't hide your emotions. You're bad at it."

"Thank you, baby." Sarcasm dripped from his tongue and I knew my efforts to avoid a fight were ultimately futile. He was spoiling to square off with someone and I appeared to be his best option.

"The more you act out, the more convinced I am that those feelings might have been reciprocated." I decided to lay it all out there. Hiding from the emotions roiling inside of me wasn't going to benefit anyone. "In that case, it seems likely I'm just a stand-in for Rain."

"Don't say that," he hissed, leaning forward. "That is not true. Why would you think that?"

"Because you're hiding something from me." I was matter of fact. "You've told me things, but you're still withholding information when it comes to Rain."

"I'm not." He was firm. "That's only happening in your head."

"I'm not an insecure person. At least I don't think I am. Right now, though, I can't help feeling that something is off here, that you're hiding things from me. I don't like the feeling."

"Well, I don't particularly like being accused of things that aren't true." His tone was gruff. "I've had a terrible morning. I mean ... terrible. I would appreciate it if you didn't pick a fight over absolutely nothing on top of everything else that's going on."

"This isn't a fight about nothing. You're hiding something from me."

His eyes flashed with annoyance. "Are you calling me a liar?"

"If that's the way you want to play it, then I guess I am."

He held my gaze for a long moment of silence. The air was thick between us. For once, the atmosphere sparked with something other than sexual tension. That's when Mable showed up to take our order.

"What will it be?" When we didn't immediately respond because we were busy glaring at each other, Mable took a moment to glance between our faces. "Is this a sex thing?"

The question was enough to draw Gunner's eyes to her. "No."

Once he'd broken the spell and I could look away from him, I realized that there was every chance that we would cross certain lines if we didn't take a break. I was agitated because he kept information about Rain from me. Whether that information would ultimately end up breaking my heart was too soon to tell. He wasn't in the mood to answer, because he'd spent the morning trying to talk down his possessed friend.

We were both walking a very fine line. If we stayed together right now, one of us would cross it.

"I'm not all that hungry," I said, pushing myself to a standing position. "I changed my mind about lunch."

"Scout ... ."

When I risked a glance at Gunner I found the anger had largely fled his features. "It's okay," I reassured him. "We're both on edge. I had a fruitless morning, and I'm guessing you had the same. I need some air."

"We should talk about this," he argued. "It's not good to let it fester."

"I agree, but if we talk about it right now when we're both raw we're likely to explode for no reason. We need to let it settle."

"But ... where are you going to go?" He obviously wasn't content to just let me walk off into the sunset. "You're not going back to the house, are you?"

"No. There's someone else I want to see."

He was quiet for an extended moment. "I'm going to see you again in a few hours, right?" He looked legitimately frightened that I might answer to the contrary.

"You are," I reassured him. That's when it hit me that we were both a little raw around the edges when it came to relationships. Neither of us was an expert and we both had fears — and ridiculous doubts — fueling us. On impulse, I reached over and squeezed his hand. "I don't want us to say things we're going to regret. I'm in a bad mood because of the barrier ... and I feel vulnerable emotionally because of the things Bonnie told me."

"I swear it's not what you think," he protested.

"I know. I still feel it because I can't help myself. You feel as if you've been backed into a corner because of whatever Brandon said to you. We need a few hours apart. It'll be fine after."

He didn't look convinced, but it was obvious he wasn't going to put up a fight. "Try not to get into too much trouble, huh?"

The admonishment was enough to elicit a smile. "I'll do my best, but no promises."

MAMA MOON WAS IN THE YARD behind her store when I arrived. She sat in one of those canvas camping chairs, the ones with the drink holder in the arm, studying the tree line to the north of the property. She didn't even look up when I moved to join her.

"I'm surprised to see you today," she said as she sipped from a thermal mug. "I thought you would be camped out at The Cauldron trying to help Brandon."

"Oh, I'm trying to help Brandon," I intoned as I grabbed one of the other chairs leaning against a nearby fence post and unfolded it. "I don't think me being at The Cauldron is helpful for his mental state."

"Probably not," she agreed, sliding her speculative eyes to me. "You look ... discombobulated."

Despite my pisser of a mood, the word made me laugh. "I guess that's how I'm feeling."

"What did Brandon do?" She looked resigned to hearing the story. "You should know, whatever he said, it isn't his fault. He's been taken over. They're forcing him to act out of sorts. The Brandon I know is a sweet boy. He would never willingly say the things he was spouting last night."

"It's not about Brandon," I countered. "Er, well, it's not only about Brandon. It's a lot of things. I'm not going to pretend what's happening to him isn't dragging me down, but he's low on my list of priorities today." And that right there was the crux of why I was so agitated. He was important to Gunner, to the point he was struggling with a mountain of guilt. I wanted to help Brandon because Gunner needed it, but I was mired in my own sea of doubt, and I hated myself for it.

As if reading my mind, Mama Moon let out a low chuckle. "Oh, I can feel the drama seeping from your pores, girl. You might as well just tell me what's going on. The longer you drag it out, the more likely I am to lose interest."

One of the things I liked best about her was her blunt nature. That was on full display today. I expected her to drag information out of me. Now that the moment was upon me, I was torn.

"What do you know about the woman who held my position before me?"

"Rain?" She pursed her lips. "I know that Brandon brought her up last night, so obviously you've decided to fixate on her."

"That's not the only reason, though it did pique my interest."

"I can't blame you there." She rubbed the back of her neck and let loose a long sigh. "Rain was ... a wild girl who didn't believe in controlling her emotions. You remind me of her in some ways, but you're completely different from her in all the ways that count.

"You rigidly control your emotions even though you lose yourself to them occasionally," she continued. "I think your biggest fault is that you have a big heart and sometimes it takes control of you. Your head often takes a backseat."

"I'm pretty sure that's an insult."

She chuckled, amused. "Yes, well, it's not. We're all different. We all have our weaknesses. Yours just happens to be your inability to control what you're feeling. In some respects you're tightly coiled and protective of what you're feeling and thinking. In other ways it's all out there. I figure you'll grow out of some of your more peculiar leanings at some point. You're not quite there yet."

She wasn't wrong ... which only served to agitate me more. "I was actually asking about Rain."

"Because of what Brandon said or are you sniffing around for answers on other things?"

That was an interesting question. "I'm looking for insight into what happened to her." I chose my words carefully. "Bonnie let slip that she had feelings for Gunner. She says they weren't reciprocated, but when I questioned him about it he flew off the handle.

"Now, it's entirely possible that his emotions are close to the surface because he spent the morning trying to deal with Brandon, which couldn't have been easy," I continued. "I'm starting to suspect he's hiding the truth, though, and that kind of makes me want to hurt him because we promised to be honest with one another."

Instead of clucking with sympathy, as I expected, Mama Moon snorted. "Oh, I love how dramatic you two are. It's ... stimulating. Sure, it's a little *Real Housewives of Beverly Hills*, but that's not necessarily a bad thing in a boring area."

I knit my eyebrows together, confused. "I don't know what that means."

"It means that you're being dramatic for no good reason other than you want to flip your own heart," she explained. "You like the thrill of little fights and you're feeling frustrated because you're used to being the toughest chick on the magical block. Right now you're being stymied by a barrier and don't know how to fix Brandon, which helps Gunner, who you think you're mad at right now because of Rain. You really just need someone to take out your aggression on."

My mouth dropped open at the convoluted statement. "Did you just explain something?"

She laughed harder this time, which only served to ramp up my agitation. "Oh, I like you." She patted my wrist and turned her attention back to the trees at the sound of snuffling. "Come on, Barney. It's time for your breakfast."

I jerked up my head at mention of the name, my blood running cold when a huge creature — seriously, it was so big and bulky it stole my breath away — detached from the tree line and started ambling in our direction.

It was a bear.

No, it was a really big bear.

Ever since I'd first crossed paths with Mama Moon I'd heard stories about Barney. He was like a pet, but he lived in the woods and did his own thing most of the time. He apparently trotted out whenever he felt like it to hang with the former Spells Angels maven.

"He's not going to do anything, right?" I gripped the arms of the chair tightly, fighting the urge to erect a protective barrier between me and the large animal.

"He's a big baby." Mama Moon was on her feet when the bear reached us. She opened her arms and wrapped them around Barney's neck. "How have you been? I haven't seen you in days. I was starting to worry that something had happened."

If bears could look sheepish, that's exactly how I would describe Barney now.

"I guess it's okay." Mama Moon stroked his broad head. "You look pretty good. Do you want a treat?" She moved toward the box sitting next to the chair she'd just vacated. "I brought you nuts ... and honey ... and some smoked fish ... and some fresh greens."

I watched, dumbfounded, as she proceeded to lay out a feast for the bear. For his part, Barney snuffled in appreciation and rubbed his head against her side before moving toward the food. He seemed perfectly comfortable in her presence — and completely ignored me — so I started to relax.

"As for you ... ." Mama Moon's eyes were cloudy as she turned back to me. "You care about Gunner a great deal."

It was a statement, not a question, and my cheeks burned under her scrutiny. "I don't remember denying that."

"That's good, because you would look like a ninny if you tried." She returned to her chair after laying out the food, smiling indulgently as Barney moved from treat to treat. "The thing is, I don't believe you've ever been in a real relationship. There's nothing wrong with that, but it handicaps you.

"Gunner has been in a few relationships, but none were serious," she continued. "He's as out of his depth with this as you are. He might be worse because he thinks he's an expert. You're at least cognizant enough to admit you're a novice.

"You're also at a disadvantage because you've put yourself first for the whole of your life. That also isn't bad. You had no choice because of what happened to you. Putting yourself first kept you alive. While Gunner's issues were different when it came to his mother and the things she did to him, the outcome is largely the same. He put himself first after she tried to hurt him and he refused to change his ways until you came along."

I absently scratched the side of my nose as I regarded her. "You're saying that we're not capable of making this work because we're both too selfish."

"That is not what I said at all." She made a face. "You're both giving individuals who guard your hearts. You fell for one another despite the fact that you always try to protect yourselves. Your hormones were stronger than your brains, which is always something I approve of."

She laughed, delighted, as I rolled my eyes. "You two are strong together, and you're good for each other. You'll have growing pains because you both need to learn about putting someone else first. It's okay. Couples fight. This isn't the end of the world."

"But ... he's lying about Rain."

"I don't think he's lying the way you seem to think he's lying. You need to give him a chance to explain."

"But ... he won't talk about it. He's crabby and shuts down."

"I'm betting you do the same when questioned about things."

"Not really."

Her lips quirked with amusement. "Talk to him about Rain. I guarantee you'll feel better once you do. I also guarantee it's not as bad as whatever you're making out in your head."

"I guess."

"That's not the only reason you're here." Mama Moon was the sage sort and her eyes twinkled as my forehead wrinkled. "You're also frustrated with the barrier. I know because I've heard reports that you were there this morning testing it."

"You have people following me?" Anger bubbled up. "Why?"

"I don't have people following you. I have people watching the house."

"Oh." Well, crap. That made sense. "What did they say?"

"They said you kept testing the barrier and it was obvious you were agitated with what you found."

"Any magic used against it is tossed back at the person trying to cross the barrier. I can't think of a way to move past it."

"Can't you?"

"No."

"If the barrier absorbs the power and shoots it back, then perhaps you should aim the magic at someplace other than the barrier."

I frowned, confused. "What is that supposed to mean?"

"Think about it."

"But ... ."

"Think about it," she pressed. "The answer is right in front of you."

I hated it when she said things like that.

TWENTY

$\mathcal{M}$ama Moon wasn't in a giving mood when it came to information, so I had no choice but to leave at a certain point. She was much more interested in Barney — and I honestly couldn't blame her because he was magnificent — and she barely looked up when I left.

Telling me to think about the magic I was using was infuriating. I momentarily considered turning around and shaking her until she told me what to do. Instead, I pointed myself in the direction of the bluff house. It probably wasn't the smartest move, but I was quickly becoming obsessed.

I parked in my normal spot and planted myself on the ground near the barrier, my eyes focused on the house. I was missing something ... but what?"

"Twice in one day?" The morose member of Melody's unholy trio appeared from beneath a weeping willow. I hadn't seen her, but she didn't frighten me so I wasn't exactly worried about her presence.

"I'm nothing if not diligent," I agreed, igniting my fingers and trailing them along the barrier. The magic sparked and burned, but there were no signs of weakness. "Where's your boss?"

The woman tilted her head, considering. "I don't have a boss. I'm not sure what you're talking about."

"I'm talking about Melody." I lifted my eyes and studied her blank features. "I expected her to be out and about taunting me again. I'm kind of in a bad mood, so a verbal sparring match with her might be just what the doctor ordered."

"She's not here."

I narrowed my eyes. "Where is she?"

She held out her hands palms out. "I don't know. She doesn't often inform me of her plans."

The woman seemed surprisingly open to conversation. She wasn't the bitter sort and didn't immediately attack. She was a ... curiosity. That was the best way I could think to describe her. "And what's your name?"

"Does it matter?"

"It does to me." I opted for honesty. "You're different from the others. You're ... less aggressive. It makes me think you don't want to be here."

A ghost of a smile flitted across her face. "Oh, who wouldn't want to be here? I mean ... it's the middle of nowhere. There's not a cinema or mall in sight. This is ... breathtaking and beautiful." Sarcasm practically dripped from her tongue, which I found intriguing.

"A city girl, huh? I get it. I used to be that way. Maybe I still am. I wasn't exactly keen when I got transferred up here. I do like the beauty of the landscape, but there are things I miss about the city."

"Oh?" The woman planted herself on the remains of a tree that had fallen years ago and placed her hands in her lap. She sat straight, her shoulders squared, and flashed a smile that didn't make it all the way to her eyes. "What do you miss?"

"Well, I miss a good movie theater ... and the shopping here is indeed dreadful." I returned her smile. "I miss good Middle Eastern food. Oh, and Greek food. Man, I miss this little place that was close to my apartment that had the best soup."

"Is there anything you miss that doesn't revolve around food?"

"I miss Belle Isle. I used to go there sometimes in the summer. It had this ... vibe. I don't know how to describe it. There was magic there."

"I liked Belle Isle, too." Her eyes drifted to the east as she stared at ... well, nothing as far as I could tell. "I lived in Royal Oak, so it wasn't that far a drive. I absolutely loved the conservatory. Those flowers ... and the scent ... and I know what you mean about it feeling magical. I always thought that too. The aquarium especially."

Well, that was something. She'd let slip that she lived in Royal Oak. That wasn't all that far from where I used to live. Of course, this woman and I weren't likely to have run in the same circles. "I miss the lake in the summer, although they have nice lakes here."

"Is there anything you like about this area?"

I nodded without hesitation. "Absolutely. I love the quiet. I love that gunshots in the night don't wake me."

"You must've lived in a rough area. That wasn't the norm in Royal Oak."

"Probably not," I agreed. "I didn't think I minded the noise when I lived there. Now I really appreciate the silence ... except for one thing."

"What's the one thing?"

"You don't realize it when you're living there, but there's a lot of ambient noise," I explained. "The cars blocks away hum along and you absorb the sound. The streetlights actually generate a buzz that you don't notice until it's gone. The first few nights I was here I didn't know if I would ever be able to sleep without the ambient noise."

"What did you do?"

"I bought a fan. The white noise knocks me right out."

"Good idea." She plucked at her jeans. "I don't think I'll ever get used to it here."

Unlike Melody, who seemed to relish her position in the vampire world, this woman looked distinctly uncomfortable. Honestly, I felt sorry for her. That didn't mean I trusted her. Sympathy was an emotion with many layers.

"You still haven't told me your name," I prodded.

"Why does it matter?"

"Because you're the only one up here I don't want to kill, and when the battle comes I would like to be able to yell out your name so you can protect yourself." That was a lie — mostly. If she died in the battle I would suck it up, and it was doubtful I would go out of my way to warn her. Still, information was power. I wanted to know her name so I could run a background check.

"You may call me Cherise."

I waited for her to say more. When she didn't, I figured I had enough to do at least a cursory search. Cherise from Royal Oak shouldn't be that hard to track. "It's nice to meet you."

"I don't know that I can say the same about you."

"Give it time. I'll grow on you."

The joke was enough to elicit a wan smile. "If you say so. I ... ." She trailed off at the sound of footsteps.

I followed her gaze to the front of the house, frowning when I saw nothing. Then, within seconds, Bixby emerged from behind the bushes. He was so short that given my position on the ground I simply couldn't see him.

"You really should trim those bushes back," I called out. Here was a target for my mixed emotions. I didn't feel sorry for him in the least and had no problem verbally lambasting him. "Either that or you should put lifts in your shoes. That might help with the Little Man Syndrome."

He narrowed his eyes as he halted in front me. "I see you're back. Was your previous visit not fruitless enough for you?"

Honestly, he made me laugh. He was annoying to the point of making me fantasize about popping his head like a zit, but he was funny, too. Of course, he wasn't purposely funny. It was all accidental.

"I love doing fruitless things," I drawled.

"That must explain your choice in men."

My smile slipped. "Why are you out here? Are you afraid she's going to let something slip? If so, you have nothing to worry about. All we've talked about is how cool the city is."

"Yes, well ... ." Doubt was reflected in Bixby's eyes as he studied Cherise's profile. She was obviously uncomfortable under the scrutiny, but she said nothing. "You're needed in the house. We're cleaning the parlor today."

"Okay." Cherise didn't offer up a single word of complaint as she got to her feet and started in that direction. She didn't look over her shoulder to meet my gaze. She didn't apologize to Bixby for talking to the enemy. Instead, she merely hopped to her feet and trudged toward the house. I thought about calling out to her, but that would paint a more prominent target on her back. She was the only one I was likely to be able to communicate with. I needed to give it time before addressing her again.

That didn't mean I couldn't mess with the little minion.

"So, how are things?" I leaned back on my elbows and regarded him. He showed no signs of fleeing. "It's been a long time since I've seen you. How many women have you enticed to half-lives since then?"

"I have no idea what you're talking about." He imperiously brushed at invisible flecks on his jacket arm. "You have me mistaken with someone else."

"Yeah, you can spout that nonsense all you want, but I know better. I remember you."

He cocked his head to the side, considering. "Well, in that case, perhaps you're not as important as you think, because I certainly don't remember you."

I didn't believe that for a second. "Yes, you do. I could tell something sparked the moment I reminded you of our previous meeting. There was recognition there. You're good at shuttering your emotions, but you couldn't hide that."

"I think you see what you want to see, child of the stars."

The name grated. "And what do you know about the children of the stars?"

"I know a great deal. I think the question is: What do you know about the children of the stars? Not much, I think."

He wasn't wrong, which only made me want to shake him until the knowledge fell out of his head like a piñata. "I know enough to make me wonder about things. That doesn't really matter today. I'm here about you."

"Me?" His eyebrows hopped. "How ... flattering."

"Don't get too excited. I was talking about the general you, not you you."

"Was that sentence supposed to make sense?"

He was good at the agitation game, I had to give him that. I was better. "Is he in there?" I inclined my head toward the house. "The guy you were with that night. Is he the master vampire? I have to admit to being curious. I was new to the game back then and had no idea who I was dealing with at the time."

"You were a child."

It was the first time he'd openly acknowledged that we'd met before and I wanted to crow. "I don't know about that," I hedged. "I stopped being a child when I was abandoned in front of a fire station with no memory of the previous years. I had to grow up fast in the system."

"It must be difficult for you." He folded his arms across his chest. "You're powerful, something you recognize, and yet you don't know how to deal with it. You're emotionally stunted because of what happened to you, which means personal growth is out the window. You're a witch in a world full of shifters. This area is crawling with them. I can smell them at every turn." He wrinkled his nose to show his disdain. "You are one of those who don't fit anywhere."

Even though I knew he was trying to get under my skin, the statement hit true and hard ... and it hurt. "I guess that's fair." I kept my expression even, difficult as it was. "I think we probably have that in common. I remember what happened to you that night, the appearance of your friend. I remember how he yelled at you, made you seem small. Perhaps you don't fit anywhere either."

"I think you only wish that were true," he countered. "I found my place in this world long ago. I fit just fine."

"As a minion?"

His frown was pronounced. "I don't like that word."

"I don't like the word moist. It gives me the heebie-jeebies. It's still a word. You're a minion. That's what you are. You have to suck it up."

"I'm not a minion."

The way he screeched it told me I'd officially gotten under his skin. That's what I was trying to do, of course, so I was happy. "If the minion hat fits ... ."

"Oh, shut up." Bixby's expression turned dark. "You're trying to irritate me. You think that will give you an edge in what's to come. Well, I'm here to tell you something, girlie. You've already lost. You just don't realize it."

"I'm not afraid of you." My voice was soft. "I've taken out vampire nests before."

"Maybe, but the others in your group haven't. They're novices. You very well may be the last one standing by the time we're done. You won't be able to hold us off forever. Once all your friends have been turned ... ." He left the sentence hanging.

"They might not be familiar with vampires, but that doesn't mean they're weak," I argued. "They'll stand with me. Together, we'll take you down because that's what we do."

"If that's what you need to tell yourself." He cast a backward glance over his shoulder at the house. "I should probably be going. You're welcome to sit out here and stare at the house as long as you like. You'll never get through the barrier. Better witches have tried."

The comment chafed, as he knew it would. Despite internal promises to the contrary, he was getting to me ... and I hated it.

"Have a nice day," he called out, dissolving into grating giggles. He was clearly enjoying himself.

I reacted before I realized what I was doing. I couldn't throw magic at the barrier without it firing back. That didn't mean I couldn't use my magic to force Bixby to leave the safety of the magical enclosure.

"*Desisto*," I called out in Latin, ordering him to stop.

He ceased moving, though I detected a faint twitch in his fingers.

"Come this way," I sang out softly, making sure my voice didn't carry. "I think you and I should have a talk."

He fought the magic, as I knew he would. I wove a bit of karma into the spell because of it, smiling as his lips twisted into a grotesque amalgamation of a grimace and grin. "What are you doing?" He was breathless.

"You need to come with me." I doubled my magic. The way he managed to fight the influence I was projecting was fairly impressive. Of course, that could've had something to do with the barrier. At least that's what I told myself. "We have some things to discuss."

"I'm not going anywhere with you," he gritted out, opening his mouth in a wide "O." I had no doubt he would try to scream for help. I couldn't allow that.

"No, no, no." I added another spell, this one forcing him to clamp his lips shut. "You're coming with me no matter what you want. The more you fight, the itchier you'll get ... and in your private parts, because I'm mean like that."

His eyes widened, but he didn't say anything. Of course, he couldn't.

"Now, come on." I forced more magic into him.

This time he took a lurching step in my direction. He looked panicked at the prospect, which only served to thrill me.

"Come on, you little ferret." I shoved again. He took two large steps, although he was fighting the process and almost looked as if he would topple over. "I'm taking you whether you like it or not."

The terror in his eyes should've given me pause, but I was over it. I wasn't particularly looking forward to torturing him — well, not entirely — but I would get information out of him one way or another.

"Stop fighting me!" The final burst of magic I let loose was enough to cause him to freeze, which wasn't my intention. He went ramrod straight, his eyes frozen in a silent plea, and then he slowly toppled forward. By the time he landed, only his head and shoulders were clear of the barrier. That was still plenty of minion for me to work with.

"I don't know why you had to make this so difficult," I grumbled, grabbing him around the shoulders and tugging until he was completely on the other side of the magical wall. "I figured you guys were immune to the barrier so you could run your errands. The spell wasn't directed at you, so you were free and clear. I wasn't firing physical magic at the barrier, so my mind magic was clear to work despite the boundary. Really, it was an ingenious little plan."

I was mostly talking to myself. He couldn't respond and I had no intention of loosening his lips until I'd removed him from the premises.

"You're heavier than you look," I complained, grunting as I shifted to throw him over my shoulder. I was strong, but he was dead weight ... and my back was going to punish me for what I was about to do. "Okay, we're out of here. Unfortunately, I only have my bike. That means I'll have to tie you over the back rack. It won't be comfortable, but if things go as planned you'll survive the trip."

He made a protesting sound deep in his throat, but no words escaped. "Don't worry. I'll fix the frozen thing and the talking thing when I get you where I'm taking you. You don't have a thing to worry about. I've got everything under control."

They were bold words, but they felt like a lie. I had absolutely nothing under control. I had made a move, though, and it was too late to take it back. My only choice was to move forward.

TWENTY-ONE

J took Bixby to the cabin. That was the only move I had. He remained frozen and silent until I had him securely tied to the same chair I'd harnessed Brandon to the previous evening. When I removed the magic binding him, a torrent of obscenities flew out of his mouth.

"You really know how to sweet talk a gal," I drawled, swiping my forearm across my forehead as I sank into one of the other chairs.

"I will kill you," he seethed, spittle forming at the corners of his mouth. "I will rip your tongue from your mouth and use it as a lapel."

"That's some vivid imagery." Now that I had him, I was at a loss for what to do with him. I'd acted on impulse — he really was a little worm and had it coming — but I'd set in motion a chain of events that were likely to backfire on me. It probably wasn't a smart move, but it was too late now. "Tell me what your master has planned."

"I won't talk. You can torture me all you want, but I'm loyal."

"Uh-huh." I pursed my lips, considering. "Is it the same master as before? Is it the guy I saw you with?"

He didn't answer, instead staring into nothing.

"I don't want to hurt you," I said. "I'm not keen on torture unless I have no other choice. You're backing me into a corner."

"You're the spawn of Satan," he shot back. "I'm sure you'll get great joy in torturing me, because that's what you do."

"Actually, you'd be wrong on that." I folded my arms over my chest and glared at him. "You're little. I mean ... tiny. You're like a small child. I don't want to torture a small child."

He turned haughty. "I'm a grown man."

"You're a little person. Wait ... is that the right term? Ugh. Now I have to look it up." I pulled out my phone and started Googling. "It says you need to be four-foot-ten or shorter to be a little person," I said after a bit of research. "How tall are you?"

The look he shot me could've been deadly if he had access to magic. "I'm not having this discussion with you."

"I could get a tape measure."

"Go ahead. Then you'll have to untie me."

"True, but I would just freeze you again so I could measure you. Is that what you want?"

"I really am going to kill you."

It was going to bug me if I didn't know. "Hold on." I disappeared into the bedroom, returning with my sewing kit in hand. I rummaged inside until I came up with my tape measure. "This will just take a minute."

IT TOOK CLOSER TO TWENTY MINUTES because the tape wasn't long enough to run his entire length. It took effort to stretch him out on the floor, and then I had to measure him five times before I was satisfied. Then I had to move him back into the chair, rebind him, and unfreeze him.

In the end, I wasn't sure it was worth the effort. Still, I had my answer.

"You're four-foot-eleven," I announced. "You're technically not a little person."

"I hate you!" His eyes were wild. There was no doubt the indignity of being placed on the floor and measured had driven him to the brink. In a way, it was an effective torture technique. I was fairly proud of myself.

"That's good. Use your anger." I grabbed a bottle of water from the refrigerator and returned to my chair. "Are you still with the same guy?"

"My master is going to rip your heart out and drink from it while it's still beating!"

"Can I take that as a yes?"

"He's going to remove each and every one of your fingers and feed them to his shadow beast."

I stilled. "He has a shadow beast? Is that like a dog?"

"It's a minion from Hell!" he screamed. Thankfully I didn't have neighbors. I could continue to verbally torture him until I lost interest, which wasn't likely to happen because he was such an easy mark.

"But you're the minion."

"Stop using that word. You don't know what it means."

"It means that you're his personal whipping boy. I remember you two together all those years ago. He treated you like an annoying child. Does he still act that way?"

Bixby lowered his voice to a threatening whisper. "He's going to bathe in your blood."

"That sounds gross. I ... ." The sound of a motorcycle engine outside the cabin caught my attention and I internally cursed. "Crap."

"Who is it? Is it my master? He's come to exact bloody revenge."

"It's the middle of the day," I reminded him, slowly getting to my feet. "It's likely someone for me, not for you ... unless you think your master is willing to turn himself into ash to save you. No? I didn't think so." I moved to a spot where I could look through the front window, frowning when I recognized Gunner's tall frame. "Oh, no."

"Who is it?" Bixby was a little too eager. "Is it the Devil come to reclaim you for his army?"

"It's my boyfriend."

Bixby looked perplexed. "Is he the Devil?"

"No, but he might as well be." I rolled my neck and shifted my eyes to the minion. "We have a problem. He's going to be angry if he knows I took you."

"Good. Maybe he'll be smart and take me back. He might recognize that's the only way to save himself."

"He's not going to take you back. He's not an idiot. He is going to yell at me, though, and I'm not in the mood to be scolded. It's already been a long day, and I didn't even get any lunch. Now I'm crabby and he's going to pick a fight. This really is a terrible day."

"He's going to release me." Bixby was adamant. "I know. I have faith that my master has corrupted him exactly as he said he would."

I shot him a sidelong look. "I'll kill your master before I ever let him touch Gunner. I promise you that. As for you ... zip it." I magically gagged him again and then moved toward the door. I would've preferred Gunner wait until later to argue. Now things were going to be ... unpleasant. I wasn't in the mood for unpleasant.

"Hey." I opened the door the same moment he raised his hand to knock. I'd pasted what I hoped was a friendly smile on my face. "I thought we agreed to take a little break today." It wasn't the most auspicious of greetings, but I was on a timetable.

"Hello to you, too." His gaze was speculative as he looked me up and down. "You seem ... different."

I didn't know what to make of the statement. "Well, I'm having a quiet day. Maybe that's what's different."

"I don't know what that means. What's a quiet day?"

"It's a day when I contemplate the meaning of life and my place in this world."

"Swell." He dragged a hand through his hair and regarded me with unreadable eyes. "I came to apologize."

That was so not what I was expecting. "I ... you did? I thought you were angry."

"I was, but not at you. I'm angry at the situation. Brandon was ... harsh ... this morning. He was saying things he knew would upset me, things about my mother and what happened."

My heart gave a little heave. Gunner acted tough and strong, but he was still haunted by the things that happened in his past. I recognized that because I was the same way. "I'm sorry. You have to know that the real Brandon would never do that. He's being controlled. His knowledge of your past is being used as a weapon, but it's not your friend wielding that particular sword."

"I know. It's just ... hard." He reached out and wrapped his hands around my wrists. "What I said to you wasn't fair. I was angry and took it out on you. I'm sorry."

"It's okay." I meant it. Now, given a few hours of perspective, I recognized that he had been lashing out and hadn't meant what he said. "I wasn't exactly at my best either."

"Yeah, well ... it still wasn't fair to you. I'm sorry."

"I'm sorry, too. I might've been looking for a fight at lunch. I was annoyed because I couldn't break down the barrier. I don't like to think I have a big ego, but I totally do. I thought I could waltz up to that thing and rip it down without issue. When I couldn't, I turned into a big baby."

A small smile played at the corners of his lips. "I think we were both babies." He leaned forward and rested his forehead against mine. "I don't like fighting with you. After you left, I felt like an idiot, but I still proceeded to pout and think bad thoughts about you for a good hour. Then I realized I was the one being a jerk and knew I needed to apologize. I wanted to give you a little time."

"I'm okay." I slid my arms around his neck and gave him a hug. "I was feeling sorry for myself, too. I hung out with Mama Moon for a bit. She essentially told me I was being an idiot."

"She's good that way. I've lost track of all the times she's called me an idiot."

"I got to meet her bear."

"Barney?" He pulled back, his features already lighter. "Cool, huh?"

"He's a little terrifying, but totally cool." I ran my finger down his cheek. "I'm sorry. I knew you were struggling with the Brandon stuff. I shouldn't have pushed you about Rain."

"I wasn't keeping it from you," he insisted. "I just didn't see the need. She went a little crazy at the end. I think it was whatever was being done to her. At least that's what I like to think. Either way, she's gone."

"Okay."

"I didn't have feelings for her," he stressed. "I don't want you thinking that. I do feel guilty because it seems I was at the center of her meltdown, but I didn't have feelings for her. Those are all reserved for you."

The sentiment was so heartfelt I could do nothing but smile. "Thanks. That's nice to hear."

He drew me close for another hug and then sighed before releasing me. "So, that was our first big fight. I believe that protocol suggests we need to go inside and make up now."

I blinked several times in rapid succession. "I ... you mean ... ."

He waggled his eyebrows. "I could use a little downtime. I was thinking we'd make up and then take a nap. Neither of us are getting anywhere on the investigation. Recharging can't possibly hurt."

It was a pleasant idea. There was just one little problem. "Um ... ."

He narrowed his eyes. "You're still angry."

I vehemently shook my head. "I'm not. I promise. It's just ... ."

The roar of a vehicle engine cut me off, and when I lifted my eyes I saw a pickup truck barreling down my driveway. I didn't recognize the vehicle, but the woman behind the wheel was another story. "Ugh. This just isn't my day."

Confusion etched across Gunner's face. "Is that ... ?"

"Melody," I confirmed, bobbing my head. "She's probably going to accuse me of something wacky. Before you jump to my defense, just be aware, it's totally true. We need to wait to fight about it until after they leave, though. We need to put up a united front."

His eyes turned accusatory. "What did you do?"

I held up a finger to quiet him and adopted a bright smile, one that was meant to completely derange the blonde menace hopping out of the truck. "What a beautiful day for a visit ... only you weren't invited. I'll have to ask you to leave until I have time to send a formal invitation."

"Oh, you're so funny," Melody drawled, her hands landing on her hips. "I can't tell you how funny you are ... except you're not. There's nothing funny about you."

I shifted my eyes to Cherise, who was hopping out of the passenger seat. The third half-vampire was with them, but she looked more confused than anything else.

"Good afternoon, ladies. It's a wonderful day for a drive in the woods."

"It would be better if we were in the city," Cherise countered. Her expression was cloudy, but I almost thought I saw a hint of amusement lurking in the depths of her green eyes. "This place is ... kind of a hole."

"It's home." I folded my arms over my chest and regarded Melody with a stern glare. "What do you want?"

"Are you joking?" Melody's eyebrows hopped so high they almost disappeared into her hairline. "We want our ... butler ... back."

"Butler?" That was beyond amusing. "I think you should call him your minion ... and I have no idea what you're talking about."

"Oh, don't do that." Melody wagged a finger as she made a face. "I know you took him. He was outside with you, on the other side of the barrier, and now he's gone. Somehow — and I still don't know how, but somehow — you convinced him to cross the threshold and then you took him."

"Oh, geez," Gunner groused under his breath. "Are you serious?"

I ignored the question. "I don't know what you're talking about. I think you should leave now."

"Not without our butler."

"I don't have your butler."

"Then I'm sure you won't mind us searching your shack to be sure." Melody moved to climb the steps to the porch, but I unleashed a torrent of magic at her feet, igniting the grass in blue flames and causing her to hop back.

"You're not invited," I stressed.

She fumed as she gripped her hands into fists at her sides. "You can't keep him. That's ... kidnapping. It's against the law."

"Report me."

"Maybe I will. In fact, no, I definitely will." She dug in her pocket and came back with a cell phone. "I'm calling the police."

Her response made me laugh. "Fabulous idea. I'll wait here."

"I'm totally doing it," she warned.

"And I still maintain it's a fabulous idea. Go ahead."

Gunner leaned close to whisper so only I could hear him. "My father might not take your side on this."

"It will be fine." I kept my smile in place as Melody danced around with the phone. "Go ahead. I think a police presence will do all of us some good." She made no move to press a button. Of course, I knew she wouldn't. "Oh, was that an empty threat? I'm shocked, I tell you. Absolutely shocked."

"Ugh." She stomped her foot and growled. "Why must you be such a pain? We can't leave without our butler. It's not going to happen. So ... ." She threw up her hands when I didn't respond. "Andrea, get him!"

The third half-vampire seemed surprised at the order. Her eyes widened as she glanced between Melody and me, as if she expected me to somehow countermand the order. Instead, I remained rooted to my spot.

"Are you suddenly deaf?" Melody challenged. "Get Bixby. I'm sure he's inside."

"But ... ." Andrea gnawed her bottom lip. "What about her?" she asked finally, inclining her head in my direction. "I don't think she's going to just let me go inside of her house."

"We won't know until we try," Melody replied pragmatically. "Now ... do it."

"Don't do it," I warned when Andrea moved toward me. "I promise you won't like what happens if you do."

"I ... have ... to." Andrea almost looked tearful. "I'm sorry. If you would just hand him over to us I wouldn't have to hurt you."

I wasn't worried about her hurting me. "Listen ... ." I didn't get a chance to finish the warning. I wasn't sure what I was going to say. She broke into a run much faster than I expected. Her plan appeared to consist of barreling me over. I reacted out of instinct, raising my hands and shooting out a bolt of green magic.

It hit her square in the chest, freezing her in place. I recognized the moment when she realized it was over. There was a split-second of regret and then her face went slack as she flew backward and hit the front of the truck. By the time she crumpled to the ground, she was dead ... and I was left to wonder if that had been a necessary move. It might've been too much power, especially given the circumstances.

"What the ... ?" Melody's eyes were the size of saucers as she scrambled to check on her friend.

For her part, Cherise simply stared.

"She's dead," Melody announced after a beat. "I ... you killed her!"

Now was the time to bolster my reputation. "You guys need to realize something. You're not in charge. I'm in charge. Don't come back here. If you do, the outcome will be the same ... only bigger."

Gunner remained silently poised for action at my side.

Melody's expression was impossible to read as she slowly stood. There was anger there — a lot of it — but there was also fear. "You're going to regret doing that," she hissed.

There was every possibility she was right, but I knew better than to acknowledge that. "Don't come back here. If you do, I'll burn your whole house of cards to the ground. You've been warned."

TWENTY-TWO

$\mathcal{W}$e had a dead body and no way to get rid of it. That meant Gunner had to call his father, which wasn't something either of us were looking forward to.

"I don't even know what to say about this." Graham stood next to the body, hands on hips, and shook his head. "I just ... don't even know what to say."

I pursed my lips and blew out some air. "To be fair, they came here and attacked me."

"Yes, I got that." He pinned me with a dark look. "But why?"

"Why what?"

"Why did they come here and pick a fight in the middle of the day?" he pressed. "It seems like a stupid move given the fact that they're protecting vampires. Why wouldn't they wait until the vampires could come with them?"

"You'll have to ask them."

Gunner cleared his throat from the chair at the end of the porch. He hadn't said much since Melody and Cherise fled, instead opting to pet Merlin while waiting for his father's arrival. I expected him to unload on me regarding the minion still tied to the chair in my kitchen. He'd been reserved, though, which told me that an argument was still coming.

Graham pinned his son with a questioning look. "Do you have something you want to say?"

"No," I answered for him. "He's just ... enjoying his time with the cat. He's a good cat daddy that way."

Gunner rolled his eyes. "Yeah, I wouldn't go there right now if I were you. As for the motive ... I don't think this is something you'll be able to keep on the down low for an extended period. You have a guy tied to your chair, for crying out loud."

I briefly pressed my eyes shut as Graham let out a snaking breath. "You just couldn't keep your mouth shut, could you?" I groused.

"There's a guy tied to your chair?" Graham was incredulous as he pushed past me and stormed into the house. Rather than follow him, I simply waited until he returned. "There's a midget tied to a chair in your kitchen!"

Well, that was uncalled for. "You can't say the M-word," I chided, shaking my head. "It's like the R-word or the F-word. It's banned."

"What's the R-word?"

"Don't ask," Gunner said. "I agree you can't say the M-word, though. It's derogatory. The correct term is 'little person.'"

"Actually, he's not a little person," I countered. "I looked it up. You're only a little person if you're an adult who stands four-foot-ten or shorter. Anything above that and you're just short. He's four-foot-eleven, so he's not a little person. He's just a short pain in the behind."

Graham worked his jaw. "You actually measured him?" he finally asked.

I nodded. "It was bugging me."

Graham threw his hands in the air and stalked away. He didn't seem happy with life this afternoon. I figured it all couldn't be because of me, but I decided to let it go.

When I risked a glance at Gunner, I found him bent over, his shoulders shaking with silent laughter. At least he no longer looked angry.

"This is not funny," Graham barked.

"You're right." Gunner sobered and lifted his hands, making sure the cat didn't move to try to jump from his lap. "It's not funny. It's serious. There's a dead woman in the driveway."

"You're darned right it's serious." Graham's eyes practically glowed red. "If you laugh, it just encourages her. Who is that guy?"

"He's a minion," I replied, ignoring the muffled complaints Bixby tried to shout from the kitchen. "He doesn't like that word. He thinks it's offensive."

"Like the other M-word?"

I took a moment to consider the question. "I think it's offensive in a 'I'm the big bad and you need to tremble before me' way rather than the other way."

I heard Gunner laughing this time, so I made sure not to glance in his direction and incur Graham's wrath.

"Okay, let's start over." Graham flashed a smile that was more deranged than understanding. "Who is that guy?"

"He hangs out with the vampires and does their dirty work during the day," I replied. "He's like a creepy little sidekick. I also think he might be perverted, but no one else agrees with me on that so I've decided to let it go."

"Uh-huh. And how do you know he works for the vampires?"

"Because he hangs around the house on the bluff all the time. They call him their butler, which is just laughable because that house is barely standing and there's nothing to buttle. Also, I ran into him when I was a teenager, and he was hanging around a creepy guy then, too. I'm guessing he's still working for the same creepy guy, but I haven't seen him yet."

"Wait ... you know the little guy tied to the chair from when you were a kid?"

"He accosted me on my way home one night."

"Define 'accosted.'"

"He hid in the bushes, but I sensed him there and called him out. Then the other guy showed up and said I was fine to go home. Ultimately it wasn't a big thing, but I still think he's a dirty pervert."

Graham shook his head and turned to his son. "Do you want to explain this?"

"Oh, don't look at me." Gunner leaned back in his chair. "She did this on her own." He turned to me. "I'm still confused about how you got him back here. I get that you went back to the house on the bluff even though you promised you weren't going to do that."

"Oh, geez," I muttered.

"I don't get how you managed to transport him back here," he continued. "I mean ... did you enchant him and make him climb on the bike with you? How did you get him to cross the barrier, by the way? Did you hide in the bushes and jump him when he left?"

"Of course not." That was the most ridiculous thing I'd ever heard. Well, maybe not ever, but at least in the last hour or so. "I don't hide in bushes. That's what skeevy perverts like him do. I used my magic to propel him over the line."

"What does that mean?" Graham pressed. "I thought you couldn't penetrate the barrier with your magic. That's what Bonnie said."

I knit my eyebrows. "When did you have time to talk to Bonnie?"

"When I stopped in at The Cauldron to check on Brandon. I'm fond of him. He's been a good friend to Gunner. I don't want anything bad to happen to him. What does that even matter?"

"I was just curious." I held up my hands in mock surrender. "I thought maybe you guys were seeing each other on the sly or something."

"Oh, my ... ." Graham pinched the bridge of his nose. "Why are you so obsessed with my personal life?"

"Because I think you need a girlfriend," I replied without hesitation. "You seem lonely. I think that's why you pick on Gunner the way you do. If you had someone else to focus on you'd be nicer to your son."

"She has a point," Gunner offered.

"Shut up." Graham jabbed a finger in his son's direction but kept his eyes on me. "Stay out of my business. I want to know how you got the little guy to the cabin."

"It wasn't that hard. The barrier was designed to keep offensive powers out. Like ... if I wanted to send a bolt of magic through to fry the little pervert I couldn't. I watched it in action. It was kind of like a fishing net — or even a dreamcatcher. It retracted when I shot magic on it and then spit it back. But there were small gaps, so I could ease my mind magic through. I made it so he had no choice but to cross the barrier."

"That's actually ingenious," Graham noted, rubbing his chin. "I can't believe you thought to do it, but it was smart."

"Yes, she's brilliant," Gunner drawled. "That's one of the reasons she's so full of herself and drives me crazy."

"You'll live," Graham said. "You controlled his actions, so you forced him to ride on the motorcycle with you?"

I shook my head. "I could've tried, but he was pretty good at fighting the magic. I had to expend a decent amount of energy. It was easier to freeze him so he couldn't move and then just tie him to the bike. He's short, so I kind of draped him over the back seat and then tied him in place." I leaned over to demonstrate.

"So, you turned him into a human Popsicle, tied him to your bike, and then drove him here?"

"Pretty much. I also cast a spell so he couldn't talk because I was afraid he would start screaming and draw attention. He's under it again because I didn't want Gunner finding out I'd performed a kidnapping before I was ready to admit it myself."

"Well, that makes sense." Graham rolled his eyes. "How do you put up with her?"

Gunner shrugged, noncommittal. "I think she's kind of cute."

"And I think you're both idiots." Graham threw his hands into the air. "I just ... this is unbelievable."

"He's fine." I waved off his concern. "I haven't even tortured him yet, but he probably thinks that thing I did while measuring him was torture."

"Well, that's something." Graham pressed the heel of his hand to his forehead. "I don't think I've ever been speechless. I'm speechless right now. I mean ... completely and totally speechless."

"And yet you're still talking."

Perhaps sensing that his father's fix on reality was fraying, Gunner coughed to get my attention and then jerked his head in a "come hither" manner. "Baby, I think it's best for everybody if you come up here."

"I definitely think that," Graham growled.

"Fine." I stomped up the steps. "This isn't my fault. They pushed me to the point of no return."

"And how did they do that?" Gunner asked as I sank into the chair next to him.

"They taunted me."

"And?"

"They tried to keep me out."

"And?"

"That's pretty much it, but they were diabolical with the way they carried it out."

"Uh-huh." He pressed his lips together.

"Don't look at her that way," Graham ordered, fury evident. "I know what you're thinking, boy, and now isn't the time."

"What are you thinking?" I asked.

"That you're cute and it's a waste of time to try staying angry with you." He leaned forward and gave me a quick kiss. "You've had a full day, huh?"

"Yeah. And I'm not done. We still have to torture the minion."

"That's something to look forward to." His smile was bright until he glanced at his father. "Oh, don't give me grief. At least she was proactive. We need to move on these jerks if we expect to get Brandon back."

Graham's expression softened, though only marginally. "Son, I get that you're upset about Brandon. I am, too. He's a good man. But this ... ." He gestured toward the body. "I have a dead woman here. How will I explain that?"

"Why do you have to explain it?" I queried. "I mean ... can't we just dump her in the woods or something?"

"She probably has a family looking for her," Graham argued. "Do you think it's right to leave those people wondering for the rest of their lives?"

"Sometimes not knowing is better."

"Really? From the girl who can't remember her past and has no idea where she came from? Is not knowing really better?"

He had a point, though I was loath to admit it. "What do you suggest we do?"

"Move the body so someone else can discover it. There are no marks on her. It's not as if you'll be a suspect."

"Oh." I hadn't even considered that. "I guess that's a good idea."

"Yes, I'm full of them." He leaned over and studied the woman's face. "Do we have any idea who she is?"

"They said her name was Andrea. That's all I've got."

"Well, that's better than nothing. Come on, Gunner. I need your help moving the body."

Gunner balked. "I don't want to touch a dead body."

"Do you want your girlfriend going to prison? Your only option is to help with the body or be separated from her on visiting days by bulletproof glass. Which sounds better?"

"You should definitely help move the body," I offered.

"And what are you going to do?" Gunner challenged.

"I'm going to question the minion."

"You mean torture him."

"Pretty much."

"Well ... at least nobody can say we're not an interesting couple." He planted a kiss on my lips and handed me the cat. "I'll want dinner once we're done dumping the body. Don't get bloody or anything."

"Don't worry about me. I don't torture with sharp implements. I use my mind." I tapped my temple for emphasis.

"You really are cute." He gave me another kiss and then shot his father a dirty look when the older man began miming throwing up over the body. "I'm coming. Stop acting like a child."

"Just as soon as you get your hormones in check, I'll stop acting like a child."

"Whatever."

. . .

BIXBY LOOKED AS IF HE'D BEEN FIGHTING his predicament when I returned to the kitchen. I'd watched Gunner and Graham load up the body and then turned my attention to important things — like torturing the minion and getting him to admit he was a dirty pervert.

"So, that was exciting, huh?"

Bixby made muffled noises behind his sealed lips. I couldn't make out a single syllable.

"Oh, right." I released the spell and smiled. "How are things?"

"I'm going to rip your entrails out, cut them open, and send a snake up through your body to kill you from the inside," he threatened.

"That was a good one," I acknowledged, smiling. "You're creative when you have a little time to think. By the way, I'm not sure you're aware of what's going on out there, but Andrea is dead. I kind of did it before I realized what I was doing and now I'm a little sorry."

"Oh, you're going to be sorry."

I ignored the threat. "The thing is, she hadn't really done anything to me. She was only acting on Melody's orders. She's the one I should've killed. Too late now, though."

Bixby fought against his restraints and leaned forward. "The master will make your blood boil from the inside. You will scream in pain, cry out for relief, but he will just watch ... and laugh."

I blinked a few times as I regarded him. "Does this master have a villain mustache? I mean ... it doesn't matter if he's clean-shaven or anything, but I picture him with one of those mustaches that curls at the corners. It would help if you could paint me a picture."

Bixby was beside himself. "I will cut off your ears and feed them to monkeys."

Oh, well, that was a new one. "Why monkeys? Where are you going to find these monkeys? Michigan isn't exactly a hotbed of monkey activity. We have some zoos, but if you get caught trying to feed a monkey at a zoo you'll totally go to jail."

Bixby let loose a scream that shook the walls. "Let me go!"

"Yeah, that's not going to happen." I crossed my legs and offered him a smile. "So, we need to talk about your torture. I'm not one for

213

jabbing bamboo shoots under fingernails or branding anyone with hot metal. That seems unnecessary ... and a little gross. So I'll have to torture you in a different way."

"And how is that?" Bixby sneered.

"Well, have you ever watched *Keeping Up with the Kardashians*? I swear there's no better form of torture."

Bafflement swamped his pinched features. "You're going to make me watch television as torture?"

"Oh, this isn't television. This is like being trapped in the world's sweatiest armpit. Everywhere you go, there's no escape ... and the scent is so overpowering — like uselessness and inflated egos and asses — that you're likely to pass out."

"Is this a game?"

"No, but I am going to win."

"I'm not afraid of you."

"You will be by the time I'm done. I promise you that."

TWENTY-THREE

*B*y the time Gunner returned, Bixby and I had taken it to a whole other level.

"That's how a proper minion works." I leaned back in my chair and focused on my screen. "See. He's doing his master's bidding. I bet you're just like that."

Bixby's expression was dark. "I do not eat bugs." He was positively apoplectic. "I don't understand why you're so stupid."

"I think this is exactly how it's done." I refused to back down, instead keeping my eye on the television as an old *Buffy the Vampire Slayer* episode rolled. "What do spiders taste like, by the way?"

"I will shove my hand through your chest wall and rip out your beating heart and show it to you before your death!"

I flicked my eyes to Gunner when I heard his shoes on the floor. "Hey."

"Hey." He leaned against the door jamb, glancing between Bixby and me. "How are things going?"

"Not well. He won't play by the rules."

"And what rules are those?"

"I've tortured him with Kardashians, those Honey Boo Boo people, and now old episodes of Buffy featuring minions. He won't tell me what I want to know."

"And what's that?"

I skirted my eyes to Bixby, who was glaring in such a manner I was certain he was envisioning me on fire. "What their plan is."

"I will die before I tell you anything of the sort," the minion hissed.

"That can be arranged."

Gunner watched us stare at each other for a moment and then shook his head. "You need a break from this, Scout. I need to go to town. Come with me."

The demand threw me. "What?"

"Town," he repeated. "I need to go there, and I don't think it's wise to leave you here."

"I can handle this little ferret."

"I think we should talk about strategy. I don't want to do it in front of him in case he's got a psychic pipeline to the vampires."

"Oh, he has a pipeline." I extended my finger so it was only an inch away from Bixby's face. "I shut it down when I took him. He can't communicate with the others."

Bixby's eyes bulged. "Is that why they don't answer me? I thought they'd abandoned me. You did this." He struggled against his restraints as I continued to taunt him with the finger that wouldn't quite touch him.

"Baby, this isn't going to work." Gunner said. "I know you don't want to torture him because you feel it's somehow wrong given the fact that he's a little person, but I don't see where you have a choice."

"He's not a little person," I reminded him. "I measured him and everything. He's technically a normal, grown adult."

"And yet you haven't cursed any part of him to fall off. To me that says volumes."

To me it said that I was turning into a big wuss — and I didn't like it. "Why do you have to go to town?" I asked, hoping to give myself a little breathing room to decide what to do.

"Brandon is having issues. They say he's sick ... and asking for me. I have to go."

That made sense. "You can go. I'll stick close to our friend here. Something will eventually break him."

"I have no doubt. You're tenacious enough to break him, even if you have to whip out old *Hee-Haw* episodes."

"What's *Hee-Haw*?"

"Something my father used to watch ... and love. It doesn't matter. I would prefer you come to town with me. Given the previous attack, I think it's better if you're not out here alone."

"I won't be alone. I have this idiot." I jerked my thumb toward Bixby. "We haven't finished bonding yet."

"I'm going to grind your bones into a powder and put it in my pancakes!" Bixby screeched.

"See. We're making headway."

Gunner's lips quirked. "This place was attacked. I'm doubtful it will happen again during daylight hours, but I want you with me. It would make me feel better."

"But ... ."

"If you don't come with me I can't go. I won't leave you. If I don't go to him and something happens to Brandon ... ." He left it hanging, but I could read between the lines.

"Fine." I stood. I could see the hints of hope lurking behind Bixby's eyes. "Don't get too excited. I'm freezing and gagging you again and making it so anyone who tries to cross the cabin wards immediately goes up in flames. No one is coming to rescue you."

Bixby worked his jaw. "I'm going to pull off your big toe and shove it down your throat. Then, when you're choking on your own bile, I'm going to do the dance of the dead and celebrate as you're prostrate on the floor. Then I will desecrate your body by hanging it in a tree and allowing the birds to pick your bones clean."

I hunkered down and stared into his eyes. "I'm going to make you watch old episodes of *Dawson's Creek* and then sing the theme song. We'll see who outlasts who."

. . .

GUNNER AND ROOSTER WERE NEAR THE bar when we walked into the Cauldron twenty minutes later.

"What's happening?" Gunner asked. I could feel the concern rippling through him. "Your text was kind of vague."

"We have a problem," Rooster replied, grim. "Brandon is sick. Like ... legitimately sick. I think he might be dying."

My stomach did a long, slow heave as Gunner immediately headed for the storage room. "What aren't you saying?" I asked, studying the two grave faces. "You're leaving something out."

"I think ... I think he's starving," Rooster replied. "He's pale and hasn't eaten a thing since we took him."

"So give him a sandwich or something."

"He refuses to eat. Besides that, I don't think he can eat regular food. He's so pale he's nearly transparent and he keeps making these noises while smacking his lips. I think he needs blood."

My mouth dropped open. This day kept getting worse. "He's still human."

"He is, but what if part of being a half-vampire is keeping him on a blood diet? I mean ... it kind of makes sense. Either way, he's really sick and I'm afraid."

I shifted my gaze to the hallway. "Well ... then we'll have to feed him."

"Oh, yeah?" Whistler arched an eyebrow. "How do you suggest we do that? I don't know anyone who will let him ... suck blood from them." The look of distaste on his face was evident.

"No," I agreed. "If I have to go and snag another one of those half-vampires from the bluff, then I will. I'm not going to let Brandon starve." I stalked to the storage room, pulling up short when I found Gunner sitting next to the cot. He looked lost and sad ... and more than a bit terrified.

Brandon was indeed pale. He was also clammy and breathing in shallow gulps. I stopped by the cot long enough to press my hand to his forehead and frowned.

"He feels cold," I muttered.

"He's dying," Gunner volunteered. "You can say it. I can see it happening. We're going to lose him."

I shook my head. "We are most certainly not going to lose him. I won't let that happen, so you need to chill out."

"Look at him!" His eyes flashed. "He's sick. He's going to drift away right in front of us."

I was afraid enough to start thinking outside the box. Brandon looked as if he had only a few hours left.

"He's going to be fine," I said finally, swallowing hard. "I have an idea."

"You have an idea?" Gunner was dubious. "And what's that?"

"It's better that you don't know."

I PLANNED TO TACKLE THE PROBLEM ALONE, but Rooster refused to allow it. Gunner needed someone to stick close to him, so I insisted Rooster stay behind. Whistler couldn't move fast enough for what I needed, and that meant Marissa was officially my partner in crime for the evening.

"What are we going to do here?" Marissa looked at the slaughter-house with dumbfounded disbelief. "You don't expect me to go in there, do you?"

"I'm sure you're having *Texas Chainsaw Massacre* flashbacks," I said dryly as I grabbed three plastic containers from my storage bin. I'd stopped at the market long enough to buy a pack of recyclable food storage containers. "You don't have to worry. That's not going to happen to us."

Marissa was incredulous as she shifted her eyes to me. "Excuse me?"

"This isn't Texas," I reminded her. "I'm pretty sure if there was a family of cannibals hanging around we would've heard about them."

Marissa stomped her foot as she dismounted. "Why would you tell me that if you didn't want me to freak out?"

"I was trying to reassure you that wouldn't happen."

"Well, good job." She flashed an enthusiastic thumbs-up. "I can't tell you how thrilled I am now that I know that's not going to happen."

"It is a tremendous relief," I drawled, bobbing my head. "Let's go." I started toward the front door. This wasn't a task I was looking forward to, but it had to be done. I couldn't sit back and allow Brandon to die if there was something I could do about it. Unfortunately, this was the best option I'd come up with and I wasn't exactly happy about it. Still, it was our only shot that didn't involve someone slicing open a vein ... and that simply wasn't going to happen.

"How are we even going to get in here?" Marissa had done nothing but whine since Rooster called her to meet up with me. I was over the sound of her voice. "We should go back to The Cauldron and rethink this."

"Brandon needs blood. Well, at least that's our belief." I extended my fingers and pulsed a bit of magic toward the lock. "We can't let him starve while we're figuring out how to take down the vampires." And Gunner will forever blame himself if his friend dies, I silently added.

"Hey, we're not the ones who fell in with the wrong crowd." Marissa's eyes flashed with wild panic as I pushed open the slaughterhouse door. Getting in was ridiculously easy. I mean ... who takes the time to try to keep people out of slaughterhouses? It's far more likely that nobody would want to remain inside. "This is on Brandon. He fell for Honey."

"Yes, and her body is now missing from the morgue." I slid through the door and ignited my fingertips to illuminate our way. "She's running around out there right now ... or the vampires took her body for some reason that I can't quite figure out. I think it's far more likely that the former is true."

"So ... she's a vampire." Marissa didn't look particularly bothered by the statement. "That's not our problem. We're not a part of this."

I shot her an incredulous look. "Our entire job is to protect the unsuspecting souls of this area from monsters. If Honey is a monster she falls under our purview. We can't just ignore the situation."

"No, *you* can't ignore the situation. I'm perfectly fine pretending nothing is happening. But I guess that's just me."

"It definitely is." I took a moment to study the facility map on the wall before continuing down the hallway. "Gunner loves Brandon. They're friends. I think Brandon did his best to help protect Gunner from his mother when they were kids. Gunner is wrecked over what's happening. We have to fix this."

"And what if we can't fix it?"

"I happen to believe this can be overcome."

"Because your ego won't let you lose?"

"Because I need Gunner to be okay," I replied. "He needs Brandon. What's happening isn't Brandon's fault. If we take out the vampires, we should be able to fix this ... at least in theory."

"Okay, but that doesn't explain why we're trying to steal animal blood from a slaughterhouse."

"Brandon needs sustenance. It's not as if I can wrestle down some random person and steal blood from him or her. This is our best option."

"Or we could've just gone to the blood bank and stolen a few bags of blood. It would've already been in containers."

I paused. "Oh, well, crap. Why didn't I think of that?"

"Probably because I'm the brains of this operation."

That was a frightening thought. "Okay, new plan. We're going to that clinic out on the highway and stealing some bagged blood."

"Too bad you couldn't have decided that before you told me that horrible story about the cannibals."

"Yes, well, you only live once, right?" I clapped her hard on the shoulder. "Let's get going. This was a stupid idea. I can't believe you came up with it."

THE REST OF THE GROUP HAD ARRIVED TO lend Gunner support by the time Marissa and I returned to The Cauldron. Doc sat at a booth, steadily typing on his computer. I had no idea what he was researching, but I figured it would be helpful.

"Did you get it?" Rooster asked, glancing up from the bar.

I held up the bags and nodded. "Put two of these in a cooler so they don't go bad." I handed them to Whistler, who made a face. "If this works, we'll probably have to steal more."

"And what happens if the state inspectors show up on a whim and look in my coolers?" Whistler challenged.

"That would suck," I replied. "If that happens we're royally screwed. That's true for a lot of stuff, though, so something tells me we'll be okay."

Whistler mumbled something under his breath that I couldn't quite make out. I didn't have time to mess with him, though. I had other things to worry about.

I carried the remaining bag of blood to the storage room. Gunner remained on the floor, holding his friend's hand. He looked lost, but his eyes were hopeful when he registered my presence. "Anything?"

"I certainly hope so." I flashed a smile for his benefit and dropped to my knees next to Brandon. He didn't stir. "This is the best I could do." I held up the blood and then looked around, confused as to how I could get the liquid from the bag to his mouth. "Um ... we need a funnel."

Gunner's eyes went wide. "You're going to use a funnel to get that in him?"

"Do you have a better idea? He can't swallow. I don't want to waste the blood by dumping it down his throat because it could spill everywhere."

"It makes sense." He rolled to his knees, sliding close enough to press a kiss to my cheek. "Thank you for at least trying. I know this couldn't have been easy."

"It'll be okay." I squeezed his wrist. "Get the funnel and we'll get this in him. I don't think we should wait much longer."

"I'm on it. Um ... thank you."

I was never comfortable with gratitude. It made me squirm. This was no different. Still, there was only one thing to say to move this along. "You're welcome."

· · ·

"I'M NEVER DOING THAT AGAIN!"

I was beyond talking by the time I finished with the funnel. Brandon revived within seconds of the blood hitting his system and then proceeded to steal the bag from me so he could suck it dry. During the process, blood splattered on my shirt, and I thought there was a genuine possibility that I might throw up.

"He's obviously doing better," Rooster noted as he appeared in the doorway, his eyes appraising as he watched Brandon lick the bag while glaring at me. "His color is back."

"It was like magic," Gunner enthused. "He was back almost right away."

"Well, that's one crisis averted." Rooster winked at me. "Now we have to decide the best way to end all this."

I'd been thinking about that and was at a loss. "I think I'm going to have to torture the minion with actual knives or something," I admitted, morose. "Under normal circumstances I would be fine with that, but ... he's tiny. It's going to feel like torturing a child."

"I don't see where we have much choice," Rooster pointed out. "We need information and he has it. I can come to the cabin and do it for you. If that's what you want, I mean. I think you've done your duty for one evening."

It was a sweet offer, but I couldn't accept. "No, this is on me. I took him. I have to be the one to break him."

"Let us know when you get anything. We'll be ready to move."

I nodded with what I hoped was enthusiasm. "I'm really looking forward to the torturing. Just you wait. It'll go swimmingly."

Gunner slid me a sidelong look. "This is going to turn into a thing, isn't it?"

He had no idea.

TWENTY-FOUR

I was exhausted by the time we returned to the cabin. All I wanted to do was climb into bed and shut out the world.

Gunner agreed that torturing Bixby would go smoother after a good night's sleep, so I at least managed to put that off. But that left us with another issue.

"I can't sleep with him in the house." Gunner was adamant as he folded his arms over his chest and glared at Bixby, who was still frozen in place.

"It's not as if he can do anything," I countered. "He's frozen to the chair."

"I don't care. He's right outside the bedroom door."

"Well, what do you suggest we do with him? It's not as if I have another place to stash him. Besides, the wards only protect the cabin. We can't exactly plant him in the yard. And if he's out there the birds are likely to crap on him and the scavengers might be bold enough to take a nibble."

Bixby whined and his eyes bulged, but he couldn't move.

"Scout, I'm exhausted," Gunner implored. "I cannot sleep with him right outside the door. There must be something we can do with him."

"Like what?"

"I don't know." He dragged a hand through his hair, frustration evident. "Wait ... there's that old shed out back. Can't we shove him in there? The wards can be extended to cover the shed, right?"

"I think there are rats in that shed."

Bixby made another noise.

"Well, that will teach him to withhold information from you," Gunner said pragmatically. "We'll move the chair out there, leave the spell on him, and take that portable television and plug it in. You can torture him with something truly awful and we can crash for a few hours."

It was an enticing option. "Well ... okay."

Bixby whined. I almost felt sorry for him.

"This is your own fault," I said as I grabbed one side of the chair. "If you would just tell us what we want to know we wouldn't have to do this."

Gunner grunted as he lifted. "If you would just torture him like a good girl we would already have the information we need. Come on. The sun is setting. I want to get him outside before we run the risk of the vampires showing up."

I slowed my pace. "Maybe we should keep him with us. You know, just in case."

"I need sleep."

"We might not get it anyway. I guarantee the vampires are going to come sniffing around." I dropped my side of the chair and planted my hands on my hips. "He can't go in the shed."

Gunner threw up his hands. "Well, that's just great. Every muscle in my body hurts and my brain is tired from the longest day ever."

Bixby started making noises again. I took pity on him and removed the gag spell.

"What?" I barked.

"I have to go to the bathroom," he announced.

I stilled. That was so not what I was expecting ... and something I hadn't considered. "Oh, no way."

"Yes." He bobbed his head. "As part of the Geneva Convention, you must provide me with acceptable facilities with which I can relieve myself."

That sounded like a load of hogwash. "I'm pretty sure the Geneva Convention is for prisoners of war."

"What do you think we're about to embark on?"

He had a point, but still ... . "You'll have to handle his bathroom needs." I pinned Gunner with a no-nonsense look. "He has to remain mostly frozen, which means he'll need help with his ... you know. It can't be me."

Gunner, who had sleepy bedroom eyes only moments before, was suddenly alert. "Oh no! Not me!"

"You're the only option."

"How do you figure? There are two people in this room."

"But I'm your girlfriend. You shouldn't want me to ... touch ... another guy's equipment. I mean ... that has to be a rule or something."

"Are you trying to get me to kill you?"

"No. I'm trying to get you to handle his bathroom needs."

"No."

"Someone has to do it."

"I said no."

I jutted out my lower lip. "Please."

His expression turned colder. "Oh, no. That's not going to work on me. That little girl thing is completely out of your wheelhouse. There's nothing on earth that you could offer to get me to babysit him while he does his business."

I pressed the heel of my hand to my forehead and heaved out a sigh. "Fine." I started toward Bixby, who looked legitimately terrified. "If you tell me what I want to know I'll let you go to the bathroom yourself. If you don't ... well ... you won't like the alternative."

His response was a horrified squeak. No words, just the shrill sound of terror.

"Fine. But you asked for it."

. . .

GUNNER WAS STILL LAUGHING when he crawled into bed an hour later. We'd skipped dinner — neither of us were particularly hungry after the bathroom incident — and the setting sun meant he was ready to crash. Apparently he was over the fact that Bixby was tied to a chair and immobilized in the other room.

"I still can't believe you did that," he said, chuckling as he closed his eyes. "I mean ... you brought a doll to life to go to the bathroom with him. That was ... terrifying."

"It was a marionette," I countered. "It's not mine. I've never had a doll and I don't intend to start a collection now. It was in the shed. I guess it must've belonged to Rain."

He cocked an eye. He was exhausted, but he wasn't quite ready to give up the ghost. "Do you still want to talk about Rain?"

"No." That was the truth. Er, well, mostly. "It doesn't matter if you were dating her or not."

"I wasn't. She had a crush on me that turned weird. That's all there was to our relationship."

"It doesn't matter," I repeated. "What's in the past is in the past. I would prefer looking forward."

"So would I. That doesn't mean you're not allowed to ask questions."

"I might have questions," I admitted. "I think it's best if I ask them down the road. We have things we need to focus on here."

"Like the minion tied to a chair in the other room?"

"That would be one of them," I agreed, rubbing my forehead. "We need to figure this out ... and soon. I got enough blood to get Brandon through tomorrow, but if this lasts much longer I'll have to break into another clinic. And I really don't want to do that."

"It's better than the slaughterhouse."

"Yeah, but I keep wondering if I'm shorting someone else blood by stealing those three bags. What if the clinic doesn't have enough tomorrow and someone dies?"

"I'm pretty sure the clinic overstocks blood. You know, just to be on the safe side."

"Probably," I agreed, sinking lower on the bed. I was suddenly as tired as Gunner. "Maybe the answer will come in my dreams."

"Maybe," he agreed, brushing his lips against my temple. "We'll talk about it in the morning. I have a feeling we'll be up early thanks to your friend in the kitchen."

I WAITED UNTIL I WAS CERTAIN HE WAS OUT and then muttered a spell to make sure he stayed that way. Should the vampires come calling, I didn't want him panicking and rushing headlong into danger in an attempt to protect me. I wanted him to get the rest he needed. If I had fanged visitors I would handle them ... and I expected that would be the case before the night was out.

I managed to sleep for a few hours. Sometime after midnight, my eyes snapped open and I was instantly awake. I hadn't heard anything. The house was quiet, Merlin completely conked out between Gunner and me. I had felt something, though. A presence ... and it was trying to probe my unconscious mind.

I checked Gunner, who was still sleeping. He would be angry when he realized I'd cast a spell to extend his sleep. It would probably result in an argument. It was better for him this way. Brandon's transformation had taken a lot out of him. If he wasn't rested, he was liable to make a stupid mistake. I wanted to ensure that didn't happen.

I followed the feeling to the front porch, quietly easing the lock and slipping outside. I made sure the door was properly latched so Merlin couldn't sneak out before scanning the darkness for a hint of movement. I was rewarded within a few seconds.

"So, we meet again," a gravelly voice said.

It took me a moment to isolate the individual I was talking to, but I finally found a silhouette on the lawn. It was difficult to make out features, but there was something familiar about the presence. I was certain we'd crossed paths before.

"I know you."

"You do?" The vampire moved to a spot directly under the moon, where tree branches didn't obscure his features, and smiled. His fangs were creepy under the limited illumination. "And where do you think you know me from?"

"Nine Mile and Little Mack."

He obviously wasn't expecting such a specific location. "I ... don't believe I'm familiar with that intersection."

"It was actually about five hundred feet from the intersection. I was walking after dark. Your minion tried to jump me. I called him on it. You showed up and got annoyed that he wasn't stealthy enough to take down a teenaged girl."

The vampire's lips curved. "Ah. I do remember you." He lifted his nose, as if scenting the air. "You're a child of the stars."

"Yes, and everyone keeps mentioning that without expounding on it." I slid into one of the chairs and crossed my legs. "You could save me a lot of grief if you would just tell me what that means."

"Don't you know?"

"Nope." I shook my head. "I grew up in the foster care system. I knew I was magical at a relatively young age, but I kept it to myself for obvious reasons."

"What happened to your family?"

"I have no idea."

"How ... terrible for you." He made a tsking sound and shook his head. "I can't imagine not knowing where I came from. I'm not always happy with my origins — family is always the bitterest pill to swallow — but at least I'm not swimming in questions."

"No." I studied him up and down. "You're a born vampire."

"That's very good." His smile was congenial. "Most people don't know the difference between the two. You, however, seem knowledgeable."

"I like conducting research. It's weird, but there's nothing that I love better than a good history book. Well, maybe chocolate. When you combine the two, though, I can entertain myself for hours."

"How ... pedestrian."

"Maybe." I exhaled heavily through my nose. Trying to poke around inside of his head was a wasted effort. He shuttered better than most mages I'd come across. He obviously wasn't worried I would somehow find a way past his barriers and get a gander at his plans. "What's your name?"

"Armand. And yours?"

I sat there a second, surprised ... and then I burst out laughing. "Armand? You're full of it. That's the name of the vampire in that Anne Rice book."

He frowned. "How do you know that? The book was released decades before you were born."

"True, but when you grow up in the foster care system you get used to old things. One of those old things was a movie collection that consisted of titles people donated when they were tired of the flicks. *Interview with the Vampire* must've been a popular title at one time because pretty much every group home I was ever in had a copy."

"Ah." He nodded once. "Well, I prefer Armand to my real name."

"What's your real name?"

"I don't want to tell you."

"It must be really embarrassing."

"Oh, it is." He was silent for a beat and then shook his head. "Adolph. That's my real name. I refuse to answer to it."

"Oh, that totally sucks." I felt legitimate sympathy for him. "You're a bloodsucker who was named after a guy responsible for mass genocide. That's, like, the most hated name in history."

"Hence the reason I go by Armand."

"Yeah, but that's a name for a tool."

His face remained blank. "A tool? Like a screwdriver?"

I considered explaining but opted against it. Nobody had time for unnecessary conversations, which was pure torture for me to admit, even to myself. "What's the deal, Adolph? Why are you here? What's your ultimate plan?"

"Armand."

"Yeah, I'm going to call you Adolph."

"I'd prefer you didn't."

"I prefer you hadn't done many things. Like, for example, I wish you hadn't killed Honey. Where is she, by the way? Did she rise? Is she one of you? If not, I have some questions about her body. If you're a skeevy pervert who loves cozying up to corpses we're going to have issues."

"Why do you care what we're planning?" He folded his arms across his chest. "It seems to me that there should be a happy medium here. You can have your half of the town. We'll take the rest."

"Oh, that sounds lovely," I drawled. "Can we get some brightly-colored tape and put a line down the middle of Main? That's what they did on *The Brady Bunch* and it absolutely worked without a hitch."

His expression never changed. "What is it you want from me, witch?"

"I want you to leave."

"We went through a great deal of effort to set up shop here. We're not going to turn around and leave."

"Then I'll have to kill you." I delivered the line with brutal calmness. "I can't allow you to stay, especially when you're killing people ... and possibly turning people ... and definitely enslaving people."

Amusement glinted in the depths of his eyes, which looked onyx under the limited light. "Is this all about your boyfriend's mate? We can come to an agreement if that's the case. I'll release Brandon from his blood bond. You can hand over Bixby. Then we'll divide the territory and draw up a map. This need not result in war."

"Oh, it's going to be a war." I lifted my feet and rested them on the other chair. He kept pacing the ward line. It was obvious he was looking for a way across. He was bound for disappointment. "There's no way across the wards."

He snapped up his head. "I have no idea what you're talking about."

"Listen, it would probably be best if we didn't lie to one another. Things are bad enough without adding ridiculous crap to the mix. You're angry that I took your minion. I'm angry that you infected Brandon. We'll never come to agreement on those two things."

"So, what do you suggest?"

"You leave my town."

"It's your town, is it?" He looked haughty. "My information tells me you are a newcomer. This might not be my town yet, but it's certainly not your town."

"And yet I'm the one who is going to take control of this situation." I refused to back down despite his obvious annoyance. "This place is magical. I sense it. I'm sure you do. There's already a mystical population here. There's no room for you."

"There could be ... if the area witches weren't so territorial."

"No."

"So, only witches are allowed in Hawthorne Hollow. Who established that rule?"

"I don't know, but it's not only witches. I don't really care who settles here ... as long as it's not vampires. The other factions can coexist without killing one another or running roughshod over the human population. You guys refuse to live by certain rules."

"And why should we? We're above humans. They're a food source, nothing more."

My stomach twisted, but I kept my face impassive. "I could kill you right now." My voice was barely a whisper. "I have the power."

"You have a dark wave of fire that you unleash without considering where you cast," he corrected. "It was an interesting trick ... once. We've taken precautions to make sure you can't use it again."

"Oh? What precautions?"

He lifted his hand in the air and made a fist, causing me to narrow my eyes. When I glanced around, a bevy of flashlights clicked on almost simultaneously. There, in the heart of the beams, I found faces from town. Most I'd never talked to, but I recognized them. They had the same glazed look as Brandon, which meant they'd been taken over. But more than that, they were now being used as human shields.

"If you let loose that spell again, you'll destroy the precious humans you're trying to protect," he said in a low voice. "Is that what you want?"

It took everything I had to keep from reacting. I wanted to lash out, ignite him in fire, but that wouldn't solve the other problem. For each of the humans, there was a vampire counterpart, more than twenty of them. And while I had no doubt they were bitten and not born, that didn't mean they weren't dangerous.

"You're powerful, witch," Armand noted. "In fact, you're so powerful I can feel the magic oozing out of you. But you're not powerful enough to defeat us."

I swallowed hard. "What is it you want?"

"I want my butler back. I want you to mind your own business. I want you to stay away from us. Can you agree to those terms?"

Honestly, no, but I had to buy time. "I need to talk to my people."

"I thought as much." He looked triumphant as he took a step back. "For now, as a sign of good faith, I want my butler back."

"I'm not giving you anything until we hammer out a deal," I countered. "It will be on paper ... and signed in blood. There will be no breaking the agreement. If there is, you'll die. I'll make sure of it."

"And what if I don't agree to your terms?"

Ultimately it didn't matter. I wasn't going to agree to my own terms. He didn't need to know that, though. "Then we'll have to go to war."

"Are you willing to make the sacrifices? You'll lose all of these people." He gestured at the blank human faces. "That goes against everything you stand for, doesn't it?"

"It does, but we're realists. Sometimes you have to pull a *Star Trek* and worry about the good of the many rather than the one."

"That seems callous."

"Really? I think it's practical." I pushed myself to a standing position, hoping he didn't recognize how badly I was shaking. "Come back after dark tomorrow. We'll hammer out the details."

"How can you be sure that your people will agree?"

"Do they have a choice?"

"Fair point. I'll return tomorrow." He started to disappear into the darkness, but then stilled. "No tricks, witch. If you try to double-cross me you'll be the first one I kill."

I wasn't afraid of him. He was a small man who thought he had unlimited power. I planned to show him otherwise. Still, I had to play the game ... for now. "Tomorrow. I'm sure we can come to some sort of agreement."

"I'm sure we can. It was a pleasure doing business with you."

He laughed all the way to the tree line, filling me with anger. He might've thought he'd won, but he was nowhere near claiming the trophy.

TWENTY-FIVE

I was relatively assured Armand wouldn't be a problem for the rest of the night — even if he wanted to break the temporary truce, he couldn't cross the wards — so I crawled into bed next to Gunner and almost immediately passed out. When I opened my eyes the next morning, I found he was already awake and smiling at me.

"Good morning, Sunshine." He swooped in and gave me a long kiss before I could even wrap my head around greeting a new day.

"Good morning," I managed when we parted, my cheeks flushing as I struggled to get control of my hormones. "Somebody's in a good mood."

"I slept hard."

That was partially due to the spell, though I opted to refrain from admitting my part in his extended slumber until I had some coffee. If we were going to fight, I was going to need caffeine.

"You look good."

"So do you." He tapped the end of my nose. "I take it you slept as hard as me."

"Mostly."

His smile dipped. "Mostly?"

"There's probably something we should talk about." I refused to lie to him. That didn't mean I was ready to volunteer information that would cause us to snipe at each other for the rest of the day. "I would like to do this for five minutes before that happens." I rolled closer and rested my head against his chest, briefly shutting my eyes as the sound of his heartbeat filled my ears.

"Wait ... ." His hands were on my shoulders and I knew he was going to push me away and demand answers.

"Not yet." I held tight. "I want five minutes of peace before we fight." When I risked a glance at his face, he looked conflicted. "Please. The argument will be waiting for us when we're done."

He growled but acquiesced and wrapped his arms around me. "Whatever you did, I'm going to kill you. Just so you know."

"How do you know it's a killing offense? I could've done something as simple as paint your toenails while you were asleep."

His feet shifted next to mine, as if he was trying to feel for polish, which caused me to smile.

"I'm guessing you don't care enough about nail polish to risk doing that," he said after a beat, his hand stroking the back of my head. "I'm going to be angry in a few minutes, aren't I?"

"Yup."

"I wish you would stop doing things to tick me off."

"Right back at you."

"Hey, I don't do half the annoying things you do. I'm the good one in this relationship."

"Yeah. You're a virtual angel." I kissed his strong jaw. "I guess that makes me the devil, just like Bixby thinks."

"Screw him. Although ... ." He shifted again and craned his neck in an attempt to look down the hallway. "Have you checked on our friend? He's been tied to that chair a good ten hours. We should probably get him up for another bathroom break."

"Probably," I agreed. "Just three more minutes."

His hand returned to the back of my head. "It might make you feel better to tell me what you did. Waiting will only make things worse."

"In theory, that's true. In practice, I know better. I want a few minutes of time with you before ... well, before you start stomping around and saying I'm giving you an ulcer."

He was quiet a moment while the soothing motion of his hand continued. "I've changed my mind on that. My father says I have an iron constitution. I can pretty much eat anything ... except for sushi. I freaking hate sushi."

"Who doesn't? I mean ... it's raw fish. That's disgusting no matter how you dress it up."

I felt his lips curve against my forehead. "I do think it's likely you're going to give me an aneurysm, though. One of these days you'll pull some shenanigans and I'll completely lose my mind. My brain will explode and that will be all she wrote."

He was dramatic sometimes. For some reason, I found it cute. "What a way to go, though, huh?"

He clutched me tighter. "Yeah. I guess it's okay."

We finished our three minutes and I graced him with a soft kiss before rolling out of bed. "I need coffee before the yelling commences. Also, I need to deal with the little minion."

"Okay." He didn't push me, instead dragging a hand through his hair as he padded into the kitchen behind me.

Bixby, his gaze murderous, glared at me as I crossed the kitchen to grab a can of soft food for Merlin, who had started screeching the second we climbed out of bed. He knew his routine. He got hard food every other time of day, but mornings were for Fancy Feast ... and he couldn't get enough of it.

"Hello, little minion." I patted Bixby's head in a condescending manner after giving Merlin his breakfast. Gunner was already busy in front of the coffee pot so I left him to the brewing and leaned over so I was at eye level with Bixby. "If I remove the gag spell, do you promise to be pleasant?"

He nodded, although his eyes said otherwise.

"You're a total liar." I released him from the spell anyway. I figured it was cruel not to. He started spewing curses and threats the second he regained control of his tongue.

"I'm going to shove a sword through your heart and leave it there so you can feel my wrath for all eternity!"

Gunner slid me a sidelong look as I sauntered over to him. "Do you think this is what it will be like to have kids?"

The question threw me. "I ... what?"

His eyes lit with amusement at my obvious discomfort. "I don't mean now ... or even two or three years from now. I mean eventually."

"I don't know." I hadn't really considered having kids. After growing up a ward of the state, I was fairly certain I was missing any and all maternal instincts. Those seemed like learned traits — and I'd never learned them.

"Calm down." He brushed his fingers over my cheek. "I wasn't suggesting anything. My father says I was a terrible human being between the ages of twelve and fifteen. For some reason, listening to that little monster made me think of that."

"Oh." Well, that wasn't as frightening as I initially thought. "I've never really liked kids, so I don't know what to think about it." The statement might've sounded brutal to an outsider, but it was important for Gunner to know where I stood. "I don't really see myself as a mother."

"Oh, yeah?" If he was bothered by the statement he didn't show it. "See, I think you would be a great mother. I wasn't sure at first, but the way you handled Raisin's crisis with the costume made me believe otherwise. You're really good with her. I'm not sure how you would be with little kids — you seem more the type teenagers would love — but it's something to think about down the road."

He was so blasé with the observation it made me uncomfortable. "I don't know how to be a mother."

"You can learn."

"I don't think I want to learn."

He shook his head. "I get that. In fact, I'm right there with you a good fifty percent of the time. Not about being a mother, mind you. I can't help but wonder if I have some of my mother in me, and it makes me fearful.

"Either way, it doesn't matter," he continued. "We're nowhere near considering any of the big questions in life. We can barely handle the little things right now. For example, making coffee pretty much has me at my limit this morning. Perhaps we can put off the deep discussion for another time."

My mouth dropped open. "You're the one who brought it up in the first place."

He snickered. "I'm not sure that's how I remember things. I guess it doesn't matter." He reached for the mugs on the counter. "Tell me what you did last night that's going to infuriate me."

I was just about to do that when something occurred to me. "Wait. You did that on purpose."

"What?"

"You did the kid thing to throw me off my game. You want to rattle me so you have the upper hand when we start arguing."

"That sounds like a diabolical plan and nothing like me."

"No, no, no." I wagged a finger. "That's definitely what you're doing."

"Well, you figured me out." He poured a mug of coffee and handed it to me. "Talk."

I accepted it with both hands and inhaled the heavenly aroma before taking a long sip. Once the caffeine hit my system, it was time. I would never be ready for the argument that was to come, but we needed to put it behind us if we hoped to move forward and come up with a plan.

"I had a visitor last night."

He arched an eyebrow as he poured his own mug. "I'm guessing it wasn't Santa Claus."

"It was my master," Bixby cackled. "He came for me. He smacked the witch down, told her who was boss. He's coming back to claim me tonight."

Gunner's expression was hard to read. "The vampire came here?"

I nodded. "It's fine. We had a perfectly reasonable conversation. He couldn't cross the wards. There's nothing to worry about."

"Yeah, but ... I didn't wake up. You would think I would've woken up. Even if you talked quietly, I usually know when you're in bed with me."

Here was the part I was dreading. "I might've cast a spell to make sure you would sleep." I immediately took a step back when he started swearing. I thought about apologizing, but in truth my heart wouldn't have been in it. Instead, I decided to let him rant.

"I can't believe you did this." He kicked one of the chairs, sending it careening across the room.

"You're in trouble now," Bixby sang out. "The shifter is going to rip your throat out. I won't even have to wait for my master to come and save me. You'll be dead before you can complete the deal you promised."

Gunner swiveled quickly, his eyes dark blocks of ice. "What deal?"

"He has a bunch of townspeople under his control. They're like Brandon. He showed them to me last night. He insinuated that he took that particular step because of the spell I unleashed outside the high school."

"But ... ." Gunner's mind was clearly busy.

"He wants to make a trade. He'll release Brandon from the blood spell if we give him the minion."

"Butler!" Bixby snapped. "I'm a butler, not a minion."

I pretended he hadn't spoken, though I did jab a warning finger in his direction. I would gag him again if necessary. "He also wants us to come up with a line of demarcation. We stay on one side and they stay on the other."

Gunner was flabbergasted. "We can't agree to that. If we do, the people on their side of the line will be nothing but food and playthings."

"He says he'll kill the people he's already claimed if we don't agree."

"Well, that's just great." Gunner strode to the sink and upended his coffee. "It sounds like you two have already come to an agreement."

"He's coming back tonight to discuss the details. We need to talk to Rooster."

"Rooster won't agree to this. In fact ... I don't agree with it. I can't believe you struck a deal with that fiend. What is wrong with you? And that's on top of casting a spell to make me sleep. We've talked about this. You cannot use your magic on me."

"You were exhausted."

"So were you."

"Yes, but ... you've had more emotional upheaval the past few days. You needed your sleep."

He stomped toward the bedroom. "I'm taking a shower. Alone. I'll be heading into town when I'm done. I'll be doing that alone, too. You can do whatever you want, but I'm going to sit down with Rooster and come up with a plan. This agreement you've roped us into won't stand."

He was angry. I didn't blame him. He thought I was willing to cede half the town to the vampires in exchange for a handful of residents and Brandon's freedom. I couldn't argue the point in front of Bixby. Even though I'd shut the minion off from the vampires, that didn't mean he couldn't make life difficult for us before the end. I couldn't risk that.

"Gunner."

"No." He shook his head. "I just ... no. I'm angry with you. You used magic on me. Again. You said you wouldn't. This agreement, that's even worse. I don't understand how you could possibly think it was okay. You are so not who I thought you were."

I remained rooted to my spot as he stalked into the bathroom, my shoulders flinching as the door slammed. He was shutting me out. Literally. I couldn't blame him. Giving voice to my actual plan in front of the minion wasn't allowed. He needed to think there was a fissure in our group.

So ... mission accomplished. I'd done exactly what I needed to do.

So why did I feel so crummy?

I DIDN'T BOTHER TO GET INTO THE SHOWER until after Gunner left. Once it was just the two of us, I gagged Bixby so I wouldn't have to listen to him and then released the clamp I'd put on his brain just enough so a few stray thoughts could leak out.

He was gleeful to the point of giddiness. He thought the vampires had won. While he couldn't fully communicate with his master, the easing of my control on him allowed his emotions to drift across miles. Armand would bask in the glow of his minion's happiness ... right up until the point I pulled the rug and upended the entire thing.

"Oh, you look sad," Bixby chortled when I removed the gag upon dressing and pulling back my hair in a loose bun. "You lost the big, bad wolf and now you have a broken heart."

"I haven't lost him." I decided some bravado, however false, was in order. "He's just angry. He'll get over it."

"Oh, I don't think so." He made a clucking sound with his tongue. "The wolf is mad. He has ethics and morals. Even when you were a kid I knew you were devoid of those. That's why I was tracking you."

I slid my gaze to him. "Why were you following me that night?"

"I could smell the magic. But I thought you were just a normal witch. I didn't realize you were more than that."

"When did you realize?"

"When my master told me."

"And what did he say about me?"

"That you were a child of the stars and should be avoided. He said you were powerful, but you don't seem all that powerful now. You've been defeated. How does it feel?"

It didn't feel very good. Sure, it was all an act, but Gunner's anger had been real. Worse, the betrayal he felt had been brutal. He thought I'd turned on him, or at least was showing the vampires my tender underbelly. He couldn't know otherwise. I'd arranged it this way for a reason. Still ... I felt bereft. I already missed him.

"You were going to attack me that night," I pressed. "You seemed surprised when I called you out. Why did you specifically choose me?"

"You were alone."

"I'd understand that if your master only wanted a meal. He seemed to want something more from me. Selecting me felt ... deliberate."

"My master likes magic. He absorbs it. Not all vampires are that powerful, but my master is. He's stronger than everybody, including that little ragtag group of shifters and witches you run around with."

Whether he realized it or not, he'd let something slip. The master vampire was more than the sum of his parts. He had special abilities. But how? I'd never heard of a vampire being more than one thing.

I held back a sigh and then turned my full attention to Bixby. "I have to run to town. I have to explain the trade. Gunner can't be relied upon to do it correctly."

"Because he's a dirty dog."

I wanted to shake the little heathen until he stopped talking. Instead, I merely nodded. "I'm keeping you frozen, but you can scream to your heart's content. Nobody will come for you. Even if they do, the wards will hold. They kept your master out last night."

"Or he only wanted you to think that."

I thought back to the way Armand circled the barrier I'd erected. "No. He couldn't cross." The wards held and even though Armand had magic at his fingertips he couldn't break the protection I'd wrought. That was something to consider. "I'll be back before nightfall."

Bixby's expression fell. "Hey! You can't leave me here all day tied to this chair. That's inhuman ... and mean ... and just plain rude."

I managed a legitimate smile. "You should've thought about that before aligning yourself with vampires. You deserve a little inhumane treatment."

He was back to being morose. "I'm going to rip off your arm and beat you to death with it."

"Well, doesn't that sound fun?"

TWENTY-SIX

I was uneasy when I let myself into The Cauldron. The number of bikes in the parking lot told me that we had a full crew. Numerous sets of accusatory eyes landed on me when I entered, and a shiver of discomfort forced me to fold my arms over my chest and stare down the friends who had suddenly become enemies.

"I'm sure Gunner has told you what's going on," I started.

"He has." Rooster's eyes were cold. "We're not sacrificing half this town so we don't have to fight with the vampires. You had no right to broker that deal. We won't agree to it."

"We won't," Marissa agreed. She looked almost gleeful as she ran her hands over Gunner's arm and tried to soothe him. "Because you're so far removed from this team I think you should probably go."

"I'm not surprised you think that," I offered, sliding over to the bar and rubbing my forehead as I got comfortable on a stool. I expected this meeting to be difficult, but it felt somehow impossible. "We only have until darkness falls to figure out a way to take out the vampires. That's when he'll come to finalize the deal."

"I thought you wanted to negotiate with the vampires," Rooster challenged.

"No. But I need the vampires to think that's exactly what we're doing. We need time to figure out a plan ... and this is it. We have eleven hours."

Roster cocked his head to the side. I could feel his eyes roaming my face. "Gunner said you were talking to him as if you agreed with the vampire. Why would he say that?"

"I was talking as if I agreed." There was no sense in lying. It was time to lay it all out for the group. "We had an audience."

Gunner raised his chin, surprise washing over his face. "Wait ... what are you saying?"

"The minion. I took him. I got fed up yesterday and he was out there, so I forced him to cross the barrier and took him. He's spent the better part of the last twenty hours tied to a chair in my kitchen."

"But ... ." Gunner slid away from Marissa, his mind clearly busy.

Rooster cleared his throat to get my attention. "I thought you told Gunner you cut off the minion from the vampires. At least, that's what he said. If that's true, they can't know what he's thinking or feeling."

"I did do that ... until this morning when I let the spell slip just a smidge. I need Adolph to believe that I'm going along with the plan if we expect him to walk into a trap."

Rooster's expression relaxed. "That actually is very smart. If the information comes from an outside source — one he trusts — he's more likely to believe it."

"I wanted to tell Gunner what I was doing, but there was no way without tipping off the minion. I ... *oomph*." I lost my breath as Gunner yanked me into a tight embrace. His mouth was hot on mine before I could question him about what he was doing.

"I'm sorry," he said when he'd finished kissing me.

My eyes were wide as I studied him. "For what?"

"I shouldn't have jumped all over you. I should've understood what you were doing. I couldn't believe what you were saying. I didn't even think about the minion. I just ... ." He broke off and smoothed my hair. "I won't doubt you again."

He looked so earnest I wanted to melt. Then I remembered we

were in a room full of people and we had a job to do. "I wanted to tell you." I squeezed his wrist in a reassuring manner. "I couldn't. We have only one shot of selling the narrative to the minion. I had to make sure he believed."

"Yeah." Gunner stared directly into my eyes. "I'm still sorry."

"You can pay me back with a nice dinner and a massage or something."

"Oh, I'm going to do way better than that." He gave me another kiss that was so soft it nudged out a sigh. The moment was interrupted by the sound of someone clearing a throat. "Well, this is just lovely," Marissa drawled. "I can't tell you how happy this entire thing makes me. Oh, wait ... it makes me want to throw up all over both of you. But I don't have time for that, because apparently we need to take on an army of vampires."

I managed a smile despite the dire circumstances and slid from Gunner even though every fiber of my being wanted me to stay and continue absorbing his warmth. We had a job to do and that had to be our focus. "I'm not even sure how many vampires we're dealing with," I admitted. "The one I talked to last night ... ."

"Armand," Bonnie clarified.

"His real name is Adolph, but yes, he goes by Armand. He stole it from that *Interview with the Vampire* book, which makes him the world's biggest tool."

"Tell us what you can about him," Rooster demanded. He was all business now that he knew I hadn't brokered a deal to sacrifice half the town to the appetite of monsters.

"He acknowledged meeting me when I was a teenager."

Gunner's eyes flashed. "Wait ... he did? I thought you were confusing the minion with another guy."

"He's hard to confuse with anyone else. I mean ... could you confuse Danny DeVito with someone else?"

"If Danny DeVito was a normal person, yeah. He stands out in Hollywood for a reason."

"It doesn't matter. I recognized him from the start. He said he was searching for magic that night." My mind was busy as I drifted away from Gunner. "The master vampire is different from any other I've crossed paths with."

"How so?" Whistler asked. "By the way, you've got one over on us when it comes to any and all vampires. This is shifter territory. The vampires usually stay away. They don't like the area, especially how cold it gets in the winter. This nest you've uncovered is a first for us."

"Vampires aren't usually difficult to destroy," I offered. "They're susceptible to sun, fire, and beheadings."

"What about stakes to the heart?" Bonnie asked. "Do they die when you stake them in the heart like in the movies?"

I had to smile. She almost seemed enthusiastic, which cracked me up. "They do die when you stake them in the heart," I supplied. "They don't turn to dust like that, but they do if you burn them. That's my preferred method when it comes to vampires."

"Not all of us have elemental fire magic at our disposal," Gunner reminded me. He looked much more relaxed than when I had first entered. "You're unique."

"Wait ... can't you just do that spell you let loose at the high school the other night?" Marissa looked hopeful. "That killed a few of them. Just do it over and over until they're all gone."

My heart gave a little heave. I was expecting the question but didn't have a ready answer. "Here's the thing ... ." I licked my lips and searched for the right words. "That spell isn't technically sanctioned."

"I don't know what that means," Gunner said.

"It's something I read about and adapted for my needs. It's dangerous."

"How so?" Rooster pressed. "It might be dangerous but it's also effective. We're going to be outnumbered. We might need that spell."

"I can't control who gets hurt with that spell," I pointed out. "That spell ... can hurt humans and paranormals alike. I unleashed it the other night because I wasn't thinking. What would've happened if teenagers were hiding in the woods making out? The spell doesn't differentiate between who it burns."

Pale realization washed over Rooster's features.

"I could've killed innocent people." And that reality made my stomach so upset I squirmed and moved away from Gunner when he reached for me. "I didn't think. We lucked out that nobody was hurt, but the vampires have found a way to eliminate that spell from my repertoire."

"And how did they do that?" Marissa demanded. "Great job on ticking off the vampires so they cut off our best weapon, by the way."

"Leave her alone," Gunner snapped, his eyes flashing. "I don't see you sticking your neck out to fix this situation. She's at least trying to come up with a solution."

"I am trying," I agreed. "But if I use that spell I'll be putting several people at risk, including Mable's daughter." Mindy was one of the faces I recognized the night before. I hadn't yet mentioned it to anyone, but it was time. "Armand basically laid it out for me last night. He's going to use those people as fodder and put them directly in front of me so I have no choice but to cut them down if I go after the vampires."

"And we obviously can't risk that," Rooster mused.

"That's not my first choice," I agreed. "The thing is, we can't allow them to get a bigger foothold. Then we'll lose even more people."

"Are you suggesting we sacrifice the people he's already enslaved?"

"I'm suggesting that we come up with a plan that saves everybody. Barring that, we have to be willing to make hard choices."

Rooster's expression was unreadable. "And do you think you can make that choice?"

"I don't see that I'll have a choice. I still think we can come up with a plan that saves everybody."

"And how are you going to do that? I say 'you' because ultimately this falls on your shoulders."

"I have an idea." I flashed a rueful smile. "But I need to visit Mama Moon. You guys need to stay here and brainstorm. If I can't carry out what I have planned we'll need another avenue of attack ... and we don't have much time."

Rooster nodded. "Okay. Keep in touch."

I switched my attention to Gunner. "Before you even start, we're fine. You can't come with me, though. I need to try ... something ... and it's best if I'm alone while doing it."

"You just said you were going to see Mama Moon. If you're with her, obviously you won't be alone."

"No," I conceded, "but she'll understand what I'm trying. I need you to stay here. It's safer. I'll be back as soon as I can."

He didn't look happy with my decision, but he nodded. "If you're not back in two hours I'm coming for you."

"Fair enough."

MAMA MOON SAT ON HER FRONT PORCH as I dismounted my bike and pulled off my helmet. She didn't look surprised to see me. Of course, she rarely showed her cards when it came to unexpected visitors.

"I figured you'd show up eventually." She smiled. "You want to know how to get past the barrier. Well, I have a few ideas."

"I have an idea, too," I admitted. "I want to slide between planes, like I did with George, and cross the barrier that way."

Her eyes widened. "I thought you were going to try to get me to help you break down the barrier."

"That would be great." I kept my expression blank. "Can you do that?"

"Given enough time."

"We don't have time." I decided to be blunt and laid everything out in precise detail. When I finished, she looked flummoxed.

"How many people are we talking about?"

"My guess is they have more than they showed, so more than twenty."

"And you think the vampires will sacrifice them to prove a point."

"The vampires realize that we stand in the way of what they want. If we're gone, they'll have an open playing field. I think they're going to try to double-cross me."

"Just like you're going to double-cross them. How will they work it?"

"I don't know. I need to get into that house before dark. I need to get on the other side of that barrier so I can walk all of those people out before burning it to the ground."

"Is that your plan? You're going to burn the house down?"

"Do you have a better plan?"

"I ... guess not. What made you think of slipping between planes?"

"No matter how much energy I throw at that barrier it's always going to ricochet back. I guess there's a possibility that we could come up with a potion to weaken it, but we don't have time. I need to get across it in the next few hours."

"Fair enough." She drew in a deep breath. "When you did it before, I helped. Someone will have to stay on the other side of the barrier to serve as an anchor. That means you'll be going in alone. Can you handle that?"

I nodded without hesitation. "Yeah, because the other Spells Angels will be there to serve as backup. All I have to do is find Armand ... and end him. He's the one providing the magic."

"How can you be sure?"

"It's the only thing that makes sense. Bixby said that they were waiting for me because they were looking for magic. I think that Armand has been fortifying his power base through his victims for years."

"How?"

"I don't know. Maybe there's something about the blood."

"If there is, I've never heard about it. What if you're wrong and Armand isn't supplying the power?"

"I'll have to deal with that if it comes to pass. Right now I need you to give me a refresher course on walking through planes. I wasn't really in control of what happened last time. That can't be the case this time."

She was contemplative for a moment. "Okay. I don't know that I agree this is a smart move, but we don't have many options."

"You need to show me, stick with me until I get it right, and then we'll collect the others. Gunner will put up a fight when he finds out what I have planned. I don't see a way around that."

"I agree. Come on. We'll go to the field to practice. That way you won't accidentally trap yourself in a wall or anything."

I balked. "Is that possible?"

"Anything is possible, my dear. You need to practice."

AT THE END OF TWO SOLID HOURS of practice I was able to successfully travel between planes. It wasn't the smoothest of rides, but I was comfortable enough with what I had to do that I was reasonably assured of a successful outcome.

Now I just needed to convince the others.

"Let me do the talking," I insisted as Mama Moon followed me to the door. "They're going to argue, and Gunner might actually stomp his feet, but in the end this is our best option. We need to get someone on the other side of that barrier and I'm the only option."

"I could do it," she pointed out as she followed me. "Maybe I should be the one to cross over."

"And then what?" I stilled and fixed her with a pointed look. "Can you call elemental fire energy and burn the house to the ground?"

"I ... no."

"Then I think it has to be me. I'll need you on the other side to help the half-vampires when things start falling apart. That's going to be your job."

"Fair enough." She held up her hands in a placating manner and followed me through the door. "You're a bossy little thing when you want to be, aren't you?"

"I am definitely bossy," I agreed, pulling up short when I got a gander at the bar. It was utter chaos. The chairs were overturned. The bottles behind the bar had been smashed. There was blood smeared on the countertop.

And there wasn't a person in sight.

"What the ... ?" My heart hammered so hard I thought I might pass out.

"What happened here?" Mama Moon looked bewildered. "Was there a fight?"

My gaze slid to the counter, to the stool Gunner had been resting on when I'd left. It had been overturned ... and the blood was close to it.

"They sent the half-vampires to take them," I replied grimly. It was the only thing that made sense. "They took them by force."

"That means they're in the house." Mama Moon's tone was grave. "You were right about them double-crossing you. They think they have the leverage to control you now. You know what that means."

"Yeah. I'm going to burn that house to the ground and enjoy doing it."

"No." She shook her head, firm. "It means that they have specific plans for you. I don't know if this Armand is really an energy-sucking vampire, but he's going to try to take what you have."

"He's already taken the most important piece," I muttered. Gunner. "We have to get them back."

"And you still want to go after them yourself?"

"We don't have a choice."

"Then let's go."

"We have one stop to make first."

TWENTY-SEVEN

*B*ixby was still tied to his chair when I stormed into the cabin. If the half-vampires had tried to cross the wards and take him they weren't successful. At least I'd done one thing right, even though it felt like a hollow victory given everything that had happened.

"Get up," I ordered as I stomped to a standstill in front of him. "Get up right now, you little maggot."

Behind me, Mama Moon cleared her throat.

"What?" I exploded. I was in no mood to be lectured.

"He's tied to a chair, dear," she said pragmatically. "He can't get up."

"Oh, right." I waved my hand to release the bindings.

Bixby let out a relieved breath as he started rubbing his wrists. His eyes, however, never left my face. "What's wrong with you?" He looked a little too gleeful, tipping his hand that he knew exactly what had happened earlier. "Nothing gone wrong, I hope?"

"Yeah." I made sure the pipeline to his mind was completely shut off. It was probably too late to matter, but I wasn't giving Armand leverage of any sort. "Your little buddies took my friends."

"Oh. Imagine that." He feigned sadness. "I wonder why they would make that move."

"The same reason I'm about to make a move of my own. Come on." I grabbed him by the ear and dragged him through the kitchen as he fruitlessly swatted at me.

"Where are we going?" he whined. "You're supposed to wait here for my master."

"Haven't you heard?" I knew my smile was biting, but I didn't care. "Things have changed. You're going home now."

"I ... but ... ." He narrowed his eyes. "What are you doing?"

"What I should've done days ago. We're going for another ride on my motorcycle."

THE HOUSE ON THE BLUFF LOOKED SILENT from a distance when I parked on the other side of the trees. They would expect me in the spot from which I'd previously approached. This visit would be a little different.

"Are you sure about this?" Mama Moon had mostly been silent. Despite my threats regarding the motorcycle, she took Bixby in her truck for the drive — I froze him again just to be on the safe side — and now he was trussed and spitting at our feet. "You can still change your mind. You have people you can call for backup. Maybe you should do that."

"No." I was firm as I checked the sheath on my calf. My favorite dagger was there — sterling silver, eight-inch blade, lethal — but I would need it only if everything else I had planned failed. "They won't get here in time. If I don't agree to the treaty tonight he'll kill someone as a message." What I didn't add was that I had no doubt that Gunner was the one he would kill. That was the one thing that would hurt me most. Of course, that would turn me into a bloody and merciless revenge machine. "It has to be now."

Mama Moon's mood was pensive, but she nodded. "What do you want me to do?"

"Kill him if the half-vampires come out."

"That's it?"

"There's nothing else you can do."

Bixby made a muffled protest at my feet. It took everything I had not to kick him. My rage was in high gear. Still, he was prone and defenseless. He might've been on my list, but that didn't mean I was a monster.

"Well, I guess this is it then." She rested her hands on my shoulders and leaned forward to press her lips to my forehead, a muttered spell on her breath. I couldn't make out the words, but a warm feeling cascaded over me. "The Goddess will watch over you."

"I hope so." I exhaled heavily and then turned toward the trees. "I'll send them out if I can. Try to watch for them, protect their flanks. There's more than one vampire in there."

"Yes, but if you find the right one the others will likely flee."

"They can't flee into the day."

"I ... very good point."

"Once I get all the humans out I'll torch the place. Try to keep the fire department away."

"What if you don't come out?"

I'd already asked myself that very question. "Let it burn. Our goal is to save as many people as possible. That doesn't necessarily include me."

She hesitated. "Scout ... ."

"No." I was firm when I grabbed her hands and squeezed. "This is the way it has to be. I'll do my best to get out, but ... ." I didn't finish. It wasn't necessary.

She nodded. "Okay. Good luck."

"Fortune favors the brave, right?" I took a moment to stare down at Bixby. There was murder in his eyes. I didn't remove the magical gag as I hunkered over and met his gaze. "I brought you so you could watch it all burn. I hope you enjoy the show."

He made muffled sounds behind his sealed lips.

"I'll see you soon ... hopefully."

I MADE MYSELF INVISIBLE AS I PASSED through the trees. It was something I'd been able to do since I was a small child. It was one of the first bits of magic I'd mastered. While locked in rooms with adults I now know were trying to help me (but at the time terrified me), I often wished I could disappear. One day that became a reality — and it had been a useful trick ever since.

Unfortunately, it was also draining. That's why I hurried to make it to the magical barrier. Once there, I glanced around to make sure I was really alone — as far as I could tell there was nobody hanging about, but that didn't mean there weren't eager eyes watching from above — and then closed my eyes.

Slipping between planes wasn't easy. With a little more practice, I knew I would become adept at it. I didn't have time for that practice, so my attempt was clumsy. I just needed to be able to cross the border.

I only went one plane over. That was more than enough to trick the barrier. When I opened my eyes again, I found I was in a shadow world. Nothing had a fully formed shape. I didn't think too much about it as I crossed the line.

There was no warning burst of magic or alarm. Absolutely nothing changed. That's how I knew I'd been successful.

I stayed in the shadow world until I reached the back of the house and then phased back. I had to blink several times as my eyes adjusted to the bright sunshine, but once I'd acclimated I headed for the back door. My fingers were extended and I had every intention of storming inside when I thought better of it and moved to the window at the end of the porch. I squatted down, peered inside, and used my magic to lift the glass panel. No one raced to intercept me, and I poked my head through the opening.

The house was as rundown on the inside as it looked from the outside. Apparently the vampires didn't care about keeping the humans in their employ comfortable. I was about to burn it all down anyway, so it hardly mattered. Still, I made a face when the musty odor of neglect assailed my olfactory senses as I climbed through the window.

The hardwood floors sagged. They'd lost their shine years ago — maybe decades. I tested my weight a few times to make sure I wouldn't fall through before striding forward. I was in and now I had to find my friends.

I reached out with my magic, carefully searching the first floor for signs of familiarity. I didn't find anything as I combed through the rooms, but I did bounce against two other minds ... and I knew exactly who they belonged to: Melody and Cherise. They were on the main floor. I wasn't sure where, so I draped myself in invisibility before moving to the next room.

I heard low murmurs at the front of the house and picked my way through a large dining room to listen.

"Do you think she'll come?" Cherise asked. She sat on a couch that looked newer than the rest of the furnishings. "I mean ... she would have to be an idiot to come."

"She's not very bright," Melody sneered, causing me to bite the inside of my cheek to keep quiet. Now was not the time for a verbal spat regarding my intelligence. "She'll come. She won't be able to get past the barrier. We can go out there and taunt her when she gets here."

"But she has to know she can't get beyond the barrier. Why would she come knowing that?"

"Because we have her boyfriend." Melody's smile was sly as I peered around the doorjamb and found her perched near the window. They were obviously watching for me. "I mean ... she has to be ticked. Armand promised that nobody would make a move. Even if she did think he would double-cross her, she wasn't expecting it during the day — and not at the bar. Now that we have all the helpers from town it was so easy to wander in there and just take them. They didn't even realize what was happening until it was too late."

I felt sick to my stomach. If I'd been there I could've fought them off. Regret burned like acid in my esophagus and I had to swallow hard to keep from blurting out something hateful.

I turned my attention to the staircase. My friends were either on the second floor or in the basement. The vampires were likely sleeping in the basement, so I figured the second floor was my best bet. The stairs were rickety and gave me pause, but I elicited only a single squeak as I climbed. I froze to see if it would draw Melody's attention, but she was too busy gazing out the window watching for me.

Once out of her line of sight, I started scanning the hallway. There were four doors, all of them closed. I knew my friends were behind one. I could feel Gunner. He was furious, and maybe slightly injured, but he was alive. I had every intention of keeping him that way.

I found them in the back room on the right. The door was locked but it wasn't difficult to use my magic to open it. I sucked in a breath when I took in the scene. They were all there. Rooster and Gunner sported bruises on their faces and Whistler cradled his arm, making me think it had been broken in the attack. Bonnie looked dazed, as did Doc, who probably wasn't used to seeing real action. Marissa sat on Gunner's left, leaning against him, staring into nothing. I probably shouldn't have been bothered that she chose to snuggle with my boyfriend given the circumstances, but I was annoyed enough to growl.

"What was that?" Rooster instantly raised his head. "Did you hear that?"

"Yeah." Gunner nodded and lifted his nose, as if scenting the air. "It's Scout. I can smell her." He moved to scramble toward the window, but Marissa grabbed his arm to keep him still.

"Don't go over there," she complained. "Stay with me. I ... this could be our last few minutes of life. I think we should spend it together."

Oh, well, that just figured. "Nice," I announced, dropping the invisibility shield and glaring at the morose menace. "I'm so glad that you used a crisis to move on my boyfriend."

"Scout." Gunner grunted as he tried to get to his feet, making a face when he couldn't move more than a foot. That's when I realized they were all magically tethered to the floor.

"Well, that's a new wrinkle," I said as I moved closer to him, mustering a smile. "Is everybody okay?"

He nodded as he pulled me in for a hug. "I was so worried that they'd found you. I was afraid you wouldn't let them take you alive."

"Oh, they haven't taken me." I hunkered down to get a better look at the rope. The magic looked mundane, which made me think there had to be a trick to it. "Did Armand cast this spell?"

"We haven't seen any vampires," Rooster replied. "The spell was cast by someone else."

"And who would that be?"

"Some woman. I didn't recognize her."

"I guess that means I have another battle to fight." I pursed my lips and extended my fingers, pulsing a bit of magic toward the tether. Nothing immediately happened, but after a second jolt the rope gave way.

Gunner tested his range of motion and then moved in for a proper hug. "I can't believe you're here. How did you know where to look?"

I gave him a moment before pulling back. Now was not the time for schmaltz. "I narrowed my list of one possible location ... and here I am."

"Very funny." He looked wiped, as if he'd been through a battle and barely come out the other side. "I was afraid for you."

"Yeah? I was afraid for you, too." I shot Whistler a rueful look. "Your bar is a mess. I locked up, but it's going to take some elbow grease to get it looking like it should."

"I think we can manage that." He was pale but looked ready to fight his way free. "Is there a reason we're still sitting here gabbing? Let's get out of here."

I hesitated.

"Spit it out, Scout," Rooster ordered. He looked as anxious as Whistler. "What aren't you telling us?"

"I didn't exactly take down the barrier."

"Then how did you get inside?" He narrowed his eyes, suspicious. "You made a deal with them after all, didn't you?"

I shook my head and tried to refrain from allowing my anger to show. We'd been over this. The fact that he was still jumping to the worst possible conclusion irritated me no end. "I shifted planes and crossed the barrier that way. It wasn't easy — in fact, it was a little messy — but I made it. That's not an option when we leave. Neither is making us invisible, because it drains me and I need my magic for what's to come."

"And what's that?" Rooster held out his cuffed hands and I hit the links with a bolt of magic to free him. "What are you going to do?"

"The best way to eradicate all the vampires is to burn this place." I was matter of fact. "The problem is that we don't know where the half-vampires are. Melody and Cherise are in the living room. I haven't seen the rest of them."

Bonnie stirred. "I heard them talking when they were bringing me in. They expected you to move on the house. They were waiting for you on the main highway. Did you not see them?"

Laughter bubbled up as I swallowed the mad urge to start chortling, which would've been a mistake because it clearly would've drawn people to us. "I came in from the back. I figured they would be watching the front. I didn't think there would be a highway ambush, but that makes sense. I came in through the trees."

"And they obviously weren't expecting you." Rooster grinned. "It seems you're smart even when you're not trying."

"Yeah. That's me." I rolled my neck and moved to Bonnie next. "If the rest of the half-vampires are on the road, that's actually a lucky break. Then all we need to do is get Melody and Cherise out. Then I can burn this place to the ground and take out every vampire inside."

"How can you be sure that you'll get them all?" Whistler asked, grimacing as I carefully removed his chains. Up close, his elbow appeared to be dislocated, not broken. There was no time to fix it now. "They're underground. They'll be safe there as long as there's no sunlight penetrating."

I flashed a playful smile. "Leave that to me."

Whistler held my gaze for a long beat and then nodded. "Okay. You've managed to pull this off so far. What's your plan?"

"You need to go downstairs, lure the two dimwits in the living room outside, and leave the basement for me. That's it."

Gunner immediately started shaking his head. "No way. I'm not leaving you to do this on your own."

"It's the best way," I insisted. "I have elemental magic to call on. I can burn the basement and escape up the stairs."

"And what if someone comes up behind you? No." He was adamant as he shook his head. "I'm not being separated from you again today. We're doing this together."

I thought about arguing, but there wasn't enough time. "Fine." I held up a finger to keep him from smiling in triumph. "You have to do what I say, though. I'm the boss. No ifs, ands, or buts about it."

"That sounds like an intriguing game." He winked as Marissa groaned.

"Maybe we'll play that game later. We have to move. It's still relatively early in the afternoon and we have a window here. I want to use it."

"Then let's do it." Rooster was grim. "We all owe these bastard vampires a little payback. It's time to get it done."

TWENTY-EIGHT

J took the lead going down the stairs because the rest of my team was battered and bruised. They would fight, but the initial play would be mine.

I wasn't surprised to find Melody and Cherise still focused on the front approach. I stood in the open archway for a long time, waiting for them to turn. When they didn't, I cleared my throat and pasted a "You've screwed up and now you must die" smile on my face.

"Oh, my ... ." Cherise visibly paled — which was impressive given the fact that she was practically transparent as it was — and shrank away from me.

Melody, on the other hand, was positively apoplectic. "What are you doing in my house?"

I wanted to laugh. The statement was so absurd that was the only acceptable reaction. "I was just taking a tour." I pointed toward the front door so Rooster could lead the others to it. The barrier was designed to keep people out. There was nothing stopping them from crossing over to freedom. "This place could really use a spruce."

"You're not supposed to be in my house," Melody complained, petulance on full display. "It's not allowed. You broke the rules."

"Don't talk to me about breaking the rules." I narrowed my eyes.

"Your little boyfriend broke the rules when he sent his cadre of human sacrifices to hurt my friends. Now he's going to find out what a real rule breaker looks like."

"What is that supposed to mean?" Melody planted her hands on her hips. "You need to leave right now. I'm serious."

"Oh, she's being serious," Bonnie drawled. "I bet that terrifies you, huh, Scout?"

"Yes. I'm quaking in my boots."

"Get out!" Melody stomped her foot. "You're going to ruin everything. In fact ... ." She dug in her pocket for a cell phone and held it up, as if I was somehow expected to applaud her ingenuity. "You're in trouble now. Just you wait."

I waved my hand and flung the phone out of her hands, smirking when it smacked into the wall, the screen shattering. "I think you need a time-out."

Melody's mouth dropped open and venom swirled in her eyes. "What did you just do? That phone is brand new. It's the expensive new model. What were you thinking?"

"I was thinking that I'm not going to allow you to call the half-vampires on the road and let you draw them into this."

She wrinkled her nose. "Actually, I was calling the police. You're trespassing and I'm going to have them arrest you. That's the absolute least you deserve."

I was caught off guard with the response. "Seriously?"

Gunner snorted. "Well, the chief of police is my father, so I don't think that would've worked out for you. Now I'm kind of sorry that Scout broke the phone. Seeing my father's reaction would've been funny."

"Especially because he can't cross the barrier and get me," I added.

"There is that."

Melody jutted out her lower lip. "I can't believe you did this. You ruined everything. Well, fine!" She threw her hands in the air, reminding me very much of a terrible teenager with an attitude problem. "Go ahead and take your friends. We'll just capture them again and then you'll be sorry."

And that was what I was determined to stop from happening. I slid my eyes to Rooster. "Just take them. Get them out. I thought you might have to entice them to leave, but they're not smart enough. Drag them over the line."

A muscle worked in Rooster's jaw as he nodded. "Gladly. Are you sure you don't want help with the rest of this?"

"There's nothing you can do." I flicked my eyes to Gunner. "Besides, I have backup. We'll be right behind you."

Confusion etched its way across Melody's face. "What are you doing? Where do you think you're going?" she called to my back as Gunner and I cut through the house. The basement door was in the kitchen. I saw it on my initial run through the house. There was only one place left to visit ... and I was more than ready to end this.

EVER THE MACHO TYPE, GUNNER tried to cut in front of me for the descent down the stairs, but I shoved him back — lightly of course — with my magic and practically skipped down the cement steps in front of him. I was feeling energized, ready for action, and extremely protective. I would do whatever it took to keep him safe.

The stairwell was dark so I had to create my own light source. I conjured three swirling light beacons and sent them ahead. The first chamber was illuminated when we reached the final step.

"Son of a ... !" I was awed as I looked around the room. Here, the vampires had spared no expense when it came to improvements. Someone had built vaults — much like at a morgue — with doors built into the walls. I had no doubt there were sliding trays inside every door, and a vampire sleeping on every tray.

"How many is that?" Gunner asked, breathless.

"At least thirty. If they're all full."

"What are the odds they're not full?"

That was a good question. I held my hands out and shrugged. "I have no idea. I ... ." The sound of footsteps on cement drew my attention to the far end of the room. There, situated against the back wall, was another door. I held my breath as it opened and then frowned when I didn't recognize the individual sliding into the room.

"Hello." She was young — under thirty — and well-dressed. She wore tweed pants, what appeared to be a cashmere sweater, and the necklace hanging around her neck looked ornate. It also looked familiar, though I couldn't quite place it. "You must be Allegra."

I exchanged a quick look with Gunner, confused. "Not last time I checked," I said finally. "I take it you're expecting someone else."

"That's the witch who bound us," Gunner warned in a low voice.

I held the woman's gaze. "And who are you?"

"Emmeline. You may call me Emma. I gave up my formal name years ago because people kept mispronouncing it."

"That must suck." Really, what else was I supposed to say? "May I ask why you're hanging out in the basement guarding a bunch of vampires?"

"You may ask."

I waited for her to answer. When she didn't, I frowned. "Seriously, what are you doing down here?"

"I am a guardian of sorts," Emma replied. Her face was remarkably smooth and pale. She didn't look like the other half-vampires. She didn't look entirely human either. "Someone needs to watch the master during the day to make sure he's safe."

"Isn't that the little minion's job?"

Her forehead wrinkled. "I'm not sure who you refer to."

"Bixby." I was quickly running out of patience, but I couldn't shake the feeling that this conversation was important. "I thought he was the butler."

"He is. That doesn't mean he's important."

"He seems to think he is."

"He's always been a bit full of himself." The smile she graced me with was unsettling. "It's been a long time."

"Excuse me?" I felt completely out of my depth. "What's been a long time?"

"Us being together. More than twenty years now ... and still we're right back where we were."

"I ... ." My heart rate picked up a notch as I tried to sort out what she was saying.

"You know Scout?" Gunner asked, his hand automatically going to my back. "How is that?"

"Oh, we go way back." Emma's gaze was keen. "I don't think you remember those days, do you? I'd heard rumors. I couldn't track you down myself because they hid you. I got close a few times ... including a few months after your eighteenth birthday. I tracked you into the city ... and found other people."

A sick feeling filled my stomach and the musty smell of the basement made me think I might actually throw up. "You ran into Bixby and Armand when you were looking for me."

"I saw you on the sidewalk and was following because I wanted to talk to you. They intercepted me. And now here we are."

I wasn't sure I could untangle all the threads in my head. "Have you been with them ever since?"

"Not by choice, but I have a job to do."

My lips parted as I tried to figure out what to say. There was so much going on in my brain I swore I could hear buzzing ... and I was hoping it wasn't my sanity as I struggled to maintain control of my emotions.

"Who are you?" Gunner challenged. He remained close to me, his warmth serving as an anchor. Shifters ran hot, something that caused us to sleep with a fan every night, but I welcomed that latent heat now.

"I just told you. My name is Emma."

"Yes, but who are you?"

"It's really none of your concern." The look she shot Gunner was dismissive. "This conversation has nothing to do with you."

"Well ... I'm here, so I beg to differ."

I put my hand on his wrist to still him. It felt as if something very important was happening, but that didn't change the fact that we had a job to do. "Do they make you stay with them?" I asked finally.

"They're not about asking politely," she replied. "They believe in enslaving people, which is why they're basically the dregs of the paranormal world. I knew the moment I saw them they would be trouble. Unfortunately, Armand is stronger than I imagined. I thought I could take him down, but he took me down instead.

"Don't get me wrong, I'm not bitter or anything," she continued. "I've learned invaluable lessons during my time with them."

"So ... you're loyal to them?" I asked.

"On the contrary, I suggested we move up here because I knew you were my only way out of this situation. Armand was hiding in the tunnels of Detroit, living like a rat. I filled his mind with delusions of grandeur.

"I told him the hills of Hawthorne Hollow could be great for his kind," she continued. "He didn't bite on the bait right away. It took a few months for him to acquiesce. I used my magic to ply him with dreams and he eventually came around to my way of thinking."

"You played him," I said, things finally clicking into place. "You were looking for me. You got enslaved for ten years because of it. Somehow you found out where I was and you manipulated him into bringing you up here. I'm still not sure why."

"I just told you. I knew you would be their downfall. Why do you think I convinced them to grab him?" She jerked her head in Gunner's direction. "I've been watching you — at least on the few occasions when I could slip away without anybody noticing. I wanted to approach you in private, but you were never alone."

Gunner leaned close so he could whisper. "I think she's saying we're codependent."

I managed to swallow a chuckle, but just barely. "What is it you want, Emma? Why were you looking for me ten years ago? Why did you seek me out now? Other than to free you from the vampires, I mean. Whatever hold they've got on you, I'm more than willing to set you free. Step out of the way and I'll kill them right now."

"I expect you will, which is exactly why I came to you. As for what I want ... just to talk. But this is not the time. We have things to discuss, but it's a conversation that will have to wait until this deed is done."

I wanted to press her. I wanted to dig deep and demand she give me answers about my past. She seemed to know things I didn't. But I didn't have the time. It was time to rid the world of a certain scourge ... and it would require fire to do it.

"Do you have to stay here and witness it?"

She shook her head. "I only remained behind long enough to speak to you. I wanted you to be aware of my presence and know that there are things we need to discuss."

"Well, great." It was a surreal conversation to be having in the middle of a roomful of drawers of sleeping vampires. "So ... I guess you should be going?"

A small smile played at the corners of her mouth. "Yes. I'll be going." She gave me a wide berth as she passed. "I'll be around once things have settled. Have fun burning down the house."

"That's it? Don't you want to say goodbye to your master?"

"Oh, it took everything I had not to tip my hand and bid him farewell this morning. He was crowing about fooling you. I knew better. I recognized what you were doing. He didn't."

"And yet you still suggested that the half-vampires kidnap my boyfriend in the middle of the day." My voice was like ice. "I think we'll be talking about that, too."

"Oh, don't get your panties in a twist." Her tone was dismissive. "I made sure no harm came to them."

I gestured toward Gunner's bruised face. "He looks harmed to me."

"He put up a fight. Had he simply surrendered as instructed he would've been fine. They all put up a fight. They made things more difficult than they had to be."

"Yeah, well, that's what we do."

Her smile was back. "I really must be going. Freedom awaits. It's been so long ... and I have so many plans."

That sounded ominous. Part of me thought I should end her right here. It was likely she was as dangerous — if not more — as the vampires. I couldn't, though. Not when she could supply answers. "Have a hot fudge sundae for me."

She looked confused. "Why would I have a hot fudge sundae?"

"To celebrate."

"Oh, well, I'll give it a try."

I heard her footsteps on the stairs as I sucked in a breath to steady myself.

"That was weird, right?" Gunner asked once she was gone.

"That was definitely weird."

"Do you think we should follow her?"

"I think she's going to find us when she's good and ready." I focused on the door. "We have other things to worry about now. She can wait until later."

"If you say so." He flexed his arms and glanced around. "How do you want to do this?"

"I want you to go back to the stairs and wait. I'm tackling the master first. He's the one we have to get no matter what. Then, when I'm leaving the room, I'll make sure this space is engulfed. I'll implode the building once we're outside to make sure there's no escape."

"That sounds ... loud."

"And messy."

He flashed a grin and leaned close. "I'm sorry for all of this. I'm mostly sorry for this morning. I should've trusted you. The thing is, when we were taken, I knew you would come. I never had a doubt. Still, I feel guilty about what I said to you this morning. It wasn't fair."

"We've already talked about this. You don't need to apologize. I was playing a part. I expected a certain reaction."

"Still, I was cruel ... and disloyal. I hate being disloyal."

I managed a smile. "We can be loyal together tonight. We'll take a long bath, order some pizza, and shut out the rest of the world. There won't even be a minion tied to the chair, so we'll both be able to sleep."

"That sounds heavenly." He planted a kiss against my lips. "Finish it. I'm ready to get out of here."

That made two of us.

TWENTY-NINE

*T*he master vampire didn't stir when I let myself into the back room. He was in a coffin — I mean, how cliché — his arms crossed over his chest. There were no lights in the room, so he was perfectly safe ... at least for the next few seconds.

I knew Gunner wanted to follow me, stick close and serve as some form of protection should something go wrong, but I needed a few minutes to collect myself. I was about to end thirty lives. Sure, they were vampires and they had it coming, but that didn't lessen the weight I was carrying.

"This kind of feels wrong," I admitted to the sleeping vampire. "You don't have a way to defend yourself. Of course, the part that bothers me most is that you're not awake for me to gloat.

"I actually believed you last night, at least to a certain extent," I continued. "I expected the double-cross to come with the darkness. I didn't think you would move on me during the day. I thought allowing Bixby's emotions to run free would buy me the room I needed to plan. You'd already ordered the half-vampires to grab my friends, though. Emma might've given you the idea, but you carried it out.

"I don't know why you were looking for magical beings," I said finally. "I have a few ideas, but none of them are good. I'm sure Emma will be purposely vague when it's time, because that's how things roll in my world. Still, despite all you've done, it seems as if you deserve a better death."

I was contemplative for a moment and then shook my head. "This is the smart way to go. After what you pulled last night, you have this coming. I'm not sure where Brandon is — he wasn't in the storage room when I checked — but if something has happened to him and he's not simply hanging out with the other half-vampires I'm going to wish I'd been more brutal.

"Either way, it's time to go." I drifted back toward the door, not stopping until I was at the threshold. I watched the sleeping vampire for what felt like forever. In real time it was probably only five seconds, but sometimes seconds can feel like hours. "I'm not really sorry about this. I don't want you to think that. It's just ... it doesn't feel honorable.

"I have to protect my friends, though. I have to protect the people of this town. I get that you were manipulated and probably wouldn't have come up here if not for Emma. I don't know what her plan is and I'm doubtful she's up to anything good. Despite all that, I can't let you live.

"A message has to be sent here today — and I'm the one who needs to send it. You marked me as your equal, so it's my response that counts."

I didn't wait any longer. I filled the room with fire. Gunner was waiting at the stairs and I started burning the second chamber as I moved toward him.

"Ready?" he asked, forcing a smile as I focused an extended blast at the morgue drawers.

"Ready. Let's get out of here."

WE WATCHED FROM THE TREES AS THE house burned. Graham showed up not long after the fire started and his fury was evident. He talked in low voices with Rooster for several minutes before sitting back to watch the show. He did not call for backup ... or fire engines.

"How do we know that they're not just waiting it out in the basement?" Marissa demanded as she gave Gunner dirty looks for rubbing his hand over my back. "I mean ... fire kills them most of the time, but they might survive. Then all they have to do is wait until dark and make their escape. If you ask me, this is a stupid plan."

"Hey!" Gunner's eyes flashed. "She saved us. You should show her a little gratitude."

"What good is any of it if they come looking for us after dark?" she shot back.

"They won't come looking," I promised, weariness temporarily taking over. "I've already thought that through."

"Oh, yeah?" Marissa cocked an eyebrow. "How are you going to make sure it doesn't happen?"

As if on cue, the roof of the house collapsed. The entire building caved in with one fluid motion.

Marissa narrowed her eyes. "There's still debris over the basement."

"It won't last long," Rooster pointed out. "This fire is meant to burn until there's absolutely nothing left. It will be fine."

"Oh, well, if you say so."

Gunner slid his arm around my shoulders and drew me close. He seemed unusually protective, though that could simply have been my exhaustion talking. "We don't have to stay," he noted.

"I know. I just ... ." I flicked my eyes to Graham as he approached. "If you're going to give me grief for this, can you wait until tomorrow? I'll be a lot more fun to fight with when I have a bit of pep in my step."

His lips curved. "I'll keep that in mind for tomorrow. For now ... ." He looked conflicted. After a few seconds, he collected himself and straightened his shoulders. "So, I thought you should know that a group of people were picked up on the highway. They seemed out of it ... and confused ... and even a little dehydrated. They're being transported to the hospital for observation."

I perked up. "Was Brandon with them? He wasn't in the storage room at The Cauldron and I wasn't sure if they ... well, if they did something horrible."

"Brandon *was* with them." The smile he shot me was reassuring. "He's being checked out even as we speak. You don't have to worry about him. He seems back to normal. A little confused."

"What about the others? Melody? Cherise? The little minion?"

Graham didn't crack a smile at my weak joke. "Melody and Cherise are in custody. Cherise is talking, says she wants to go home. Melody is giving us fits. We've called her husband. I figure she'll be his problem soon enough."

That probably wasn't the end she was looking for, but I couldn't muster much sympathy for her. "I guess that's the end of that." Even as I said the words I knew that wasn't true. Emma was still out there and her motivations remained murky. I worried things would get worse before they got better, but for now at least they appeared settled. "What about Honey? Her body went missing from the morgue and we never saw her again. Do we know what happened to her?"

Graham shook his head. "I'm assuming she's in one of the vaults Gunner described to Rooster. You didn't check them?"

I shook my head. "We didn't. She could've been sleeping the day away for all we know."

"And yet you don't look like you believe that." Graham folded his arms over his chest and pinned me with a probing look. "Why can't you just take the win? You singlehandedly ended all the vampires. Somehow you got across that barrier and you saved your friends. Why can't that be enough for you?"

"I didn't say it wasn't enough." He was starting to irritate me so I took a step back. "I just ... wish I would've thought to check. It's better to know than wonder."

"Where else would she be?"

He sounded so reasonable that I opted to check my attitude. "She was probably in the basement," I agreed, a hint of movement catching my attention over his shoulder. There, Mama Moon stood next to Bixby's forlorn figure. The minion was on the ground, free of the spell even though I'd forgotten to release him, which made me think Mama

Moon handled that particular task. Tears coursed down his cheeks. He looked legitimately broken-hearted. "Excuse me for a second."

Gunner followed. It was obvious he had no intention of letting me out of his sight. It would take more energy to argue than I had, so I didn't mention it. Instead, I hunkered down in front of Bixby and waited until he met my gaze.

"You killed them." His tone was accusatory as he sniffled.

"I did," I agreed. I wasn't going to apologize. Still, part of me felt sorry for him. A very, very small part. "You're free of whatever blood bond you shared with them. You can go and ... start a new life."

"And what if I don't want to start a new life? What if I want my old one back?"

"Then you're doomed to disappointment."

He narrowed his eyes. "I'm going to rip out your intestines and use them as a straw."

I couldn't stop myself from smiling. "That sounds fun." I patted his shoulder and stood. "I'm not going to kill you — at least not now — but I don't recommend staying in town. You need to get out of here and find someplace new to hang your hat."

"I don't wear hats. They're undignified."

For some reason that made me laugh. "Well ... then find a new home where you don't have to wear a hat and your services will be appreciated. That's not Hawthorne Hollow."

He was suspicious as he looked me up and down. "That's it? You're just going to let me go?"

I nodded. "There's no reason for you to stay. But if you return I won't hesitate to kill you. You need to go ... someplace else."

"And you need to do it today," Gunner added. "I need some sleep and that won't happen with you tied to a chair in the kitchen."

"That was not my choice," Bixby sneered, shaking his head. He pushed himself to his feet, taking a moment to glance around as he brushed the leaves and twigs from his coat. "So ... I can just go?"

"On your way."

"We'll be watching for your return, though," Gunner warned. "You might want to think long and hard before you get involved with vampires again."

"Oh, you needn't worry." Bixby's smile turned smarmy. "You'll never see me again. I promise you that."

"Good. Get out of here." Gunner slung his arm around my shoulders as we watched Bixby scamper into the trees. He stopped at the foliage line long enough to glance over his shoulder, his eyes finding me. There was hatred there, maybe something worse. I thought he was going to say something, but he disappeared into the trees.

"Do you think that was a good idea?" Mama Moon asked.

I shrugged. "I don't know. I can't kill him and I'm over keeping him captive. I guess we'll try it. If he comes back, we'll handle the problem then."

She was quiet as she turned back to the fire. "You did good work today. You saved your friends. You saved the half-vampires. It was a good day."

"Yeah, but speaking of that" — I craned my neck and searched the field — "what happened to Melody and Cherise? Graham said they were in custody, but I want to make sure they're not out causing problems."

"They tried to flee when the fire started. They knew what it meant. Cherise thanked me for helping. She seemed legitimately relieved for this to be ending. Melody was furious. She could be back to cause trouble down the road, depending on what happens when she's reunited with her husband."

"We'll handle it when it happens," Gunner replied, tugging me tighter against him. "For now ... I think we've done all we can do here. What do you say to pizza in bed and however many bad movies we can find on Netflix?"

The invitation was warm, friendly, and exactly what I needed. "Can we get ice cream on the way home, too?"

"Absolutely."

"Then that sounds like the best offer I've had all day."

"It's a date then." He pressed his lips to my forehead and then looked around. "I don't have a way to get out of here unless we ride together on your bike."

"I think we can make it work."

"Yeah, but ... I need to drive. I can't be on the back. That's the chick seat."

Oh, well, now this conversation revived me. "It's my bike," I noted as I led him toward the trees. "I'm not sitting in the chick seat on my own bike. You have to do it."

"No. I draw the line there."

"Then you're walking home."

He exhaled heavily. "Maybe we could flip a coin or something."

"Sure. Tails you lose, heads I win."

"I already won when you moved to town."

That was unbelievably sweet, but there was no way I was falling for it. "I'm driving and that's all there is to it."

"This day just sucks."

Actually, the day hadn't ended too badly all things considered. More trouble would be calling in the form of Emma eventually, but for now we could rest and recuperate.

Rooster called out to us before we got too far. Every muscle in my body ached for whatever he was about to say.

"I don't want to keep you when it's obvious you need a break." He closed the distance between us and kept his voice low. "I just got a call, and I thought I should make you aware."

I waited, bracing myself.

"It was Drake. His sister is ... better. I won't say she's good because I'm not sure that's happening anytime soon, but he feels safe enough to leave her for a bit. He's on his way back —and he wants to set up a time to talk to you."

My heart gave a little jolt. "Today?"

"No. It will still be a few days. He just wanted you to know he hasn't forgotten about you."

Everything was coming together at once and I wasn't sure how to feel about it. "Well ... then I'll be waiting when he gets here."

"I'll tell him." Rooster flashed a smile. "You guys should get some rest. You've earned it."

"That's the plan," Gunner reassured him. "We're just arguing about who will do the driving on the way home."

"I'm driving," I said automatically. "It's my bike."

"I think we should arm wrestle for it."

"Fine. Absolutely. That sounds like a great idea."

He narrowed his eyes. "You can't use magic to cheat."

"Oh, no. That wasn't part of the challenge. I'm totally using magic."

He was silent for a beat and then he exploded. "I'm not riding on the chick seat!"

"Do you care to place a wager on that?"

Made in the USA
Monee, IL
20 March 2020